LADY MAGE

SERVING MAGIC
BOOK TWO

TONI CABELL

CHAPTER 1

Linden sidestepped left, blocking the downward thrust of her opponent's sword as it whooshed past her hip. Pivoting on her right foot, she used both hands to swing her sword in an upward arc. Her adversary leapt backward, temporarily out of reach. Linden exhaled, slowing her heart rate and waiting for him to rush her.

Light on his feet, he danced just outside the range of her sword, almost beckoning her to charge him. *Two can play at this game*, she thought, as they moved in a tight circle around each other, looking for any opening to attack. Linden's father, her first fencing coach, had taught her well; despite her tendency to act first and think later in most things, she'd learned to bide her time whenever she held a sword.

She narrowed her eyes and considered her options. Given her opponent's size—he towered over her—and his skill with the sword, her best course was to wait until he grew weary of the cat-and-mouse game and then make her move. Linden had enough experience fighting larger opponents to know they generally tired first, or grew impatient first, attacking with less precision than they possessed.

The strategy worked once again. Growling in frustration, the swordsman lunged toward her. She counterattacked, surprising him with her speed. Backing him against a hedgerow, the tip of her blade aimed squarely at his chest, she shouted, "Drop your weapon!"

Her opponent threw down his sword. Whipping the fencing mask off his face, Stryker said, "Queen's Crown! You don't ever tire, do you?"

Sheathing her sword, Linden pulled off her mask, smiling. "Of course I tire. You're just impatient to be done." Her stomach still lightened whenever Stryker looked at her that way, as if he couldn't wait to take her into his arms once more. He wore his dark hair Valerran style, shorter than most Faymons, and when he became frustrated, he'd run his hands through his hair, making it stand up in little spikes. Linden used to joke he had the longest eyelashes she'd ever seen, but she didn't tease him so much anymore. His dark brown eyes had become more guarded over the past few months, more watchful and less playful.

Stryker reached her in one stride and drew her into his arms. Weaving her shoulder-length hair through fingers that had gripped a sword moments earlier, his other hand slipped around Linden's waist. "I'm impatient to be doing this," he murmured, sealing his lips over hers. She leaned into the kiss, Stryker pulling her closer with a raspy sigh.

Linden heard footsteps approaching her private garden and broke away first. Although everyone knew they were betrothed, she refused to be the source of gossip and giggles. Stryker let her withdraw from his embrace reluctantly, sliding an arm around her shoulders as Reynier, her cousin and second-in-command of the Faymon clans, approached them. Linden smoothed her ankle-length maroon skirt, tucking a loose lock of hair behind her ears.

Reynier cleared his throat, so like Matteo, her brother, who would clear his throat to stall for time whenever he had something unpleasant or difficult to discuss. A sharp pang of longing for her Valerran family, scattered, lost, some long gone, settled in the pit of her stomach. Reynier, his dark brown hair lightly salted with bluish streaks, looked more like another older brother than her cousin. A long scar bisected Reynier's left eyebrow, a constant reminder of the many battles he'd witnessed and survived.

"I'm glad I've found you, my Liege. I've been looking everywhere for you. I believe you may have accidentally cast a privacy screen around your garden." Reynier glared at Stryker pointedly.

Linden raised her shoulders slightly. "I'm finding my private garden isn't very private after all, so I've improvised." She glanced around the walled garden outside her suite of rooms in the longhouse where she lived. Roses, bougainvillea, and hyacinth bloomed in every corner of the garden, the bright flowers a cheerful reminder to be thankful for everything, and everyone, she had left after fleeing war-torn Valerra. A few benches were scattered about the garden, placed beneath fruit trees—plum, pear, and apple—offering shade from the midday sun. A water fountain occupied the center of the garden, spouting water from the mouths of five fish, each fish colored with different tiles that sparkled brightly in the sun.

"By magically blocking even the Faymon Elder?" Reynier referred to himself by his official title, drawing his brows together. Linden had to tread carefully. After all, she needed Reynier perhaps even more than he needed her. Together, they led the prickly, rebellious, and magically gifted five clans of Faynwood. Plus, he'd just conjured the magical key to unlock her most recent privacy spell, which meant she'd have to return to *Timely Spells*, her spell book, to find something more foolproof if she wanted any alone time with Stryker.

Reynier constantly interrupted them, explaining there were important visitors, or there was some huge problem that only the Faymon Liege herself could sort out. Queen's Crown, if she'd known what she was getting herself into, she'd never have...what? Wouldn't she have fled to Faynwood anyway, home to her father's side of the family? With Valerra overrun by Glenbarran troops and grihms, their wolf-man crossbreeds, she'd had little choice. Mage Mother Pawllah, her mentor, had instructed Linden to find her second family, and she had—as the Faymon Liege, she was related by either blood or magic to every Faymon—and she'd soon discovered the challenges of leading such clannish, magical, boisterous people. Without Reynier, who'd ruled the clans before she'd been crowned the Faymon Liege, she'd never have survived.

Linden looked at her cousin, his eyes clouded with worry, and said, "I'm sorry. I have so many official duties that sometimes I need a little escape. Besides, Stryker was helping me with my sword fighting." She avoided any explanation of the real reason for casting the privacy screen; she'd been hoping to spend some uninterrupted time with Stryker.

Reynier arched an eyebrow. Linden could tell he knew she'd just told a white lie, but Reynier wasn't about to call her out on it. Thankfully, Reynier was too classy or maybe too respectful for that. "Aye, my Liege. Unfortunately, we have urgent business to attend to. Pryl and one of his scouts have arrived with news from Glenbarra." Clearing his throat again, Reynier spoke in the ancient buzzing language of the fays, a language that Linden was attempting to learn but had little hope of mastering.

A mist rose from the water fountain in the center of the garden and stretched toward where they stood. As vaporous tendrils groped along the ground, two forms strengthened and solidified within the mist, until a fay man and woman stepped into the afternoon light. Linden recognized the fay chief, Pryl, but not the young woman who traveled with him. A tad shorter than Pryl, she wore her vivid blue hair in a side braid that dangled down her left shoulder. When she smiled, her dark eyes danced with mischief and intelligence. Linden decided she liked this new fay scout and hoped they could spend some time together.

Bowing deeply, Reynier offered to interpret, but Pryl raised his hand. "There is no need, Elder. We will speak in your tongue." Inclining his head toward Stryker, Pryl added, "Forgive me for the intrusion, Tall Warrior." Tall Warrior was Stryker's nickname, since he stood half a head taller than most Faymons, and he loomed above Pryl. Despite the fay chief's outward appearance—slight of build, thinning blue hair, and an anxious expression most of the time—he was an extremely powerful mage, scholar, and leader of the Fay Nation.

Unlike Faymons, whose blue highlights ran through their base hair color of black, brown, red, or gray, the fays had bright, eye-catching blue hair through and through. Even a half-Faymon, like Linden and her brother Matteo, had the telltale blue running through their hair. Although Linden's blue-streaked black hair had been the source of much teasing as a child in Valerra, she was unashamed of her mixed heritage—equally proud of her Faymon father and Valerran mother.

Pryl ran a hand through his blue beard and waited. Stryker hesitated, and then bowed. "Of course, I can see this is official Faymon business." He leaned over and brushed his lips against Linden's, causing Reynier's scowl to deepen. Linden made a mental note to remind Stryker about respecting Faymon customs, which meant limiting public displays of affection to handholding.

Despite Reynier's assurances that her friends from Valerra would be treated as befitting the Liege's companions—which had been true for Jayna, Mara, Toz and Remy, Linden's friends who'd traveled with her to Faynwood two months earlier—her cousin couldn't seem to accept that the Faymon Liege would be marrying a Valerran soldier.

Pryl waved his hand at the pretty fay scout by his side. "Wreyn comes from Glenbarra with urgent news."

Wreyn stepped forward and blurted out, "Mordahn is alive."

Linden gasped, "Impossible! I saw Mordahn die, my sword stuck in his chest." Linden shuddered involuntarily at the memory of her showdown with Mordahn, the master of Fallow magic. He'd pursued her across Valerra, finally catching up with her aboard the ship carrying her and her friends to the shores of Faynwood. Mordahn's dark magic, coupled with his hatred of her and her bloodline, terrified her. She still had nightmares about their battle, a wild combination of magic and sword fighting, and she carried the scars he'd given her. That she'd survived at all had been a miracle; in the end, Mordahn had tripped and fallen onto her sword.

Wreyn bowed. "Aye, my Liege. Many witnessed his

death onboard the *Aurorialyss*. Do you recall what became of Mordahn's body?"

Linden's brow creased as she tried to remember. Shaking her head, she said, "I was injured and focused on the search for Mara and Fen, who'd gone overboard during the battle. I remember Captain Raff—you know him as Raffindor—retrieving my sword from Mordahn's body." She gave another shudder. "The captain wiped off my sword and handed it back to me. But I don't remember anything more about Mordahn after that."

Pryl glanced at Reynier and said, "The after-shades of Fallow sorcery. Mordahn would have cast multiple protection charms."

"What are you saying? That Mordahn didn't die? But I saw his appearance change from that of a young man to an old one, his face and body withering, his hair graying as he took his last breath," said Linden.

Reynier turned toward her, his face partially hidden by the shade cast from the plum trees overhead. "My Liege, did you actually see him transform?"

When Linden nodded, he asked, "Did he say anything, anything at all?"

Closing her eyes to recall Mordahn's exact words, Linden slowly repeated them. "He said, 'This is not the end.' And something else, I think it was, 'There are others.'"

Reynier glanced at Pryl, who let out a string of words in his buzzing language that caused Wreyn to blush. Linden suspected the fay chief was swearing and bit her bottom lip to keep from smiling. She sobered immediately when Reynier clutched a chunk of his hair and gasped, "A necromancer."

Linden frowned, trying to recall her lessons in the history of magic—the Serving magic that she, Reynier, and

Pryl were sworn to uphold and protect from the Fallow magic of Mordahn and his followers. "But how? The ancient scrolls containing necromantic spells were destroyed centuries ago."

The incantations for reanimating bodies with the spirits of the deceased were considered the lowest form of Fallow sorcery. No Serving mage would ever perform a necromantic spell, because of the polluting nature of the magic involved. Serving mages who dabbled in necromancy wound up contaminating their own magic; they lost their ability to conjure, unless they crossed over entirely to Fallow ways and darker magic.

Pryl had regained his composure and replied, "And yet, Wreyn spoke with eyewitnesses in Glenbarra who claim they dined with Mordahn and a necromancer not two days past."

Linden crossed her arms, her thoughts a jumble of half-formed hypotheses. "How reliable are these witnesses?"

"Very reliable, my Liege," said Wreyn. "They risked their lives to get me this information."

"Where is Mordahn now?"

"With King Roi. My informants tell me the Glenbarrans are planning another invasion."

Linden knew what the fay scout would say next—the five clan chiefs had been drawing plans for weeks to defend their provinces against an attack—but she nonetheless winced when Wreyn added, "Attacking Valerra was their warning shot. The Glenbarrans have set their sights on Faynwood, and they'll not stop until they've destroyed all of Serving magic in their wake."

CHAPTER 2

"Never!" said Reynier, shaking his fist in the air. "They'll never defeat Serving magic using Fallow sorcery and necromancy."

Linden reached out her hand to grip her cousin's arm. "That's exactly what our mages, generals, and politicians, including my own uncle, used to say. That Valerra would never fall, that Fallow magic could never defeat Serving magic. There was only one master mage, my grandmother, who foresaw the impossible, that Glenbarran troops would occupy our capital."

"The Liege is right. While we make plans to defend against an isolated attack along our border, the Glenbarrans are preparing for all-out war. We must anticipate the worst," said Pryl.

"Where do we even start?" asked Reynier.

Linden felt as if she were sitting in her uncle's study at Delavan Manor, the Arlyss family home in Valerra, listening to another round of speculations about the Glenbarran threat. Waving her hand, she said, "We need to fortify our border—our entire border. When the Glenbarrans are ready to invade, they'll exploit any weakness in our defenses there. But first they'll toy with us, try to distract us with minor skirmishes."

Pryl agreed. "We've seen more border incursions from Glenbarra during the past few months, ever since the Liege was crowned."

A vision of her crowning ceremony pulsed in Linden's mind. She paused, turning the memory over, trying to pinpoint what triggered this specific scene. Linden, wearing her crown woven of the vines, berries, and flowers of the forest, used the commanding voice of a master mage to address the large crowd gathered to see their new Liege. She called for unity between the Faymon clans, and healing after fifty years of civil war.

The memory leapt forward, to the end of her speech, when the clan chief from Arrowood stood before the gathering. According to Reynier, Arrowood had earned its reputation as the most troublesome of all the clans—due to the size of its territory, the ferocity of its warriors, and the tendency of its mages to dabble in Fallow magic.

Arrowood's clan chief had bowed low before Linden, exposing the back of his neck to his new Liege, a sign of fealty and trust. Although the Faymon prophecies all pointed to Linden as the next Liege, and most of the clans readily welcomed her, she knew that Arrowood's loyalty was not given lightly. As Reynier often reminded her, she must never take Arrowood for granted.

Linden blinked rapidly a few times to clear her head. "Arrowood is vulnerable. We must act soon." She resisted the urge to massage her temples in front of her guests. Her head always ached after she interpreted one of her visions or cast a particularly complex spell.

Not only had Linden inherited the title of Liege from her great-grandmother, Liege Ayala, she'd also inherited Ayala's skills as a revelator—someone who was both a seer and a mage at the master level. Mages had occasional visions, and seers performed basic magic, but a revelator was considered a master of both the complex gifts. Although mastering the gift of interpreting visions was less about practice and skill, and more about instinct and nuance, since the visions could be any combination of the past, present, or future. Not all visions came true, nor did they provide any sort of reliable clues to help the seer tell the difference.

As far as Linden was concerned, she often wished she could pass Liege Ayala's inheritance on to some distant Faymon cousin and go back to being simply Linden Arlyss, a not very promising mage who occasionally had weird dreams and visions. Last year, before the Glenbarrans invaded Valerra, her biggest worry was passing her school exams. Now she was the Liege of Faynwood, consulted on a multitude of issues and decisions, relying on Reynier's experience and guidance on a daily basis. Most mornings, when Linden first opened her eyes, she'd forget where she was. For a delicious moment, she'd think she was back in her old bedroom, and that her family was together and safe and home.

"Aye, my Liege." Pryl bowed, acknowledging her foresight. "You perceive the danger, which grows daily. The Chief of Arrowood requests your assistance." Turning to Reynier, he added, "And the Elder's counsel."

Reynier said, "What does Chief Haydahn seek from us?"

"Warriors and mages," said Linden, still interpreting her vision. "We must send warriors and mages to defend Arrowood."

Reynier arched an eyebrow at Pryl, looking for confirmation. When Pryl nodded, Reynier sighed. "And so it begins."

Linden half-listened as Reynier and Pryl discussed their plans. Reynier would depart in the morning, leading a contingent of warriors and mages to the Arrowood province. Pryl and Wreyn would visit the other clan chiefs to request their support.

Wreyn approached Linden and said quietly, "My Liege, something troubles you, something beyond this talk of war with Glenbarra."

Linden gave Wreyn an appraising look. "Are you familiar with the concept of *repenva*?"

Wreyn shook her head, so Linden explained, "It's a feeling that you've already experienced the present situation."

"Is it magical, this *repenva*?"

Linden smiled. "There's no magic involved. Just a feeling, although in my case, I have experienced much of this before—the threat of war from Glenbarra, the battle plans and contingency plans, and—well, I won't think about the rest." Noticing Wreyn's confusion, Linden added, "My uncle was Alban Arlyss, Prime Minister of Valerra. I lived with him and my grandmother, Nari Arlyss, during the war."

Wreyn tilted her head. "And so the feelings of *repenva* you describe, they're partly based on memories, are they not?"

"I suppose so."

"And these memories are based on what you've previously experienced?"

Linden nodded slowly. "Aye, that's true enough."

"Then I understand what troubles you, my Liege," said Wreyn. "And I am sorry."

"Sorry for what?"

"Sorry for what has passed, sorry for what is to come. "

Linden glanced at the five multicolored fish spouting water inside the fountain, each fish representing one of the clans of Faynwood. "More battles, more loss, more heartache."

"And Mordahn. You must face him again," said Wreyn.

"How do you defeat a dead man?" Linden asked herself more than Wreyn.

"By defeating Fallow magic," said Pryl, who'd managed to overhear Linden's last remark. Linden didn't know whether fays had better hearing, or their magic extended to eavesdropping. Probably both, she decided.

Reynier glanced at Pryl. "Our ancestors have been attempting to defeat Fallow magic throughout history, to no avail."

"This time we have no choice. If we do not succeed, then we will succumb. We will go the way of Valerra, and Serving magic with it," said Pryl.

"When do we ride for Arrowood?" asked Linden, deciding action was far better than words. At least she could be doing something instead of worrying.

"What do you mean, 'we?' I will ride out in the morning with our warriors and mages from Eloway, and we will gather more of our people along the way. You will remain here, in the last refuge of Serving magic." Eloway was the largest stronghold inside Tanglewood—Linden and Reynier's clan—as well as the capital of Faynwood itself. The city's central location made it highly defensible from outside attack.

Linden tossed her head. "I will ride out with you. There is nothing for me to do here that can't be done on the move."

Reynier looked ready to argue, but Pryl interrupted. "It is right for the Liege to lead us, along with her Elder. It has always been thus."

Reynier jutted his jaw out. "And if we should lose the Liege in battle, then what? We have no other heir. The Faymon clans will splinter again."

Pryl's answer sent a chill down Linden's spine. "If we lose our Liege, then we lose our last hope of defeating Fallow magic. We lose everything."

Linden had never heard the fay chief speak so plainly. He usually spoke in riddles, but then again, Reynier had always translated for Pryl. Perhaps Pryl decided that in order to be understood, he had to speak for himself. In any case, Linden had heard enough. "Thank you for bringing us this intelligence."

Pryl and Wreyn bowed and said goodbye, fading into their traveling mists.

Reynier turned to Linden, his eyebrows drawn together. "I don't like the idea of you riding with us into Arrowood. I wish you'd reconsider."

"You heard Pryl; he agrees with me. As Liege, it's my duty to accompany our men and women into battle, if it comes down to that."

"You know Mordahn and the Glenbarrans. It will come down to that, sooner or later."

Linden nodded. "All the more reason for me to be there. We'll need all the magic and swords we'll be able to muster." She added, "Now if you don't mind, I'll take dinner in my chambers. I need to prepare to leave in the morning."

"Aye, of course, my Liege," said Reynier, bowing. "I'll issue the call for warriors and mages."

"When it's just the two of us, can't you call me Linden? And dispense with the bowing?"

Reynier gave her a weary smile. "In times of peace, yes. But in times of war, I dare not slip up in front of the clan chiefs and their advisors."

Linden shrugged, realizing she'd not win this argument. "I'll see you in the morning then, Elder."

Linden instructed her maidservants to request a private dinner in her chambers and invite her companions, her Valerran friends who'd escaped with her during the final battle and later accompanied her to Faynwood. Linden wrote a short note to Stryker, inviting him to join her for dinner. She gave the note to Kal, her miniature griffin, to deliver. Kal had the face of an eagle, framed by a reddish mane, the body of a small lion, and a pair of wings that measured eight feet across when fully extended. While most of the residents of Eloway might prefer to have a servant deliver their private notes, Linden trusted Kal with her life. She knew he'd be able to find Stryker faster than any servant.

Linden bathed and dressed carefully for dinner, selecting a dark blue silk gown that she knew Stryker admired. She wanted this last evening to be special; once they were on the road, there would be even less opportunity for private time with Stryker and her Valerran friends. As she combed her hair, she heard a flutter of wings and turned around to see Kal soar through an open window, folding in his wings as he glided to a stop.

"What's that?" Linden asked, pointing at the piece of ivory vellum jutting from Kal's beak. He padded over to her on his cat-like paws, dropping the vellum note by her feet. Recognizing Stryker's handwriting, Linden's heart sped up. She tore open the wax seal.

Dearest Linden (Or should I start addressing you as Dearest Liege? Would that make Reynier like me any better?)—I'm preparing to ride in the morning, along with the other warriors in our squad, for Arrowood. I have a lot to do and will have to miss dinner with you. I'll make it up to you, my love.

~SS

Sighing, Linden tucked the note into her dresser drawer and picked up her comb. He seemed almost happy to be riding out with the squad of Faymon warriors. Stryker's restlessness during the past few months contributed to the rising tensions between him and Reynier. Until now, he'd never missed an opportunity to dine with her and their friends from Valerra.

Kal clicked his beak at her, breaking into her thoughts. She ruffled his mane and said, "We're leaving in the morning."

Kal cocked his head to one side. "Aye, you're coming with me. You're almost as restless as Stryker. An adventure will do you some good."

The miniature griffin flapped his wings once, bumping into a chair, and then settled down to lick his paws in front of the fireplace. Although the days were warm, the summer evenings came with a chill, and a cheery fire burned in the grate. She thought of her family and friends she'd lost during the last war and wondered what fresh pain this new war would bring. She still held out hope she'd see Matteo again. As a Royal Marine, her brother had been recovering from his injuries in a military hospital when the Glenbarrans overran his base. He had been missing ever since.

Jayna knocked on the door separating Linden's inner and outer chambers, calling out, "We've arrived and so has the dinner you ordered. Are you almost ready? Remy says he's famished."

Linden opened the door to her best friend and confidante, forcing a smile. "Remy's always famished."

Worry lines formed on Jayna's brow, crinkling her flawless brown complexion. "What's happened? You look like you've seen a ghost."

Linden shook her head. "Let's have dinner. We can catch up later." Linden's outer chamber contained a low, oval table that could seat ten, assorted seat cushions covered in a thick plushy gold fabric, sturdy candles for dining and reading, and one entire wall of shelves lined with scrolls and bound books. She never tired of reading something from her own private library, especially the fay history books and old prophecies. This room had become her sanctuary during the past several months, one she would miss when they left Eloway in the morning.

After they were seated and the servants had withdrawn, Toz said, "We heard Reynier is departing in the morning with a squad of warriors and mages." The first boy she'd ever kissed—secretly, and at the age of twelve—Toz had been her friend since they were toddlers. She could never deflect him for long; Toz seemed to have a sixth sense where she was concerned and sometimes was as overprotective as Reynier.

"But no one's telling us what's going on," complained Mara, tossing her honey-blonde hair. "Shouldn't we know what's happening, just like everyone else in Eloway?"

Remy cut into his shepherd's pie and waved his fork. "If it's bad news then it can wait until after I've eaten. I don't want anything spoiling my appetite."

"Nothing ever spoils your appetite." Mara rolled her eyes.

Ever the diplomat, Jayna switched topics. "I saw several carrier pigeons arriving this week. Did any carry news from Sanrellyss Island?"

Mage Mother Pawllah, an elderly prophet who led the

Sanrellyss Sisterhood, had tutored Linden and her grand-mother Nari before her. Pawllah used carrier pigeons rather than telegrams to communicate. While the telegraph was a popular means of sending and receiving express messages in Valerra, too much magic interfered with anything mechanical or electrical. Since every Faymon used Serving magic in one form or another—from simple kitchen magic that kept food warm to healing magic and the defensive spells that protected Eloway—telegraphs and locomobiles and other such devices had never found a home in Faynwood.

Linden nodded. "Mage Mother Pawllah asked after all of you, wanting to know how we were faring here, and reminding us to keep up with our magical studies." Pausing, Linden added, "She said her sleep has been interrupted by troubling dreams of late, but she couldn't make heads nor tails of them." *When Mage Mother learns a powerful necromancer is raising the Fallow dead, she might stop sleeping altogether,* thought Linden with a sigh.

Toz narrowed his eyes. "That's the third time you've sighed, Linden. Just tell us what in Queen's Crown is going on around here."

"We haven't seen this much activity since we arrived in Eloway. Something big is happening, and we know you know," Mara said, looking at Linden expectantly. "You do know, don't you?"

"I think it's probably best to tell us before our imaginations run wild," said Jayna.

Linden stopped pushing the food around on her plate and put down her fork.

She started and stopped a few times before she could say it out loud. "Chief Pryl and one of his fay scouts visited

Reynier and me today. The scout says Mordahn is alive. Several reliable eyewitnesses swear they've seen him in Glenbarra."

"No way!"

"She's wrong!"

"I saw him die on the ship."

Mara shrugged and said, "I don't remember anything other than being in the water and thinking Fen and I weren't going to make it. When Captain Raff found us, I was in shock."

Linden nodded slowly and asked her other friends. "Do any of you remember how the captain disposed of Mordahn's body? Did he have a burial at sea? Or was he transported back to his own ship?"

Toz, Remy, and Jayna looked at one another, frowning in concentration. Jayna explained she'd gone with Mara and Fen below deck to assist the healer. Toz and Remy had gone below deck as well.

"But even if we can't remember what happened to his body after he died onboard the ship, what does it matter? Mordahn is dead. Period," said Toz.

"That's what I thought too. Until Pryl told us he suspects necromancy."

Toz's face paled, and Remy choked on a forkful of mashed potato. "But that's against every known magical law of the universe. No one is permitted to practice it," said Jayna.

"Even so," said Mara slowly. "That wouldn't prevent a master of Fallow magic from resorting to the dark arts, even necromancy."

"Apparently King Roi has a powerful necromancer who's raised Mordahn," said Linden, wishing that Wreyn's informants were mistaken, but sensing the truth in what Wreyn had shared, and what Linden's vision had revealed about the threat to Arrowood. "Reynier has put out a call for warriors and mages to ride to Arrowood to assist the clan chief in defending the border with Glenbarra. I'll be leaving in the morning."

Mara glanced around the table and said, "What about us? We're all mages. We can help."

"She's right," said Toz. "We're mages, and we've fought the Glenbarrans before."

Linden looked at each of her friends, her voice shaking with emotion. "That's exactly why I didn't want to ask you to come along. After all we've been through, I can't ask you again."

Mara folded her arms. "After all we've been through, how can we stay behind? I'm coming."

"I'm in." Toz nodded.

Remy laid his fork aside, his hazel eyes glittering in the firelight. "Me too."

"I want to help," said Jayna quietly.

Linden felt her eyes welling and used her napkin to quickly swipe at them. "You're amazing friends—and mages—and I have a feeling we're going to need all the help we can get. I'm glad you're coming, but I'm also scared." Her voice dropped to a whisper. "I don't want to face Mordahn again."

"You won't have to face him alone," said Toz, reaching across the table to squeeze her hand. Linden often reflected she'd chosen her oldest friend well. His blue eyes and dimples, coupled with a general air of mischief, masked his true nature. Toz had proven himself fearless in a fight more than once, and she never doubted his loyalty to her or to their cause—protecting Serving magic whatever the cost.

Linden nodded. "I know, and thanks. I wish we could defeat Fallow magic once and for all."

"Let's focus on defeating Mordahn and the Glenbarrans," said Mara.

"And that necromancer," said Jayna with a shiver.

CHAPTER 3

"ARE YOU READY, MY LIEGE?" ASKED REYNIER AS HE DREW abreast of Linden. The processional of horses and riders, lined up in two columns, started at the Liege's residence, a longhouse constructed of wood and stone, and stretched half a mile behind them. Reynier's horse, a chestnut stallion named Hoff, pawed the cobbled street to demonstrate his impatience.

Wearing the battledress of a Faymon warrior, silver chainmail vest layered over an aubergine tunic, his riding pants tucked into tall leather boots, Reynier's resemblance to her brother jolted Linden once again. She felt certain Matteo was still alive, hiding somewhere in occupied Valerra. Some days she wondered whether it might be false hope, fueled by her dreams that they'd meet again, and not by any true foreknowledge on her part.

Linden scanned the ranks of warriors behind them but didn't spot Stryker; she'd expected to see him before they set off, but everyone was too rushed trying to depart. Jayna, Toz, Mara, and Remy were within shouting distance, riding directly behind an elite group of twenty warriors assigned to protect the Liege and Elder during battle. Kal flew in circles above them, clicking his beak.

Ashir, Linden's horse—a feisty black stallion with a white diamond above his eyes—snorted, eager to be off. Linden leaned over to pat Ashir's neck. "Aye," she replied. "I'm ready. Although I wish we could have slipped away quietly, without all this fanfare." Linden nodded at the crowd of men, women, and children lining both sides of the road. She stopped herself from waving her arm in their direction, which she'd learned from recent experience could have multiple meanings. As the Liege, she could be signaling the crowd to cheer, trill, clap, or charge. She'd trained herself to keep her arms at her sides unless Reynier instructed her otherwise.

"The Faymon Liege never slips away quietly."

Linden nodded, sighing inwardly, resigned to trying to learn the many duties and rules she needed to know as the Faymon Liege. She wore the same battledress as every other Faymon warrior and mage riding with them. The only clue to her status as Liege was her bright gold chainmail, and the purple and gold ribbons woven through Ashir's mane.

Reynier raised his hand to signal the riders behind them, and then he and Linden lightly flicked their reins. The crowd surged around them, running alongside and ahead of the horses, waving banners and ribbons, and chanting a Faymon blessing.

As they passed through the stronghold gates flung wide open to accommodate the tidal wave of people and horses coursing through, Linden resisted the urge to spur Ashir into a full gallop. She longed to feel the wind whipping through her hair, to ride until she was breathless, to be free of all the restrictions that came with being the Liege of Faynwood. Linden remembered feeling confined when she

23

lived with her uncle, the Prime Minister of Valerra, and nearly laughed at the comparison to her life now. As the Liege, she lived under a spyglass, her every comment and gesture scrutinized in case she said or did something profound, her every need met even before she could articulate it. All of the attention left her feeling exhausted.

Jayna asked her recently whether she liked being the Liege, but Reynier had interrupted them before Linden could formulate an answer. She suspected Jayna knew the truth: that Linden longed for Valerra, and her scattered, missing family, and worried that Stryker couldn't adapt to her being the Faymon Liege.

"Linden? Linden?" called Reynier above the sound of horses' hooves hitting the ground, as the cheers and shouts from the crowd faded behind them.

Linden looked at Reynier and arched her eyebrows. "I can't believe my ears. You used my real name for a change."

"I couldn't get your attention any other way. You seemed lost in fay land."

Linden smiled, remembering how Nari used to say the same thing whenever Linden's concentration wandered during her grandmother's long magic-handling lessons. "Just lost in thought. I have a lot on my mind these days."

"Anything I can help you with?"

Linden appreciated the offer. She also knew only she could solve her problems—uneasiness over Stryker and general homesickness—and the fact that she yearned for a homeland currently under occupation didn't make it any easier. "I'll let you know. And thanks."

They rode in silence for a while, until Reynier asked, "How do you really feel about riding into Arrowood to help Chief Haydahn?"

"Strange. Unsettled. Even a bit scared."

"Understandable. Our two clans don't have the best reputation for getting along."

Linden snorted. "Our two clans started the last civil war." She certainly grasped the historic significance of the Faymon Liege and Elder—the recognized leaders of Faynwood, and members of the Tanglewood clan—offering military and magical assistance to the Arrowood clan. Fifty years ago Mordahn's father, the chief of Arrowood at the time, had killed Linden's great-grandmother, Liege Ayala, sparking a civil war that had spanned the decades since then. Mordahn's nephew, Haydahn, had been leading the Arrowood clan for the past fifteen years.

"And our clans ended the civil war too. Let's not forget that," said Reynier.

Linden wondered why Reynier worked so hard to support the Arrowood clan, encouraging her to do the same. She had mixed feelings toward them, with good reason, and wouldn't be overextending herself on their behalf. Yet she knew that as the Liege, she needed to give the Arrowood clan, and this clan chief, the benefit of the doubt. Pryl certainly supported the reunification of their clans, and Haydahn had been nothing less than conciliatory since her crowning. She could almost hear Nari telling her to "wait and see."

Although they traveled all day, stopping twice to water the horses, they were still within the boundaries of Tanglewood itself when they made camp for the night. They would pass through Riverwood territory before arriving at the Arrowood province in three days, where they would travel another day before reaching the clan chief's residence deep within the forested bluffs of Arrowood.

Linden insisted that she travel like everyone else, without the ceremonial tent and trappings of the Liege.

Reynier reminded her, however, the Liege's tent served as the traveling capital of the Faymon people whenever she was outside of Eloway. She watched as four serving men unpacked the leather tent and supporting equipment, consisting of two wooden center poles, four corner poles, stakes, and ropes. The men set up the tent, large enough to accommodate twenty people for meetings and meals, in less than a quarter of an hour. Five banners, one for each clan, flapped in the breeze, with the Tanglewood banner flying from the top of the tent, and each of the others fluttering from the four corners. The serving men then added a number of finishing touches to the tent's interior, carting in furniture, wall hangings, and rugs to complete Linden's traveling home. She felt embarrassed that so much effort went into her tent, but Reynier wouldn't consider doing anything less than was customary.

Stryker wandered over and stood next to her. Bowing slightly, he said, "Evening, my Liege. Would you care to go for a stroll in those woods behind the campsite?"

Linden bit her bottom lip. She yearned for some private time with Stryker, and yet she knew she couldn't, or shouldn't, slip away into the woods without the elite escort accompanying them. Reynier would probably mount a search party, and Stryker would become even more moody and frustrated. Touching his arm lightly, she said, "Not now, I'm afraid. I've got to meet with Reynier in a little while. Come join us for dinner."

Stryker wrenched his arm away. "'Come join us for dinner,'" he mimicked, shaking his head. "Let me know when you're free, for real. When you can stop being the Liege for a while and just be Linden." He stalked away toward the woods.

"Stryker!" Linden called out, following him to the edge of the woods, but he ignored her.

"Let him go; he needs to blow off some steam," said Jayna, joining Linden. They both watched as Stryker disappeared into the woods.

"I don't understand why he's been so moody lately."

"You really don't?"

Linden squinted at the tall oak trees rimming the woods and thought about Jayna's question. "Stryker doesn't like that I'm the Faymon Liege. He protests when we're interrupted, which happens frequently, and he complains every time my 'official duties' interfere with his plans. He wants to turn back the clock."

"What do you want?"

Linden shook her head. "Sometimes I dream I'm back home, living with my family before the war, and then I wake up and remember where I am and all that's happened. I'm here, we're all here, for a reason, to protect Serving magic at all costs."

"At all costs?"

"Anything less and—"

"—and Faynwood goes the way of Valerra." Jayna had a habit of finishing Linden's sentences.

Knitting her brows together, Linden said, "Stryker knows this as well as anyone, and yet he's behaving childishly, as if our relationship is more important than what we're trying to do."

Jayna tilted her head and looked at Linden. "It's a big adjustment for him. When he left for the front, you were still in school. Now you're the Liege of Faynwood."

"It's a big adjustment for me too. I don't think he quite grasps that or is even trying to understand."

Jayna's eyes clouded over. "I know," she said softly. "But

I'm more worried about you. All this responsibility came on too quickly. You had so little time to prepare."

Linden put her arm around her best friend. "Thanks for worrying about me. I think you're the only one who does, but I'm starting to adjust."

"So am I," said Jayna, who hastened to add, "But I still think about him often, and hope that he's safe."

Linden knew she was referring to Matteo; Jayna and Matteo had started dating shortly before the war with Glenbarra broke out. "I know, so do I."

Linden looped her arm through Jayna's and walked slowly back toward their tents. "I've been thinking a lot lately, better late than never, I guess. I realize now that Nari, and even my father and mother, had been preparing me for years. I just didn't realize it at the time."

"They may have been preparing you, but you weren't a very cooperative student," said Jayna. They both laughed as Jayna recounted some of Linden's most impressive failures. "Remember when your spell backfired, and you pelted our classroom with enough fresh fruit to fill the market? You even managed to bonk Mara a few times."

Linden chuckled. "Mara didn't speak to me for a week afterward."

"It's good to hear you laughing, my Liege," said Reynier, joining the two of them.

Jayna glanced at Reynier, compressing her full lips. "I didn't think you cared whether Linden laughed or cried."

Reynier's eyebrows shot up as Linden said hastily, "Jayna, that's not fair. Reynier's been incredibly good to me, and you know it."

Reynier bowed. "Mage Jayna, I apologize if I've offended you in any way."

"I think I'd better be going now," Jayna said to Linden.

Nodding curtly at Reynier, she walked briskly toward the tent she shared with Mara.

Linden turned to Reynier. "I'm sorry. Jayna is the kindest person I know. She never has a cross word for anyone."

"I'm sure it's my fault. I must have done something to offend her."

Linden started to object, but Reynier seemed eager to change the subject. She half-listened as he discussed the latest reports from the Faymon scouts. Linden tried to work out what had upset Jayna, but she gave up when one of the serving women informed her dinner would be served soon.

Linden hurried toward her tent to change out of her aubergine tunic and riding pants. Tapestries depicting various scenes from Faynwood's history adorned the walls, and a long, low wooden table, surrounded by silken pillows, occupied the public side of the tent. A filmy curtain, strung across the center of the tent, divided the space in half. Linden's private quarters, accessible through a slit in the curtain, contained a portable bed carved from Tanglewood's famous red oaks, a chest filled with her clothes, and a basket seat suspended from one of the tent poles.

One of the servants brought her an urn of water and a linen towel, which Linden used to clean off the layers of dust she'd acquired from a full day of riding. She longed for a bath, but that would have to wait until they camped closer to a water source tomorrow. Garlan, her lady's maid, helped her into a silvery blue split-skirt, ingeniously disguised as a gown, which allowed her the freedom of movement required to ride Ashir. In Faynwood, women's attire needed to accommodate horseback riding; while farmers used wagons to cart their produce to market, the uneven terrain and thick forests broke too many axles. No one, not even a clan chief, bothered to invest in a fancy horse-drawn carriage. Garlan brushed out Linden's black-and-blue hair and draped a long silver scarf over her left shoulder to complete the outfit.

Linden scooped up *Timely Spells*, a gift from her grandmother when she turned sixteen, from the top of her chest. The book was written in ancient fay hieroglyphs, which no one, except maybe Pryl, could read anymore. But the book decided which set of spells to reveal, and when, and then translated them for the current owner. Curling up in her basket seat and using one foot to push herself into a gentle rocking motion, Linden paged through the book, searching for any new or modified spells. No new spells revealed themselves since she last read the book, so she reviewed the familiar spells to ensure she could recall every line of every incantation. She'd learned from experience the spells in her book could save lives—her own and others—and she was diligent about studying it.

Linden heard Garlan speaking softly with someone in the outer chamber and hopped off her seat to take a look. Suppressing a smile, she watched as Garlan and Kal had a "chat," Garlan reminding the miniature griffin he had to look out for her mistress, and Kal clicking his beak to acknowledge he understood. Linden pulled back the curtain and bent down to scratch Kal behind the ears. "You're going to have to be on your best behavior tonight, and every night from here on out. We'll have important guests joining us for dinner." Kal ducked his head inside one of his wings, and Linden and Garlan both laughed at him.

Reynier arrived first to help Linden with the protocols she needed to know as the Liege. Her role at the official dinners seemed pretty easy, she decided. Reynier explained that she should be seated before everyone else, as the Liege greets all the guests at the same time, after they arrived and were sitting at the table. Once the war planning began in earnest, she would participate just like everyone else, but she had to take care that she didn't appear to be commanding a particular course of action.

"In other words, I should listen more than I speak?" Linden summarized Reynier's lesson in protocol.

When he nodded, Linden chuckled. "That's the same advice my mother used to give me as a child, before one of her dinner parties."

"It is good advice for any leader anywhere," said Reynier with a smile.

Linden sat cross-legged on a gold pillow at one end of the table, Kal curled up next to her, and Reynier sat opposite her. Ambassadors from each of the clans gathered around the table, joined by Mara, Toz, Jayna, and Remy. The clan chiefs, traveling from their home bases with their armies, would be meeting them later in Arrowood.

Although Stryker declined the dinner invitation, Sergeant Desi, from Stryker's old Royal Marine unit, arrived at the tent and sat down. Linden reasoned the Faymons could learn a lot about Glenbarran military tactics from Valerran marines who'd survived the war, and Reynier agreed. They could also learn from her and her friends, all of whom had fought the Glenbarrans—first with their magic and then with their swords—during the siege of Bellaryss, Valerra's capital, now under Glenbarran rule.

Servants carried platters of food, pitchers of sweet tea, and jugs of wine into the tent. After everyone had been served, they withdrew to allow for private conversation. Linden sipped her tea, listening to the various discussions around her. Sergeant Desi described an encounter with a Glenbarran assassin early in the Valerran war. The assassin had been injured in a swordfight, and rather than allow himself to be captured, used magic to self-immolate. By the time Desi had reached him, nothing was left of the man but black sooty ashes.

The ambassador from the Shorewood clan shook her head. "That's very dark magic indeed."

Reynier said, "And yet it pales in comparison to the news from Pryl's scout."

"Necromancy," spat out Ridgewood's ambassador. "Impossible."

"Is it really so impossible?" asked Arrowood's representative. "Something's happening in Glenbarra that smacks of Fallow sorcery and secret spells, long dormant."

"But why?" asked the clansman from Riverwood. "We know Serving magic and Fallow magic have always been at odds, but why attack Valerra and Faynwood? And why now?"

Reynier waved his hand. "Why now? Think about it. Our Liege, though young, is a revelator, both master mage and master seer, a rare combination not seen in Faynwood since Liege Ayala, may she rest in love and peace."

"May she rest in love and peace," echoed everyone around the table. Linden had quickly learned this was the standard response among Faymons when referring to any honored person who was deceased.

Reynier continued. "The Glenbarrans want to stop us now, before Liege Linden comes into the fullness of her power."

"And while we're still trying to figure out how to govern ourselves again after fifty years of civil war," added the Arrowood ambassador.

"That explains their interest in attacking Faynwood. But the war with Valerra started last year, before anyone knew Linden would be your Liege," said Toz, frowning.

"Mordahn knew her bloodline," said Reynier. "He must have told King Roi. The Glenbarran leadership knew exactly what they were doing."

"And there were the prophecies," Remy reminded Toz. "Your father always believed something was different about Linden."

Toz's face clouded, his eyes turning an icy blue. "My father studied the ancient scrolls and talked about fay prophecies to anyone who'd listen. Let's hope his foolish talk never endangered Linden."

Reynier arched an eyebrow. "I believe we've established that Linden's lineage, as Liege Ayala's great-granddaughter, was not so secret as we'd believed."

Linden's head started to throb. As she rubbed her temples, she heard garbled screams and whines, clanking chains, and hobnailed boots hitting hard ground. Recognizing she was in the midst of a vision, Linden slowed her breathing, trying to concentrate. Her hands bound, she found herself in a darkened room, not unlike the dungeon at the palace in Bellaryss, but not the same. Someone was lying down across from her, probably a man by the size of him, but she couldn't see clearly in the gloom. She sensed fear in that room, seeping from the walls, surrounding both of them.

Linden told herself the vision could be foresight, a prediction of something to come, or a shadow from the past, and not necessarily her past. She blinked and glanced around the table. No one seemed to notice she'd been in the midst of a vision, no one except for Reynier, who'd been watching her, his eyebrows drawn together.

"What is it, my Liege?"

"I'm not sure." After reminding everyone the vision might not mean anything at all, Linden described what she'd seen and heard.

Mara asked, "Could it be a memory from our time in the dungeon in Bellaryss?" During the chaos following the queen's evacuation from Valerra, Linden and her friends had been tossed into the palace dungeon by the queen's crazy half-brother.

Linden shook her head. "No, this felt different, more frightening somehow, and the screaming"—she winced— "it sounded like someone being tortured."

Shivering, Jayna said, "Let's hope this isn't foresight, and that none of us will see this come to pass."

The conversation around the table resumed. Linden barely listened, convinced she'd seen an image from her future—and she couldn't run fast enough or far enough to escape its arrival.

CHAPTER 4

THE WEATHER COOPERATED. COOL DAYS WITH OVERCAST SKIES helped the horses and their riders make good time. Linden, Reynier, and those traveling with them from Eloway arrived at the stronghold of Arrowood early in the afternoon of the sixth day. While they were still some distance away, the Tanglewood guards blew their ram's horns, signaling the arrival of the Liege and Elder of Faynwood.

Chief Haydahn and twenty of his elite warriors rode out to greet them. "Well met, Liege Linden and Elder Reynier! Welcome to Arrowood," said Haydahn, attired in the ceremonial robes of a clan chief, his outer robe a tapestry of green, brown, and gold, layered over a darker green tunic and trousers. Linden appreciated the subtle reminder that he needn't dress for battle against the Tanglewood clan any longer. Although the chief's brown-and-blue hair and beard were heavily salted with gray, he held himself as erect in the saddle as any twenty-year-old.

"Well met, Chief Haydahn," said Linden.

Reynier added, "Well met indeed. Thank you for the warm welcome."

"The other clan chiefs and their warriors have been arriving over the past few days, Ridgewood only this morning. They are setting up their campsites. Let's get you settled. The entire stronghold has prepared a feast for this evening to commemorate the occasion—the arrival of our Liege in Arrowood for the first time in over fifty years," said Haydahn.

Of course it's the first time in fifty years, thought Linden. *My great-grandmother, the last Liege, was murdered in Arrowood by your uncle!*

The clan chief led them through the wooden gate separating the stronghold from the forests of Arrowood. Men and women, many clutching babies in their arms, lined the cobbled main road, clapping and waving as Linden passed them. Children darted in and out of the crowd, waving flags of green and brown, Arrowood's colors. Haydahn and a handful of guards stuck to the main road, Linden and Reynier plodding along behind them on their horses. The remainder of Haydahn's mounted patrol led the Tanglewood contingent to a clearing, where they would set up camp. Kal accompanied Garlan and the rest of the Tanglewood clan to the campsite.

"Should I wave back at the crowd?" she asked Reynier, not sure how to acknowledge the clan of Arrowood. Ever since she'd stepped onto the banks of Shorewood, the easternmost province of Faynwood, two months earlier, uncertainty had accompanied nearly every new encounter for Linden.

Smiling, Reynier nodded at the crowd. "The Liege does not wave when entering a stronghold. Smile and nod, just as I'm doing." Linden followed suit, knowing if she asked Reynier "why" the Liege doesn't wave when entering a stronghold, he'd either launch into a long historical explanation or tell her that it's simply not done. It didn't matter to her either way. Her goals were basic: not embarrass herself too badly, and not cause another civil war by inadvertently insulting one of the clan chiefs, which she'd nearly done during her first week as Liege.

Haydahn stopped in front of a longhouse, the largest in the complex, and invited Linden and Reynier to dismount. Servants ran forward to take their horses to the stable yard. Members of the chief's household stood in front of the longhouse, waiting to greet the Faymon Liege and Elder. Linden spent time visiting with Haydahn's wife and two daughters: Carissa, age sixteen, and Gisela, a young girl of seven. After making the introductions, he added, "My son, Corbahn, is expected soon. He rides from the border."

A maidservant showed Linden to a guest room, her saddlebags already stowed next to a dresser. Two other servants carried urns of water on their backs into the room, filling a copper tub in one corner. Opposite the tub sat a bed, stacked high with feather mattresses and pillows, an open invitation to a nap. A simple white robe had been left on the bed for her to wear while in the privacy of the room. But first, Linden wanted to wash off the layers of dust from her days of travel; she'd bathed once in a pond during the trip, but otherwise, she'd managed to take only quick sponge baths when they stopped each night.

When the tub was full, the servants withdrew from the room. Linden picked up a linen towel and piece of soap, lightly scented with elderflower, and climbed into the tub with a sigh. Every muscle ached from a week in the saddle. Linden lathered the soap over her arms, legs, and torso, pausing to run her fingers over the deep scar in her side, where Mordahn's dagger had pierced all the way through to her lung. Although Linden had recovered from her physical injuries, she still carried the scars and at times, the nightmares, from her last battle with Mordahn. After her bath and a short nap, one of the maidservants helped Linden change into a purple split-skirt gown, decorated with gold embellishments. The maidservant draped a lavender shawl trimmed in gold tassels around Linden's shoulders and brushed out her slightly damp hair, which fell in layers down her back.

Linden fingered the locket Stryker had given her and placed it firmly inside the neck of her gown. When he had first gifted her the necklace, she'd proudly worn it on the outside of her clothing. But lately, she'd taken to tucking it inside whatever outfit she was wearing, whether a simple summer shift, a split-skirt gown, or her battledress. Linden reasoned she was keeping the locket safe from damage. Stryker had asked her once where she kept the necklace, and when she'd pulled it out of the folds of her gown, he'd been satisfied.

Linden closed the door to the guest room. Walking toward the receiving room in the front of the house, she heard raised voices in the passageway. She hesitated, wondering whether to continue walking and interrupt them, or retrace her steps back to her room.

"I'm in no mood to play nice with our little Liege," grumbled a man, his deep voice unfamiliar to Linden.

"Keep your voice down," hissed Haydahn. "Liege Linden is our guest."

"When I think of the losses we've suffered at the hands of her clan, I don't think I can be civil." Linden knew she shouldn't eavesdrop but decided she couldn't afford not to hear what they were saying about her and her clan. She crept closer to the voices.

"They've suffered just as many losses at our hands, as

you well know. The Elder lost his pregnant wife in one of the raids led by your brother," replied Haydahn.

"Who died one week later, felled by a Tanglewood archer," snapped the man. Linden knew about the surprise attack that took Reynier's wife a few years earlier. Reynier never discussed it, but there were moments when his whole demeanor changed, when sadness wrapped itself around him like a shroud.

"You know as well as I do, without Tanglewood and the other clans to help us, we'll lose Arrowood." Linden heard the weariness in Haydahn's voice, which brought to mind her Uncle Alban, the prime minister of Valerra during the war with Glenbarra. His hair had turned silver in a matter of weeks.

The other man sighed. "If there were any other way..."

"There isn't, and you know it," said Haydahn. "More than a tenth of our clan has fallen away, and we risk losing more without outside help."

What's happened to ten percent of their clan? wondered Linden.

The man grunted. "Fine. I'll go make myself presentable."

"More than presentable," said Haydahn. His voice sounded farther away, closer to the receiving room now.

"Don't worry," the man called after him, "I'll be positively charming to the little Liege."

How dare he speak about me—about anyone—this way? Clutching the folds of her gown, Linden walked briskly down the passageway, replaying his words in her head. She rounded the corner, colliding with a large, muscular man in full battledress, his chainmail vest and riding boots grimy from travel. He held himself erect, towering a foot above her. Refusing to make eye contact with him, she caught a glimpse of light brown-and-blue hair and beard, both in need of a trim. Staring at his broad chest, she waited for him to move out of her way.

"Excuse me," he said. "Are you alright?"

Linden recognized his voice; definitely the same man who'd been speaking so rudely about her a moment earlier. She folded her arms. "I don't believe you're presentable at the moment. And I'm certainly not charmed."

"Oh no," the man groaned, running a calloused hand through his unruly hair. "I'm sorry about that. I'm in a foul mood, not fit for polite company."

Linden gave him a half-shrug. "I gathered that." The man still hadn't moved out of her way. Linden was not about to walk around him. Reynier had told her often enough that the Liege never moved aside for someone else. She must wait for others to cede to her. It had sounded like a silly rule, until now. "Would you step aside."

Instead of moving out of her path, the man took two steps back and dropped to his knees in front of her, completely blocking her way. He bowed forward from the waist, exposing the back of his head to Linden, a sign of his fealty. "I pledge my life, my home, and my mage's honor to my Liege, Linden Arlyss of Tanglewood and Valerra. Please accept my deepest apology as well."

Linden had no choice but to follow the Faymon protocols. "I accept your sworn allegiance, um...." She needed the man's name to complete her portion of the allegiance pledge.

Still kneeling, he supplied his name. "Commander Corbahn Erewin, at your service."

"I accept your sworn allegiance, Commander Corbahn Erewin of Arrowood. In return, I pledge my loyalty to you, your clan, and all of Faynwood, to fays and Faymons, to woodlands, streams, and all creatures therein."

"What about my apology?" asked Corbahn, who leaned back but continued to kneel on the floor. The man had a smear of dried mud on one cheek and a cut over his eye that needed looking after. "You need to accept my apology. Please."

Linden was about to object, until he added "please." Nodding curtly, she said, "I accept your apology, Commander."

Corbahn rose to his feet. His eyes, the color of the Pale Sea in summer, bore into hers, searching for something, sincerity perhaps, or integrity. She held his gaze. Nodding, he said, "Thank you, my Liege. And now if you'll excuse me, I'll go make myself presentable."

"And charming?" asked Linden, unwilling to let him off the hook.

Corbahn arched an eyebrow. "As charming as a hibernating bear awakened from his slumber."

"That sounds about right, based on our short acquaintance."

Grinning, Corbahn stepped aside and bowed. "It's been a pleasure, my Liege. One I look forward to repeating."

Linden had no intention of paying Corbahn Erewin a similar compliment. She passed by him without replying.

LINDEN FOUND Reynier and Haydahn in the receiving room, a large, open space with long benches lining the perimeter, and tapestries depicting scenes from Arrowood's history hanging on the walls. While they waited for Corbahn to join them, Haydahn and Reynier discussed news from the other clans, mentioning people and places unfamiliar to Linden. She found her mind wandering back to her meeting with the clan chief's son. Linden wasn't sure what irked her more, the man's rude comments when he didn't know she was listening, or his allegiance pledge that essentially required her to accept him and his apology.

Corbahn joined them forty minutes later, considerably more respectable looking. Linden reflected that if his personality underwent the same transformation as his physical appearance, he might even be considered attractive. His hair, still damp from his bath, grazed the top of his shoulders, longer than customary among the Tanglewood clansmen. Like his father, Corbahn wore a ceremonial robe in rich shades of green and brown, draped over a darker brown tunic and trousers. Despite the loss of his chainmail and battledress, his bearing was still that of a leader and commander, a man more comfortable on the battlefield than in a longhouse.

Haydahn invited them to sit on cushions scattered around a low, square table in the center of the room. Servants plied them with refreshments, honeyed wine with fresh mint, mushrooms harvested from the forests of Arrowood and stuffed with breadcrumbs and minced onion, and slender sandwiches filled with jams, cheeses, tomatoes, and thinly sliced meats.

After they'd had their fill, the servants withdrew. Haydahn turned to his son. "What news from the border?"

Corbahn stroked his beard, neatly trimmed since Linden's encounter with him. Taking a sip of wine, he put his glass down on the table in front of them. "It's not good. Grihms and Glenbarran troopers are openly amassing along our border. We've suffered a few midnight raids, mostly a lot of saber-rattling and growling, but no loss of life as yet. They clearly want to provoke an attack."

"What if we don't attack them and demonstrate our strength through defensive maneuvers only?" asked Reynier.

"I fear they'll overrun our borders either way," said Corbahn. Turning to Linden, he asked, "Did they use similar tactics with Valerra?"

Linden nodded. "It sounds like the same pattern. The Glenbarrans began with quick border raids to unsettle us and progressed to a full-on invasion when they were ready." She added, "And their magic overwhelmed our best warrior-mages."

Haydahn shook his head. "Is there no way to broker a peace with them?"

Corbahn looked at his father. "With a crazy king, his Fallow sorcerers, and our dear Uncle Mordahn, raised from the dead? What sort of terms could we possibly negotiate?" Everyone in Faynwood knew the story of Mordahn's downhill slide, from Serving mage to Fallow sorcerer, from loyal Arrowood clansman to Glenbarran military leader, bent on destroying Serving magic, even if it meant attacking his own clan. Linden agreed with Corbahn; negotiating with the likes of Mordahn would be a waste of time.

Haydahn said, "I've been hoping Pryl might be overstating the situation. He's been warning us about the rise of Fallow magic for a long time, and the dangers of allowing it to flow freely in Glenbarra, on the other side of our border."

Linden looked at Corbahn and Haydahn, recalling their earlier conversation. "Has a tenth of your clan already fallen away from Serving magic and now follow the Fallow ways?"

As Haydahn stammered, Corbahn turned to his father.

"The Liege overheard us conversing in the passageway this afternoon."

Haydahn's face turned red. He sputtered, "My Liege, I must apologize for..."

Linden held up her hand. "There is no need. The commander has apologized to me." Reynier's eyebrows rose, curiosity evident on his face. Yet Linden knew he was savvy enough to wait until a private moment to ask her about Corbahn and the need for an apology. Linden continued, "If Fallow magic has a strong foothold in Arrowood, that places all of us, fays and Faymons alike, in danger."

Haydahn expelled a puff of air. "It's true. Although the Fallow magic we're confronting today has its roots fifty years ago, well before Mordahn deserted us for Glenbarra."

Reynier leaned forward, frowning. "What are you saying? And why is this the first time I'm hearing of it?"

Haydahn shrugged. "We've been fighting with each other ever since. We haven't had the opportunity to tell you the truth of what really happened. Pryl knew, of course, which was why he pushed us so hard toward reconciliation when our new Liege"—he bowed toward Linden—"arrived in Faynwood."

Corbahn picked up the thread of the story. "Fifty years ago, Liege Ayala began to suspect something was amiss here. She rode with her husband to Arrowood to investigate complaints of Fallow spells, of clansmen disappearing under mysterious circumstances. And you know the rest. The Arrowood clan chief killed them—murdered them both —in an effort to hide the truth. He'd become a master mage, a genius in fact, but of Fallow magic. He's the one who recovered the old scrolls, long buried in the caves along the Windrun River, revealing the darkest secrets of the Fallow ways."

Reynier guessed the rest. "And Mordahn, his son, eventually followed in his father's footsteps. I suppose he brought those old scrolls to Glenbarra?"

Corbahn nodded. "He carried those everywhere with him. He discovered many Fallow mages in Glenbarra, eager to study and practice the dark arts, particularly necromancy."

Haydahn ran a hand through his hair. "Mordahn has ensured he would rise again, more determined than ever to destroy every one of us."

"Every one of us who has sworn to uphold Serving magic," said Linden. "His message is clear: either convert to the Fallow ways or suffer the consequences."

CHAPTER 5

THE FOUR LEADERS DECIDED THEY'D KEEP QUIET ABOUT THE BAD news from the border until after the feast and the upcoming magic trials, a three-day celebration of unification under their new Liege. If war was inevitable, they reasoned, then the five clans needed to bond together more tightly than ever.

Servants brought their horses around to the front of the longhouse. Haydahn and Reynier mounted first, followed by their respective guards. Corbahn and Linden rode behind them, taking a circuitous route to the location of the feast, the same clearing where each of the clans had set up their camp. Huge trees hugged the rim of the clearing, a vast basin-like opening in the middle of Arrowood. Colorful tents and campfires dotted the basin, extending as far as Linden could see. The intoxicating aroma of roasting lamb, venison, and whitefish caught in nearby streams, mixed with root vegetables and spices, scented the air around them.

"It's so beautiful here," she said, "and peaceful." The

forests of Arrowood held the oldest trees in Faynwood, some over two thousand years old.

Corbahn narrowed his eyes. "Peaceful for now. But lately, my sleep's been disturbed by visions of war, unspeakable images that I can't repeat once I wake."

"Can't repeat, or won't?" Linden asked, thinking of Pawllah's recent note, complaining of poor sleep and bad dreams.

"I won't. It's not right to burden anyone else with my nightmares. Besides, they've lifted since leaving the border." Corbahn's voice dropped. "I've known nothing but warfare my entire life. I've had my courage tested many, many times. But I'll tell you this much: we'll be facing an avalanche of Fallowness when the war with Glenbarra begins. And for the first time since I was a boy of thirteen, heading into my first battle, I'm fearful."

Her scalp tingling, Linden shuddered. "Then we must stand firm, ensure nothing and no one separates clan from clan again."

"Aye, my Liege. It's the only way we'll survive, if we survive at all."

A loud whoop went up around them, followed by wave after wave of cheering that echoed from one end of the clearing to the other. Engrossed in her conversation with Corbahn, Linden didn't realize they'd emerged from the trees and stood at the edge of the field, visible to all. Reynier called out to her, "Now would be a good time to wave, my Liege!"

Linden waved to the clans spread out on the plain below. Another round of cheers reverberated across the camps. Linden could feel Corbahn's eyes on her. "What is it?" she asked him.

"You look so serious! Aren't you enjoying all this adoration and attention, my Liege?" Corbahn said "my Liege" with particular emphasis, as if to remind her, or himself, who she was.

Linden gathered her reins to follow Reynier and the others down the rocky ridge into the field below. "Just the opposite; it exhausts me. I never asked to be the Liege of Faynwood. But I am. And I will do my duty."

Corbahn knit his brows together, seeming to be lost in thought. His horse followed Ashir down the ridge, single file, and the four descended onto the plain in silence, along with their elite guards. When they reached level ground, servants ran over to take their horses from them. Clansmen nearby blew on ram's horns to announce their arrival, and then others standing farther away took up the horn-blowing, until the entire basin reverberated with sound.

The chiefs from the three other clans, along with their commanders and ambassadors, lined up to greet Linden, Reynier, Haydahn, and Corbahn. Pryl and several members of the fay council emerged from their traveling mists to join the clans in the welcoming feast. Representatives from Linden's own Tanglewood clan bowed to her as well, part of the receiving line. Linden's head swirled, trying to keep everyone straight, even though Reynier had helped her memorize names, ranks, and clans the previous week.

The throng swept Linden and Corbahn away to the center of the clearing, where a number of campfires burned. Pots of food, the source of the delicious scents she'd detected while still in the woods, sat over the flames, stirred by menservants and maidservants. Linden sat on a floor cushion at one end of a long, low table, with Corbahn and a commander from the Riverwood clan sitting on either side of her. Haydahn, Reynier, and Pryl sat opposite them. After everyone found a seat, Haydahn raised his goblet of mulled wine in a toast. "To our Liege, Linden Arlyss of Tanglewood, to Fay Chief Pryl Orion and the fay council members, and to the five Faymon clans of Faynwood, welcome to the forests and bluffs of Arrowood! May we all, as one united people, uphold and preserve Serving magic, to the benefit of all creatures, lands, and generations." Loud cheering and trilling reverberated around the field, as everyone sipped from their mugs to mark the historic occasion.

Corbahn and the other commander were distantly related through marriage. They carried on a lively conversation about people Linden didn't know, giving her the opportunity to observe and recharge, exactly what she needed. Kal flew in lazy circles overhead. Linden knew he preferred quieter evenings, where he could curl up near her feet and allow her to scratch behind his ears occasionally. He'd be keeping a safe distance from the crowd during the next few days.

During a lull in conversation with the Riverwood commander, Corbahn turned to Linden and asked, "Can I get you anything, my Liege? Something more to drink perhaps?"

"No, thank you. I have what I need."

Corbahn gave Linden an appraising look. "Aye, I believe you do."

Linden tilted her head, wondering whether Corbahn had just complimented her. "Thank you. I think?"

Corbahn narrowed his sea-green eyes and took a sip of wine before responding. "You're not what I expected."

"And I suppose that's a good thing?"

Nodding, Corbahn said, "A definite improvement over my extremely low expectations."

"You say the nicest things," said Linden with a shake of her head. "A true diplomat if I ever met one."

Corbahn grinned. Linden thought he ought to grin more often; he looked a lot less fierce, almost handsome. "I compared myself to a bear earlier today. I'm a warrior, not a diplomat," he said, leaning closer. "In fact, I can almost guarantee my father is watching us right now, looking for any signs that I've offended you. Do me a favor and smile at something I just said. Please?"

Linden glanced down the table and saw Haydahn watching their exchange, his brow furrowed. She gave Corbahn a sympathetic smile. Linden understood what it was like to be under constant scrutiny, to be continuously corrected "for your own good."

She detected a movement out of the corner of her eye and sensed someone else watching her, beyond the flames of the campfire. The tall shadow moved again, this time receding from the crowd. She had no idea how long Stryker had been standing there. Linden pulled her shawl more closely around her shoulders, feeling exposed somehow, as if she'd done something wrong by smiling at Corbahn. She and Stryker would have to sit down and talk things out, discuss his reactions or overreactions to the many official duties that came with her role.

After hearing another speech about the importance of Faynwood unity, this time from Reynier, the crowd slowly began dispersing. The clan chiefs and their entourage returned to their respective camps, where the clan celebrations would continue, with dancing and storytelling well into the night.

Reynier escorted Linden back to the Tanglewood campsite. He took his time, and Linden realized Reynier was probably just as tired as she was. In the distance, they heard musicians entertaining their clan with old Tanglewood melodies. "You managed to charm Chief Haydahn and Commander Corbahn today, a feat I'd have thought impossible a few months ago. Well done, my Liege."

Linden knew Reynier meant well, but she cringed, nonetheless. "I hope you realize I wasn't performing today or acting any differently than I would with anyone else I'd just met. I don't have an on-off switch."

Reynier hastened to explain. "Please don't misunderstand me. They were charmed precisely because you're genuine." He stared at something off to the side, behind Linden's shoulder. When she started to swivel around to take a look, he lowered his voice. "Don't turn around. But we're being followed."

"Who?" Linden asked, but she already knew the answer.

"Your fiancé." Reynier sighed. "I've tried giving him the benefit of the doubt, but—"

"I'll talk to him, help him understand," said Linden, wondering how she could help Stryker understand, when all he wanted was to return to the way things used to be, before the war with Glenbarra, before she became the Liege of Faynwood.

"He's not even trying to acclimate to our ways."

In the past, whenever Reynier would make a remark like that, Linden would jump to Stryker's defense. She'd run out of excuses for his poor behavior. "I'll talk to him," she repeated.

"I hope he doesn't do something foolish in the meantime."

Linden hoped so too.

❧

L INDEN SAT in the basket seat inside her tent and picked up *Timely Spells*. Running her hand over the fay hieroglyphs decorating the book's tooled-leather cover, she recalled her excitement the first time she'd opened the spell book on her sixteenth birthday. Her excitement had quickly dissipated when she discovered half of the yellowed vellum pages were blank. Her grandmother had explained that Linden needed to focus her mind and her magic on those pages containing squiggles of fay symbols. Linden had concentrated on the first page with any sort of writing, beads of sweat breaking out on her brow. Gradually, the squiggles had reformed themselves into recognizable words, in an oversized font, more appropriate for a children's picture book. When she'd turned the spell book around to show Nari, her grandmother had chuckled. "*Timely Spells* is smart enough to know you need to begin at the beginning. There are no shortcuts when it comes to learning your magic, lass. Take it slow and steady, and over time the book will reveal much more to you."

Smiling at the memory, Linden reflected on how far she'd come—physically, emotionally, and most of all, magically—in the nearly two years since she'd received the spell book. She flipped through the book, each thick vellum page covered with detailed instructions in small, adult-size font. She reviewed all the spells she already knew by heart: spells for fire-building and water-dousing, protection and provocation, binding and unbinding, truth-telling and prevaricating, defense and offense, housekeeping and healing, immutability and shapeshifting. Kal slept on a cushion beside her, snuffling occasionally in his sleep.

Her index finger stopped moving down the page. A new shapeshifting spell, for master mages only, had revealed itself. The spell transformed one animate object into another animate object. Linden knew how to shapeshift inanimate objects, and she'd even shifted a sword into a snake once, but shifting one living creature into another seemed unethical to her. She read the fine print and learned this spell could only be used under extreme circumstances, such as to save a life. She carefully studied the instructions, memorizing every step in the complex incantation.

"Linden, may I come in?" Stryker called softly through the entrance to her tent. Linden glanced down at her night-dress and ran a hand through her hair. Stryker wouldn't dare come this late to her quarters back in Eloway; Garlan or another of her servants would inform him she'd retired for the evening. At first, she'd resented their intrusiveness, but over time, she'd begun to appreciate how they protected her privacy. She had no one to intercede for her that night. She'd sent Garlan and the others away to enjoy the music around the campfire.

"It's late," she said.

"I know, but I miss you. Besides, Reynier is talking to Jayna about something, so we'll have some alone time." Linden made a mental note to ask Jayna about her conversation with Reynier and to find out why her friend seemed annoyed lately whenever he was around.

"Give me a few minutes to change." Linden slipped off her nightdress and pulled on an ankle-length chambray summer shift. Grabbing a dark blue shawl to drape around her shoulders, she emerged from behind her privacy curtain to find Stryker already inside her tent, lounging on a floor cushion. He smelled strongly of spirits. Despite their betrothal, he had no right to enter her tent uninvited. He should have waited for her outside. For the first time since she'd known Stryker, she found herself uneasy in his presence.

Before Linden could say anything, he sprang up from the cushion and in two strides had drawn her into his arms. She put her palm on his chest and pushed him away. "No," she said.

Stryker stepped back, startled. "What's wrong?"

"You've been drinking, and you definitely shouldn't be here." She walked over to the entrance of her tent. "You need to leave, now."

"Oh come on, Linden, don't be like this." He reached for her again, but she slipped out of his arms and walked outside. Stryker stumbled outside behind her and hissed, "I knew it."

Linden drew the shawl around herself and took a few steps away from the tent. She didn't want to attract attention to herself and Stryker, but she didn't want to be alone with him either, not in his current state. The musicians still played, a bit frenetically now, as couples, children, and young women danced around the campfire. "Please go."

Stryker continued as if he hadn't heard her. "I knew Reynier would find a way to come between us. He's always hated me. He wants you to marry into another clan, preferably Arrowood, and what better candidate than Commander Erewin, who didn't leave your side all evening."

Linden's temper flared. She knew she shouldn't let him bait her, but he'd pushed her too far. "This has nothing to do with Corbahn or Reynier, or Faymon politics for that matter. This has to do with you."

Stryker's eyes flashed darkly, reflecting the flames of the campfire in each orb. He took a step toward her, his voice guttural. "What about me?"

A blur of wings, fur, and beak streaked out of the tent, barreling into Stryker's chest. Stryker lost his balance and toppled backward onto the ground, Kal standing on top of his chest, clicking his beak angrily. Stryker uttered an incantation in another tongue. As a "speaker," Stryker could call on any animal by command. Linden had only heard him casting this kind of spell a few times, and it always unsettled her. Dozens of bats swooped from the trees above, heading straight for the three of them.

Linden's first instinct was to run, but she was the Faymon Liege, a master mage in her own right. She'd not be running away from Stryker's magic, no matter how off-putting. She shouted, "Raise impenetrable fog with this charm, protect those within from outside harm," casting a defensive ring of fog around herself and Kal, who'd hopped off Stryker's chest to stand protectively in front of her. The bats dived toward them, and then sensing the fog, flew back into the trees above.

Stryker jumped to his feet and ran a shaking hand through his short hair. She knew he could see her image, grayed and blurry, through the fog. "Queen's Crown, I'm sorry, Linden, really I am. I shouldn't have done that."

Linden didn't answer. Her head throbbing, she was close to tears. She watched as he walked away from her, stumbling into the woods beyond the campsite. He never once looked back.

CHAPTER 6

Jayna reached Linden first, Reynier running behind her. "Linden, are you alright? What happened?"

Linden unbound the fog shield surrounding her and Kal, who clicked his beak, flapped his wings, and flew into the woods, in the same direction as Stryker. Linden suspected Kal was going to give Stryker a piece of his mind. Since Stryker not only could command animals, but he could converse with them, it was going to be quite a conversation. She wished she could eavesdrop.

Linden used the end of her shawl to wipe away the tracks of tears on her face. "Stryker has been drinking and we argued."

Reynier drew his brows together, but before he could ask any questions, Jayna put a hand on his arm. He relaxed ever so slightly at her touch. Linden decided her best friend had some pretty amazing skills, and not just as a healer. Jayna asked softly, "Why did you feel the need to cast a defensive spell?"

Linden's bottom lip quivered, and Jayna led her by the hand into the tent. Reynier followed behind them, concern etched on his face. As Linden sat down on a floor cushion, Jayna asked Reynier to fetch them some ginger tea. After he left, Linden blurted out everything, tears flowing freely down her cheeks. Jayna rubbed her back like Nari used to do, which made Linden cry harder. Not a day went by when she didn't miss her feisty, loving, fiercely loyal grandmother.

By the time Reynier returned with the tea, Linden had washed her face and felt calmer. As she sipped from the mug, she let Jayna quickly fill in the details for Reynier. He paced around the tent, waving his hands in the air. "I don't like that he can command animals. I've never encountered that gift before. More importantly, no one, and I mean no one, is permitted to cast an offensive spell around the Liege. It's a violation that's punishable by expulsion."

Jayna asked, "Expulsion from where?"

"From Faynwood. No clan would welcome him," said Reynier flatly.

Linden took a shuddering breath. She didn't want any harm to come to Stryker. She still had feelings for him, but they were a jumbled-up mess at the moment. "Stryker didn't cast an offensive spell aimed at me. He had too much to drink and was upset, not in his right mind. Kal had just knocked him over and was standing on top of his chest. Stryker called down those bats as a defensive move, to distract Kal. I'm certain he didn't intend to hurt me. He apologized immediately afterward when he realized I'd cast a defensive shield around me and Kal."

Reynier looked at Jayna and asked her, "You know him better than anyone other than Linden. Does this ring true? Do you believe he was trying to protect himself and got carried away?"

Jayna nodded slowly. "Aye, I do. Look, he's always been

hot-headed. Linden, I'm sorry to say so, but you know it's true. Stryker struggles to control his emotions." Linden couldn't disagree. Stryker had picked a fight with another guest at her seventeenth birthday party and ruined the entire evening.

Reynier took another few turns around the tent, deep in thought. Sighing, he turned to the two of them. "Alright, we will keep this incident between us, for now. But rest assured, I'll be watching Stryker closely. One more false move, and I'll have no choice but to expel him." Speaking quietly, his voice barely above a whisper, he added, "As the Faymon Elder, I have two priorities: to preserve Serving magic, and to protect the Liege of Faynwood. The two are inexorably linked."

Linden closed her eyes and thought about Corbahn's remarks earlier that day. He worried the five clans of Faynwood may yet lose to Fallow magic. She knew the only chance they had was to be unified, to fight as one nation. "I understand," she said, her heart wrenching in her chest. Somehow, she'd have to find a path forward for her and Stryker. She didn't want to lose him too.

LINDEN STOOD on a raised dais in the center of the clearing, a heavy mallet in her hands. The sun was hiding behind puffy cumulus clouds, promising a cool, comfortable summer day. A good thing too, because Garlan had insisted Linden wear the shimmery gold, purple, and red ceremonial robe, specially commissioned for the occasion. Linden tried leaving the robe and matching gown behind in Tangle-wood, deciding it was far too pompous for her taste, but Garlan had slipped the outfit back into her trunk. Her intrepid lady's maid wove summer flowers through Linden's long dark waves. Around her waist, she wore the circlet of fire opals that had belonged to Liege Ayala before her.

Raising the mallet high over her right shoulder, Linden swung it at an ancient brass gong, covered in fay hiero-glyphics and suspended from a tree branch above. The gong reverberated throughout the clearing, creating an echo-chamber effect. When the echoes subsided, she banged the gong again, repeating the ritual five times, one for each clan. On the fifth strike of the gong, each clan raised and lowered their banners in the air, creating a ripple of color across the plain that undulated in time with the echoes. First came a wave of blue-yellow, followed by green-brown, orange-white, red-black, and purple-gold.

Linden put down the mallet and took her seat between Reynier and Pryl. The three of them sat on padded chairs in the front row of the dais, ready to judge the magic trials. Directly behind them sat the other judges, the chiefs from each of the clans: Serai of Shorewood, Hemma of Ridge-wood, Orlaf of Riverwood, and Haydahn of Arrowood. As both the Chief of Tanglewood and Faymon Elder, Reynier served in a dual capacity. Linden couldn't help but feel as if her role as the Faymon Liege was merely an old-fashioned tradition. She was a figurehead only, without any real authority, especially given her youth and inexperience. Reynier, Pryl, and the other clan chiefs really ran things in Faynwood, despite Reynier's protests otherwise.

The first day of the magic trials started with the youngest magic handlers from the various clans, the mage apprentices. Linden remembered being a nervous appren-tice not so long ago, one who struggled to pass her magic-handling classes in school. She leaned forward in her chair, anxious to see how well these mage apprentices controlled their magic.

Reynier whispered, "My Liege, if you lean forward for every mage apprentice, you will exhaust yourself by the end of the day."

"And we have three full days of trials to observe and judge," added Pryl dryly.

Linden smiled. "I'll pace myself; I promise." Looking down at the mage apprentices preparing to exhibit their skills, she said, "They look so young."

Reynier laughed. "That's exactly what the clan chiefs said the first time they saw you. 'She looks so young. Can she really be our Liege?' But they no longer say that, at least in my presence."

"I'm sure it didn't help that I was born and raised in Valerra," said Linden. While the two nations had peacefully co-existed for centuries, and much intermarriage occurred between them—her parents included—old prejudices remained.

Some Valerrans complained that Faymons were tricksome and unreliable, due primarily to their fay ancestry. Although Faymons were ninety-eight percent human, their blue-highlighted hair, an inheritance from the vivid blue locks of their fay forefathers, served as a visible reminder that Faymons and Valerrans were different. Some Faymons believed Valerrans couldn't possibly be as committed to Serving magic as their Faymon counterparts.

The real sticking point, the one inescapable truth, had to do with their respective skills as mages. While both nations swore themselves to the protection of Serving magic, Faymon mages, because of their closer ties to the fays, were more powerful magic handlers. Linden's own

Faymon grandmother, Nari, had been the most powerful master mage in Valerra.

As if reading her thoughts, and Linden wouldn't put it past the fay chief, Pryl said, "All the prophecies predicted a young Liege, with ties to Valerra, would emerge fifty years after Liege Ayala died here in these very woods." Linden shivered, thinking of her great-grandmother walking into a trap set by Mordahn's father. How had Fallow magic defeated Serving magic that day? She'd asked herself the same question after the fall of Valerra.

"Linden is the Faymon Liege, by blood and right and prophecy," said Reynier.

Pryl waved his hand at the campsites dotting the plain below them. "Aye. Anyone who can read the old scrolls would not dispute her legitimacy. However, the survival of Serving magic requires more than unity among the Faynwood clans. We must look beyond our borders and build a strong alliance with Valerra."

A crease formed on Linden's brow. Pryl was sounding more like Nari all the time. As the only direct female descendent of Liege Ayala, Linden had inherited the title, the duties, and the headaches associated with being the Liege of Faynwood. "But how can we build an alliance with Valerra when it's occupied by Glenbarran thugs? We have no one there who represents the legitimate Valerran government. The queen has escaped to the colonies, and we have no means of contacting her."

Reynier leaned in, as curious as Linden to hear the fay chief's answer. Pryl said, "Our fay scouts report that resistance fighters are organizing in cells across the country. They mention a Valerran resistance leader with military training who runs a cell in Bellaryss."

"What do we know about this leader?" asked Linden.

"We know he goes by the name of Tam and suffered severe burns during the war with Glenbarra. Although military healers saved his life, Tam bears a number of scars. Resistance fighters identify him by the placement of the scars on his face, neck, and arms."

Tam's story stirred something inside Linden, whether an old memory or a new premonition, she wasn't sure. Heartened by the thought of a budding resistance movement inside Valerra, Linden looked forward to offering them assistance from Faynwood. But first, they'd have to face down their own Glenbarran threat. She said as much to Reynier and Pryl, who agreed with her.

A round of cheering and applause from the clan chiefs reminded them to pay more attention to the apprentice trials. Reynier had explained to Linden that most, if not all, of the apprentices exhibiting at the trials would advance to mage status. Based on Linden's observations of their magic handling, she had to agree. The apprentices had mastered the fundamental incantations and spells. Two girls from Tanglewood handily performed one of Linden's most challenging magic spells as an apprentice: shapeshifting a fireball into a pomegranate, reverting the pomegranate back into its original fireball form, and then deploying a waterdouser spell to control any flare ups. Linden applauded enthusiastically when the apprentices took their bow.

By the time the trials concluded at the end of the day, every apprentice had advanced. Musicians and dancers from each of the clans gathered in the center of the field for a joint celebration of their newest mages. Women and men stirred pots of food over open campfires, offering a taste of their stew or porridge to any passersby. Linden even saw some recipe-swapping between the Shorewood and Riverwood clans, long-time rivals.

Reynier encouraged Linden to spend the next few evenings visiting each of the campsites, chatting with the men and women, and getting to know their clans and customs. Jayna accompanied her to the Ridgewood campsite, where they sampled a particularly tasty meat pie.

Linden had kept an eye out for Stryker all day, but he hadn't shown up. She didn't know whether to be relieved or worried about him, which she mentioned to Jayna.

"Definitely relieved," said Jayna. "Stryker needs a couple of days to cool off before he makes a public appearance."

Thanking a woman who handed her a roasted cob of maize, Linden said, "I guess you're right. But I can't help worrying about him. He seemed so downtrodden when he left, so sad."

Jayna took a bite of her roasted maize before answering. "He should be sad, given what he did to you. Don't minimize how his behavior made you feel."

Linden appreciated Jayna's friendship and her amazing healing skills. Her friend had another quality that Linden valued. She possessed an innate understanding of what someone needed at the moment, such as the gentle touch to Reynier's arm the previous evening that had a calming effect on him.

"After everything that happened with Stryker last night, I didn't have a chance to ask you about Reynier. I'm glad to see you're getting along better. You're my best friend, and he's my cousin and advisor. It would be really awkward if you hated each other."

Jayna tossed her cob and Linden's onto one of the fires. Sighing, she said, "It's not that at all. Quite the opposite in fact."

Linden tucked a chunk of hair behind her ear and asked, "What do you mean?"

The words tumbled out of Jayna. "I've been avoiding Reynier because I've started to have feelings for him. I've been so conflicted because of your brother, and then I felt guilty about my feelings and took it out on Reynier."

Linden linked her arm through Jayna's. "I know you liked Matteo for a long time, and I also know my brother wasn't ready for a commitment. He wouldn't want you to feel guilty."

Jayna sniffed. "It's true. He said as much that last day before he and Stryker deployed. I'm sorry, Linden, so sorry about Matteo."

Linden had to change the subject before she felt any sadder. "Did you explain all this to Reynier?"

Nodding, Jayna said, "I told him everything last night, about my feelings for Matteo, and how he kind of reminded me of your brother. And when Reynier asked me if I could ever feel the same way about him, I said yes. You should have seen his face light up. I don't think I've seen that man smile like that since I've met him."

Linden tilted her head. "You mean that you and Reynier..."

Jayna smiled. "He feels the same way about me. We talked about our losses, his wife killed during a raid, and about my family. I don't know if I'll ever see my sister or mother again. He's a good man, Linden. In fact, I'd say that good men run in your family."

Reynier, who was five years older than the rest of them, had married early. He and his first wife had barely a year together before she'd been killed. Linden knew Reynier's most visible scar, which ran down his forehead and bisected his eyebrow, couldn't compare with the emotional scars he carried inside. Linden's best friend would help heal Reynier's hidden scars.

Linden gave Jayna a hug. "I'm so happy for you and for Reynier. You're perfect for each other. You balance each other out."

Smiling, Jayna waved at someone in the crowd behind them. "Speaking of which, he's heading over here now."

Turning around, Linden waited for Reynier to join them before she asked, "Do you two mind continuing without me? I'd like to slip away quietly and return to my tent."

Reynier looked like he was about to object, but Jayna said, "You do look a little pale, and we wouldn't want you getting sick in the middle of the trials. I think Linden should turn in early tonight. Reynier, what do you think?"

Reynier arched his eyebrows. "As her friend and healer, you know best. If you think Linden should have an early night, who am I to argue?"

Smiling, Linden said goodnight. She wended her way back to the tent, stopping occasionally to visit with a clanswoman or clansman, or to congratulate an apprentice-turned-mage. She decided she was going to thoroughly enjoy having Jayna run interference with Reynier.

CHAPTER 7

Linden arrived at the judge's dais for the second day of magic trials to find Corbahn sitting in Pryl's seat, and the fay chief sitting in Haydahn's spot. The morning was steamy, the sun already heating up the clearing when she arrived.

Linden wore a lavender silk gown embellished with tiny silver stars, her gauzy silver shawl draped over her left shoulder. She debated removing Stryker's locket before leaving her tent but had tucked it inside the square neckline of her gown. She feared if she removed the locket that morning, she might never put it back on.

Corbahn stood up to allow her to pass, so she could take her seat between him and Reynier. The space between the two men seemed to have shrunk, Corbahn's muscular bulk taking up considerably more area than the fay chief's slighter frame had the day before.

"Are you feeling better?" asked Reynier.

"Aye, much better. Thank you." Linden had lain awake for a long time, worrying about Stryker and their future together, but she finally fell asleep with Kal curled up on the floor beside her bed.

Corbahn's shoulder brushed hers when he sat back down. "Have you been ill?"

Linden shook her head. "After a week of travel and a full day of activities, I needed some rest." Changing the subject, she asked, "Is your father well?"

Corbahn glanced down at the field stretched below them before answering. "This is a difficult anniversary for us. Riordahn, my older brother, was slain three years ago today. Father and Mother conduct a remembrance ceremony each year."

"I'm sorry for their loss, and yours," said Linden, her heart tugging as she recalled her own losses again. "Were you and your brother close?"

Corbahn smiled. "Very close, despite the fact Riordahn was the perfect son, the better athlete, better mage, better scholar. I was the wild son, happiest outside, in the woods, preferably with a bow in my hands. Riordahn was being groomed to succeed my father as clan chief, and the plan was for me to be his commander, his war chief, which suited me just fine."

Corbahn shook his head. "But Riordahn's gone, and my poor father is trying to prepare me to lead. I'll never be the kind of leader my father is, or my brother would have become."

Linden reached out a hand toward Corbahn but let it drop onto the arm of her chair. *What am I thinking? I'm betrothed to another, but I want to comfort this man I barely know, a man who was my enemy three months ago.* "You will be the leader your people need when the time comes. Let's hope your father lives a good long life, and you can use your bow and arrow for hunting instead of fighting."

Corbahn put his hand over hers, and squeezing it gently, said, "Thank you, my Liege. Your words comfort me." He removed his hand, placed it in his lap, and stared straight ahead.

Reynier had been listening to their exchange and now he spoke up. "I am sorry as well, Commander, for your loss, for all the losses suffered by your clan."

Corbahn turned to look at Reynier. "And I grieve for your losses as well, Elder. I know your wife was slain the week before my brother." Corbahn ran a hand through his unruly hair. "We've inflicted fifty years of pain on each other, without eliminating the real enemy, the culpable party."

"Fallow magic," said Linden.

"Aye," said Corbahn, "it's at the root of all the death and destruction in Faynwood and Valerra."

"Well said," replied Reynier. "We must never again allow ourselves to forget this truth."

A cheer from the crowd diverted their attention, as a swarm of mages, more than Linden had ever seen gathered together, ran onto the field. The mages lined up in four columns based on skill level: novice, junior, senior, and master. The master mages would not compete but served as referees for mages in the lower tiers. Linden recognized a number of apprentices from the day before, standing in the line for novices.

Corbahn rose from his seat and offered her a hand up. Remembering her official role, Linden slipped past him to sound the gong again, five times for each of the clans, and once more to signal the beginning of the magic trials. The previous day had been a warm-up, not a competition so much as an assessment of the apprentices' readiness to advance to the novice tier. For the next two days, the highest forms of Serving magic would be on display. Linden took her seat, excited to be able to see Faynwood's famous magic trials. The trials had become something that old mages reminisced about, taking on an almost mythical quality, since they'd been suspended during the civil war.

Mages in the novice tier competed throughout the morning, many of them demonstrating more advanced forms of everyday spells, from a water-douser spell to mist roses, to a green-thumb spell for growing better tomatoes.

As the novices advanced to the final round, Hemma of Ridgewood said, "Watch this next one closely; she's the daughter of one of my advisors. You'll enjoy her magic." Linden noticed everyone, even Reynier, leaning forward to give the novice from Ridgewood their full attention.

The girl, who looked to be no more than fourteen, walked into the center of the exhibition area and announced, "I will shapeshift my hair. Please do not become alarmed, and do not come near me while I'm shifting."

Linden held her breath. She couldn't imagine shapeshifting her hair, and worried that a novice this young might not be able to pull it off without harming herself. The girl shook out her long auburn-and-blue hair so it fell evenly down her back and shoulders. She shouted an incantation, and her hair shifted into drops of rain, falling down her face, her back, her clothes. The judges and the crowd applauded, and her hair shifted again, this time into copper coins that fell to the ground, tinkling as they piled up around her feet. Taking a deep breath, the girl uttered her final incantation. The coins flew back onto her head and began wriggling. As they wriggled, small eyes began appearing on top of the coins, along with tiny tongues that licked the air. The wobbling coins lengthened into writhing snakes that encircled the girl's head, forked tongues darting out in every direction. Linden let out a gasp of air and began applauding, along with the entire judging area. The judges unanimously declared the novice from Ridgewood the winner in her tier.

The junior trials started after lunch and proceeded until dinnertime. Linden clapped for every junior mage, appreciating the focus and skill required to perform each of the spells. Surprised that Toz and Remy entered the junior trials, Linden tried not to show any favoritism, but was thrilled when they advanced to the final round. Their skill at magic handling put to rest any notions that Valerran mages were less adept than their Faymon counterparts.

Remy stepped into the exhibition area in front of the dais and raised his arms in the air, creating a *V* shape. He snapped his fingers, fire shooting out of his palms six feet in the air. The crowd clapped and whistled at Remy's exceptional pyro gift. Remy combined the two streams of fire into a single fireball and bounced it on the ground, dribbling around the center of the field. Grabbing the ball of fire, he flung it in the air, where it separated into a dozen smaller fireballs. Remy flicked his fingers at the smaller balls and each one of them disintegrated into a series of sparkles that fell harmlessly onto the grass. The crowd cheered enthusiastically, the judges joining in the applause. Remy bowed and returned to his spot with the other junior mages.

The final exhibitor that day, Toz carried a banner from each of the five clans onto the field. Unfurling one at a time, he walked ten feet and placed a banner on the ground, then walked another ten feet and repeated the process until he'd placed all the banners. Backtracking so that he stood in front of the judges, he raised his hands, palms outward, and shouted an incantation. Each of the five banners began vibrating, curling in on themselves, until they became cloth balls. The balls melted into the ground, and the crowd let out a collective gasp.

Green stalks sprang from the ground where the banners had laid; the stalks branched out, sprouting leaves and buds. The stalks grew into thick rose bushes, each ten feet high, the roses the same colors as the banners they'd sprung from: blue-yellow, green-brown, orange-white, red-black, and purple-gold. Now the crowd and judges were clapping and cheering, but Toz wasn't finished. He gathered blooms from each bush, creating a bouquet of rare roses that he presented to Linden with a dimpled grin. Smiling, she leaned down from her seat on the dais and accepted the bouquet.

Toz bowed, returned to the center of the exhibition area, and snapped his fingers. The rose bushes folded into themselves and shrank to the ground, where they became clan banners once again, a bit smaller than before, since some of the matter retained its alternative rose shape in Linden's bouquet. Running around the field, Toz collected the five banners, bowed one more time, and returned to his spot with the other junior mages. The crowd roared its approval, and the judges declared him the winner of the junior trials.

Linden raised the bouquet of roses to her nose and sniffed. Not only were they beautiful to look at, but they perfumed the air with their delicate scent. Corbahn said, "You seem to know that last mage quite well. Is there a special meaning in that gift of the roses?"

Linden said, "I've known Toz all my life. Our mothers were close friends, so we literally grew up together. The gift of the roses was his grand finale. Toz is a bit of a showman."

Corbahn nodded. "I'd understood you were betrothed to a Valerran, so I assumed…"

"Oh no, not Toz. He's a friend." Linden paused. "My fiancé isn't here at the moment, but I hope he'll put in an appearance soon."

Reynier and the other judges left the dais in search of dinner, but Corbahn lingered. Linden sensed he had something to say to her and remained in his seat. "Forgive me for saying this," he said, "but I don't understand how your fiancé isn't by your side. I'd never leave my betrothed, and the Liege of Faynwood no less, unattended at such an important event."

Linden's eyes unexpectedly welled up. She had no handkerchief with her, nothing but her shawl. It would look too obvious if she used it to wipe her eyes. She turned away from Corbahn, using her hands to brush the tears off her cheeks. *What's wrong with me? I'm a tangled web of emotions.*

Corbahn shuffled in his seat, then gently tapped Linden on the shoulder. "My Liege," he said, "are you crying?"

Linden kept her back to Corbahn and nodded. Muttering something about missing fiancés under his breath, Corbahn said, "Let's get you out of this public place, away from the crowd. Follow me."

Linden nodded again and turned toward Corbahn. Looking at her reddened eyes, he squared his jaw but said nothing. Instead, he rose and extended his hand toward her. She took his hand, clutching her bouquet in the other, and followed him down the steps of the dais. Corbahn hurried her away from the crowds gathered around the open fires and bubbling pots of food, leading her behind the tents. They walked in silence until they reached a modest-sized tent with Arrowood's colors flying above it. Corbahn plucked an oil lamp from the ground beside the tent and pulled aside the curtain at the entrance. "Step inside and make yourself comfortable. I'll go find something for us to eat."

Linden carried the oil lamp inside and hung it on a hook hammered into the central tent pole. The simple interior, everything organized with military precision, reminded her of Reynier's tent. A cot neatly made up, small traveling trunk, and a simple wooden chair occupied half the tent. The other half contained an oval table surrounded by floor cushions. Linden ran her hand across the surface of the black walnut table, richly inlaid with lapis lazuli, malachite, opal, and quartz. Tilting her head, she saw that the inlaid stones formed fay hieroglyphs, similar to the ancient hieroglyphs etched into the doors of the Valerran Museum.

"I see you're admiring my table," said Corbahn as he entered the tent, three servants trailing behind him. The eldest servant rapidly set the table, pulling eating utensils and linen napkins from the pockets of his robe. Placing a vase of water in the table's center, he bowed to Linden. She handed him her bouquet, which he expertly arranged. The younger servants carried steaming bowls of whitefish stew, thick slabs of bread, a block of cheese, and two goblets of chilled wine, setting them down in front of Linden and Corbahn. Bowing, they exited the tent.

Linden said, "These fay hieroglyphs look remarkably similar to those etched on the doors and columns of the Valerran Museum in Bellaryss. My grandmother used to be able to read some of the ancient hieroglyphs, but even she could only interpret a small portion of them."

Corbahn said, "I know only a few of these symbols, but I cherish this, nonetheless. It belonged to my mother's father, and his father before him."

Linden tasted her fish stew; the sauce and spices were a perfect blending of flavors. "We'll have to ask Pryl about the meaning."

Corbahn laughed. "Pryl is the one who told me what some of the symbols mean. As for the rest, he's at a loss." Corbahn took a bite of bread and chewed it thoughtfully. Glancing at Linden, he said, "As you've observed, I'm not much of a diplomat. My father despairs of me ever learning to control my tongue and blunt my words."

"I prefer frank speech, myself," said Linden.

"That's good, because I'm about to ask you a frank question." Linden bit her bottom lip and nodded at Corbahn. He continued, "I've heard rumors about your fiancé, that he drinks too much, loses his temper too often, and argues with you in public. Is there any truth to these rumors?"

Linden looked at her stew and put down her spoon. She'd lost her appetite. "The rumors are exaggerated; the truth is complicated."

"Tell me," said Corbahn.

Hesitating, Linden wondered how much to tell him, but opted for the truth. Linden explained about meeting Stryker a little over a year ago, at a dance at her brother's military college, and how they'd begun corresponding while he was away for the summer. They developed a friendship that had blossomed into something more, but before they could really explore their feelings, he was deployed to the border. Stryker asked her to wait for him. She promised, and they became betrothed. They were reunited on the day of her crowning ceremony several months earlier and had renewed their commitment to each other.

Corbahn listened carefully, not saying a word until she

finished. "And since your crowning, he's been...moody, demanding? What exactly?"

Linden blew out a puff of air. "Unhappy. Unwilling to learn Faymon ways. Always challenging Reynier, who has my best interests at heart."

"And where is he now?"

"He did have too much to drink two nights ago. We argued, and he left. He needed some time to cool off," said Linden, unwilling to share any more details about that night.

Corbahn looked at her, his sea-green eyes reflecting the light of the oil lamp nearby. "My Liege, if you ever require my assistance, you need only ask."

Her heart skipped a beat at the intensity of his gaze. Corbahn's presence, his powerful build and his commanding personality, demanded respect. She decided he would be a remarkable clan chief one day, despite his reservations. A no-nonsense man whom she could trust as her ally, and perhaps even as her friend. "Thank you," said Linden. Frowning, she added, "You think I'm going to need help with Stryker, don't you?"

Corbahn took a sip of wine. "Aye, I'm afraid so."

Linden picked up her goblet and tasted the blush red wine. "I hope you're wrong."

"For your sake, I hope so too."

CHAPTER 8

THE FINAL DAY OF TRIALS STARTED WITH ONLY HALF THE MAGES running onto the field and lining up, the senior mages who would be exhibiting, along with the master mages who served as referees. The novice and junior mages relaxed in the crowd with their clans, the competition behind them. The sun peeked from between scuttling clouds, offering periodic shade to those sitting on the field, a cooler day than the previous scorcher. Linden sounded the gong for the last time, five clangs to represent the five clans, and two more clangs to signal the second day of magic trials.

She smoothed the folds of her pale green gown, decorated with delicate ivory flowers at the hem, waist, and around the cap sleeves. Adjusting her ivory shawl, she returned to her spot on the dais between Reynier and Pryl. Haydahn, who'd returned to his original seat behind her, waved toward the senior mages below. "Corbahn's mother asked him to compete today with Carissa, our eldest daughter, and he agreed."

Reynier squinted at the mages and gave a start. He

leaned over, speaking so softly that only Linden heard him say, "Stryker is competing."

She examined the column of mages and sure enough, she spotted him, standing several inches taller than the rest of the Faymons, even Corbahn. "I don't think this is a good idea," she said under her breath.

"Aye," said Reynier, "but it's too late now."

The morning progressed quickly, Linden enjoying the remarkable display of Faymon magic handling. When Stryker stepped into the exhibition area, Linden gripped the arms of her chair, not sure what to expect. He threw back his head, shouting a series of guttural calls into the sky. A long line of white wisps formed above him. As the wisps circled overhead, Linden realized they were white doves. She heard a sharp intake of breath from Haydahn behind her. Pryl murmured something, clearly uneasy, but Linden didn't understand why.

Stryker lifted his hands, and the doves created an arch above his head, each dove carrying a small branch or flower in its beak. He spoke again, and one dove flew over to Linden, dropping a single lily into her lap. As the crowd whistled and applauded, Stryker clapped his hands, breaking the spell. Flapping their wings, the doves returned to wherever Stryker had called them from, and the crowd broke into applause. Stryker took a bow and returned to the side of the field.

"Remarkable," said Haydahn. "And unsettling."

Pryl gave a diplomatic answer. "We need to learn more."

"Why? Is anything wrong?" Linden asked.

Pryl merely said, "Let's hope not," echoing Corbahn's words of the night before. Linden glanced at Reynier, who shrugged, as clueless as she was about Pryl's answer.

Corbahn and Carissa stepped into the exhibition area, each cradling a cat in their arms. Carissa carried a white cat with black markings, and Corbahn carried what appeared to be the mirror image, a black cat with white markings. When they reached the area directly in front of the judges, Corbahn called out, "Since we are performing magic with the most sensitive of animals, please withhold any applause until we are finished. Thank you!"

The two split up, Corbahn walking ten paces in one direction, Carissa counting off the same distance heading the opposite way. Turning to face each other, they spoke an incantation. The two cats disappeared from their arms and reappeared halfway between them, facing each other and meowing. The crowd gasped in awe, but Corbahn raised his hand for silence. Teleportation was a rare skill, used by experienced master mages to relocate small objects while they were working; Nari would teleport books from the library shelf to her lab table when in the midst of an experiment. However, Linden had never seen teleportation of live animals, and rarer still, performed by senior mages. Corbahn had more magic-handling skills than he'd admitted—either that, or his late brother had been truly exceptional.

Corbahn and his sister cast another spell, and the cats were back in their arms, this time Corbahn holding the white cat, and Carissa snuggling with the black cat. They spoke again, and the cats wound up in the arms of two girls standing closest to the exhibition area. The girls squealed in delight, one of them asking her mother whether she could take the cat home. Before the mother could answer, the cats were back with Corbahn and Carissa. They'd returned to the center of the field, facing the judges. Corbahn looked directly at Linden and spoke one final incantation. The black cat appeared on Linden's lap, licking one of its paws. Corbahn and Carissa, still holding her white cat, bowed. The crowd roared and cheered, breaking into wild applause. The judges rose in their seats, applauding and declaring Corbahn and his sister the winners of the senior trials. Linden stood up, the cat purring in her arms; she kissed the top of the cat's head.

The judges took their seats again, and the crowd settled back onto the grass. The magic trials officially over, they awaited the closing ceremony. Pryl and Haydahn, as the hosting clan chief, would present the awards to each of the winners. As the winners gathered on the field, a cloud passed over the sun. The cloud darkened and spread rapidly toward them. Women and men turned their faces upward, murmuring and pointing. A cacophony of caws and screeches filled the air.

"They're ravens!" cried Hemma. "Hawks and falcons too!"

Linden's heart sank to her knees. Only one mage had demonstrated his ability to command birds, and that mage had just lost to the man he considered his rival. Linden scanned the crowd for Stryker, but there were too many assembled in the field, some beginning to gather their little ones in their arms, seeking cover from the growing black cloud. She raised her eyes to the tree line, where Stryker stood with his arms raised high, his head thrown back to the sky.

The ravens, hawks, and falcons swarmed overhead, children crying and some women screaming now. The birds formed a spinning funnel cloud above the winners' circle, preparing to dive beak-first into the group. Corbahn, Haydahn, and Pryl began casting impenetrable fog over the field, and as other mages joined them, the curling fingers of fog spread. However, their efforts were hasty and haphazard at best, offering protection for some in the crowd but missing others completely.

Linden stood, placing her cat in the seat behind her, and spread her arms wide, palms open to the sky. She visualized the newest shapeshifting spell she'd been studying and used her commanding voice to call out the words. "Shift from predator bird to butterfly, gossamer wings to color the sky." Repeating the incantation over and over, her arms grew heavy, her head throbbed, but she carried on until she heard no more caws or screeches.

"My Liege, Linden; you can put your arms down now," said Reynier, pride in his voice. "Look at what you've done!"

Linden took a shuddering breath, uttered a binding spell, and lowered her trembling arms. Where there'd been ravens, hawks, and falcons circling overhead, yellow and orange and red butterflies fluttered on the wind. Corbahn ran toward the dais and when he was a few feet away, bowed deeply. "My Liege, your magic is beautiful!"

He straightened, his gaze boring into hers with admiration, and something more. Linden, weakened from the expenditure of so much energy, swayed and tumbled headfirst out of the stand. She felt herself falling, and then a strong pair of arms catching her. As she drifted into unconsciousness, she heard Corbahn say, "Rest easy, my Liege. I've got you now, and I won't let you go."

Linden awoke to hushed voices coming from the other side of the privacy curtain inside her tent. She tried lifting her head off her pillow, but the effort left her breathless, her temples throbbing. A small black cat with white markings lay curled up next to Kal at the foot of her bed.

"Are you sure she'll recover? She seemed nearly spent," said Corbahn in a hoarse whisper.

Jayna spoke in the soothing tones of a healer, quiet, competent, and firmly in control of the sickroom. "I've seen this before with Linden. She needs complete rest for the next few days. I promise you, she'll recover."

"And her magic?" he asked. Mages who expended every last measure of their magic might never be fully restored. In their weakened condition, their magic dissipated and was lost forever.

"And her magic," replied Jayna. "It's safe to leave her with me, Commander. I will take care of her."

A man called through the tent flap, "Commander? We've found him."

Corbahn thanked Jayna and followed the other man outside, the interior of the tent falling silent. Linden heard Jayna saying to someone, probably one of the guards, "Absolutely no more visitors; the Liege must rest."

Pulling aside the privacy curtain, Jayna came up to Linden's bed and checked on her patient. Although her eyes were closed, Linden managed to croak, "Stryker—did they find him?"

Jayna placed a damp cloth, soaked in essence of lavender and mint, on Linden's forehead. "Shh. You need to rest."

"Please tell me," Linden felt the pull of sleep. She'd be drifting off in another minute.

"Aye, they found him."

Linden had nothing more to say. As she slept, several tears rolled onto her pillow.

Two days later, Linden sat at the table in her tent. Reynier and Jayna joined her for dinner, although Linden had little appetite. She could tell by the way he avoided making eye contact that Reynier brought bad news. When she could wait no longer, she blurted out, "What do you have to tell me?"

Reynier wiped his mouth on a linen napkin and finally met her eyes. "Stryker has been found guilty of misusing his magic. As you know, the punishment is expulsion."

Linden leaned her elbows on the table and massaged her temples. "What Stryker did was wrong, terribly wrong. He deserves to be punished. But no one came to harm. Can't we show him some mercy?"

"No one came to harm because of your remarkable shapeshifting spell!" said Reynier. "But it's too late; Stryker is beyond your protection now."

Linden closed her eyes. She'd known the moment Stryker called down those birds that it was over, they were over. She could never marry a man who misused his magic and risked the lives of others. "When?"

Reynier rose from the table and began pacing inside the tent. "Under normal circumstances, he would have been escorted to the nearest border by now. But Pryl discovered something that has disturbed us all, something that we believe you must hear before we expel Stryker."

Jayna said, "Reynier, please stop pacing and tell us what you know."

"I'm sorry," said Reynier, who returned to the table and sat on one of the floor cushions. "During the magic trials, when Stryker first called the white doves, Pryl and Haydahn seemed distracted. After the second incident, Pryl left to meet with several of his fay scouts. While he was gone, Haydahn told me that according to Arrowood legends, the ability to call animals—especially birds—is similar to calling spirits. In other words, it's akin to necromancy."

"But Stryker is a Serving mage; I'm sure of it," said Linden.

Reynier nodded. "We spoke with Sergeant Desi, who served with him during the war. Stryker employed Serving magic repeatedly to oppose Fallow ways. At the Battle of Wellan Pass, he and his sergeant saved countless lives."

Linden could hear the "but" in Reynier's voice. "But there's more?" she said.

"We believe he's struggling to master himself and his magic." Reynier ran a hand through his hair. "Pryl returned with astounding news; Stryker's uncle, his late mother's brother, is a Fallow mage and the highest-ranking necromancer in Glenbarra."

CHAPTER 9

LINDEN REMOVED STRYKER'S PENDANT AND HANDED THE NECKLACE through the cell bars. The Arrowood prison cell where they'd locked up Stryker contained a narrow cot, chamber pot, and wash basin. She'd begged Reynier to allow her into the cell with Stryker, or to allow him to leave the cell long enough to have a civil conversation. But Reynier refused, and given what they'd learned, she understood her cousin's reluctance. As an extra precaution, two guards and Reynier waited behind the door in the anteroom.

Stryker grabbed her hand in both of his, his twisted steel manacles clanking against the bars of his cell. Comprised mostly of iron, which counteracted magic, plus traces of carbon and fay gold to strengthen its properties, the twisted steel encircling Stryker's wrists ensured he'd not be casting any spells. His brown-black eyes, always so luminous, now had a haunted look. "Linden, I'm sorry... about everything. I never meant to hurt anybody. Please believe me."

Linden compressed her lips to keep them from trembling. She'd tossed and turned all night, and she still hadn't fully recovered from the expenditure of magical energy during the trials. "I believe you, but it changes nothing. I could never marry you, not after you endangered innocent lives with your magic, and not after learning about your uncle, the chief necromancer in Glenbarra. How could you keep something so important from me?"

His shoulders sagging, Stryker grasped the necklace from her and turned away. He sat down on his cot, his face in shadow. "Because I knew you'd react this way. Everyone seems to think Fallow magic is like a bad inheritance, something passed from father to son. It's not; in the end, it's a choice. My mother chose Serving magic when she ran away from home at the age of sixteen, after discovering her father and brother had crossed over into Fallow ways. I'm not a Fallow mage and never will become one, despite my 'gift' of speaking to animals."

Linden's heart went out to him, not because she had any regrets about breaking her engagement, but because Stryker had managed to cut himself off from everyone who could have helped him. "Where will you go?"

"Reynier secured a spot for me on a Faynwood ship. Someone by the name of Raffindor will be my captain. Apparently, his crew members are all misfits, so I ought to fit right in. Sergeant Desi is coming with me. He says someone needs to keep an eye on me, so I don't pull anymore stupid stunts."

Raffindor had captained the ship that delivered Linden to Faynwood. Stryker would be looked after; Captain Raff would see to it. She owed Reynier a debt of gratitude. Instead of casting Stryker away, Reynier had found him a home and a job, a place where he could belong. "I know the ship and the crew. You'll do well there."

Stryker stared at the floor, his long lashes fringing his

cheeks. She remembered the first time he'd kissed her on the beach in Valerra, and later, his more urgent kisses when he was leaving for the front. She'd held such high hopes for them, for their future together.

"Please go. I can't bear to see you, hear your voice, and not hold you in my arms one more time," he said.

Nodding, Linden reached out to touch the doorknob. An image came to her: Stryker onboard Raffindor's ship, laughing at something one of the crew members said. He looked happy, in command of himself. She said softly, "Peace go with you."

Stryker dropped his head in his hands and didn't respond.

As REYNIER and Linden rode their horses back to camp, Reynier explained that Stryker was just leaving the stronghold with Sergeant Desi and the guard escort. They would arrive at Raffindor's ship in the main port of Shorewood in one week. When the guards transferred their prisoner, they would hand the key to Stryker's manacles over to the captain. Captain Raff would set Stryker free after they sailed.

"Are you very angry with me?" asked Reynier, pulling Hoff alongside Ashir, the two horses plodding along, side by side.

Linden shook her head. "Not at all. In fact, I'm indebted to you."

"You could never be indebted to me."

"But I am. Your solution for Stryker is brilliant. Joining Raffindor's crew will be good for him. It'll keep him and his magic out of trouble," said Linden. "And I'm relieved Desi is accompanying him; Stryker will have a friend onboard the ship who understands him and his struggles."

"I want you to know that I tried to work with him, to teach him Faymon customs." Reynier paused. "I know you cared for him, and I didn't want to see you hurt."

"I know you tried. And I did love him. But Stryker couldn't, or wouldn't, adapt. I think I've known for a while we wouldn't be marrying. I wasn't ready to admit that until now," said Linden, realizing she'd been making excuses for Stryker for months. She should have broken their engagement sooner—and definitely after he'd entered her tent uninvited and drunk, and then called down the bats on her and Kal. The warning signs were all there. Perhaps if she'd been more honest with herself, Stryker might not have misused his magic in a desperate bid for attention.

They heard horses approaching from behind them and pulled up Hoff and Ashir to wait. As they drew near, Linden saw the riders wore battledress and flew Arrowood's colors.

"My Liege, Elder, we bring news from Chief Haydahn," said the lead warrior. "Arrowood is burning! The Glenbarrans started several fires along our western border. We need mage reinforcements, as many as can travel, to ride with us. Warriors too."

Reynier asked, "Aren't your mages skilled in water-dousing spells?"

"Aye, Elder, but the fires have overwhelmed our mages."

A chill passed through Linden, despite the bright sunshine peeking through the trees overhead. The chill sent icy fingers into her sinew and bones. Shivering, she said, "Those fires have their origins in Fallow magic. There's no time to waste. Their magic grows stronger, more tightly bound, with each passing hour."

"Ride on to the other camps and raise the alarm. We'll

gather the Tanglewood mages and warriors. We'll meet you on the plain below," said Reynier.

"We'll ensure our mages are as well armed as our warriors," said Linden, who'd learned during the Valerran war that mages needed both spells and swords during a battle. Her sword had saved her life more often than her magic.

Linden and Reynier followed the Arrowood warriors onto the field, the sound of pounding hooves managing to raise the alarm before they arrived. When they'd dismounted, Reynier said, "You're not fully recovered and in no condition to ride out. We have enough mages to douse the fires."

Linden said, "I'll ride with the rest of you. You know as well as I do that as Liege, my presence helps to rally our mages, even if I'm not casting spells myself."

"Very well, but don't overextend yourself or your magic."

"I'll be careful," said Linden, who knew from prior experience that merely being near that much Fallowness would drain Serving mages and their magic. She also knew her reserves of magic ran deeper than master mages twice her age.

Jayna and Mara ran over to her. They each gave her a sisterly hug, knowing that Stryker's behavior during the past few months, then his outrageous "trick" as Mara called it, had shredded her heart.

Noting the soldiers thundering past, Mara asked, "What's happened?" Reynier explained about the fires along the border, and they ran off to help him spread the word, going tent to tent with the call for mages and warriors. Linden knew her Valerran friends would be riding out with her. Tanglewood had become their adopted clan.

Less than an hour later, mages and warriors from the five clans, dressed for battle and bearing their clans' colors, dotted the basin-like plain. Horses neighed and stomped, ready to be off. Linden had asked Garlan to watch her cat until she returned to camp. She resolved to ask Corbahn the name of her new pet; so far, the cat seemed to answer to anyone with a morsel of food in hand. Meanwhile, Kal sat nearby licking his paws and waiting for the horses to begin moving.

Linden patted Ashir's neck, waiting for Corbahn to ride up to the front of the column and join her. Normally, the Faymon Liege and Elder led the clans into battle, however, Reynier asked Corbahn to take his place. Corbahn knew the best routes through Arrowood to the border with Glenbarra, and his land and clan were at stake.

Corbahn, his chainmail gleaming in the sun, rode up on a champagne-colored stallion. He held the reins loosely in his right hand, the fabric of his tunic straining across his muscled arms as he moved.

"My Liege, are you certain you're recovered?" Worry lines creased Corbahn's brow.

"Recovered enough," said Linden. "Thank you, Commander, for catching me and for getting me to Jayna. She always knows what to do." Jayna had told Linden that Corbahn's quick action saved her from serious injury that day. He'd insisted on carrying her all the way to her tent, shouting at anyone who got in his way, and yelling for "the best healer in yer clan."

"Of course, I'd do anything. I mean," Corbahn paused and tried again. "I'm sure these past days have been exceedingly difficult for you. If there's anything I can do, anything at all, please let me know."

Linden knew he was referring to Stryker, his trial and

expulsion, and she didn't know how to respond. Before she could formulate an answer, Reynier, sitting on his horse in the row behind her, called out, "My Liege, are we ready to sound the horns?"

Linden and Corbahn replied "Aye!" simultaneously. As a man who commanded his own army, he'd never before had to wait for a higher authority, the Faymon Liege, to give the order. Realizing his blunder, Corbahn attempted to apologize, but his words were lost in a series of blasts from the ram horns. Both Linden and Corbahn flicked their reins, and the entire contingent lurched forward. For the first time in fifty years, the five clans of Faynwood moved as one fighting unit.

Since they traveled over rough, heavily wooded terrain, they kept a steady pace, but not one that would strain the horses or cause injuries. Corbahn had told her they had a five-hour ride, which meant they'd arrive in the late afternoon.

Linden smelled the fire well before she spotted any smoke. The clan chiefs and commanders had agreed on casting a series of water-douser spells, layering the spells one on top of the other, and using master mages to bind all the spells together, but first they had to be in range. Corbahn spurred his horse forward.

Linden called to him, "Commander, wait for the others. This requires every mage among us."

"I can't wait while Arrowood burns!" shouted Corbahn, plowing ahead on his horse.

Huffing in annoyance at Corbahn's stubborn refusal to stick with the plan, she let him ride ahead. If she joined him, then the other clans would begin breaking rank and trying to follow her. When she could see the flames licking the treetops, she signaled to Reynier to sound the horns again, this time to alert the clans they were in range to begin casting spells. She grimaced at a sharp pain in her side, the result of the injury she'd suffered during her battle with Mordahn and his Fallow magic. The searing ache in her lung came on suddenly, and without warning. Gritting her teeth, she slowed her breathing and focused on the forest fires ahead. She couldn't afford to be distracted by old memories and fears.

The mages dismounted, handing the reins of their horses to servants who'd traveled along for that purpose. The horses were understandably skittish, and no one wanted to risk losing their animals to fire or Fallow magic. The servants retreated with the horses in tow, many guiding several horses at a time farther inland, where Jayna and the other healers set up triage tents to handle the injured.

The mages lined up, master mages interspersed with seniors, juniors, and novices. As the mages began casting water-douser spells, dark storm clouds formed above the trees. Thunder rumbled and the clouds burst open, spilling rain onto the flames. They conjured downpour after down-pour, watching as the flames flickered and sputtered. Some of the mages began complaining of headaches, and several novice mages passed out, healers running over to drag them out of the line. More mages collapsed, and Linden called out to Reynier, "The Glenbarrans' Fallow magic is making our mages sick, novices and juniors need to stand down, now!"

Reynier said, "Are you sure, my Liege?"

A junior mage, no more than fifteen, screamed and fell backward, blood pouring from her nose and mouth. Reynier ordered the healers to begin pulling the younger mages off the line before the Fallow magic caused more injuries. Linden ensured that Toz, Remy, and Mara retreated with the juniors. Jayna and the other healers had their hands full by then.

When Linden glanced over at her best friend, Jayna was standing in the middle of a huddled, scared group of younger mages, checking injuries and directing patients to the various triage tents. Their eyes met, and Jayna, her curly hair wild around her face, shouted, "None of our mages will be able to take much more of this Fallow sorcery. I have three young novices in serious condition. Keep a sharp eye and pull back the rest of our mages before it's too late—and that goes for you too, Linden Arlyss!" Linden arched her eyebrow at the bossy-healer side of Jayna's personality, nodding to indicate her message was received and understood.

Meanwhile, the senior and master mages pressed forward, their layered water-douser spells taking hold. Two of the fires sizzled out. A third, although contained, continued to smoke and burn. Corbahn had returned to the group by then, joining Linden and the other mages still standing. "Something about this doesn't feel right to me," he said.

"Nothing feels right about this," said Linden, coughing from the smoke in the air. "I sense Fallowness all around us."

"Aye, I sense it too, but I don't like how our numbers have dwindled," said Corbahn. Many of the warriors who'd accompanied the mages also complained of headaches and nosebleeds, collapsing as they patrolled the perimeter they'd established. "We should pull back."

Linden stopped incanting long enough to say, "And this from the man who rode straight toward the fire, not waiting for his own reinforcements."

Corbahn thrust his jaw out. "I rode ahead to scout the area. And now I can see we need to regroup."

Linden was about to agree with him, but then Carissa cried out and collapsed on the ground. Corbahn ran over to his sister and carried her off, as far behind the line as he could take her.

A different cry rang out, this one freezing the blood in Linden's veins. Grihms and Glenbarran troopers stormed through the trees, snarling and screaming. Grihms had four wolfish legs, with two hands extending from their front legs. The upper part of their faces looked human, but they had wolf snouts and muzzles. Although Linden had encountered the wolf-human crossbreeds before, she still recoiled at their gruesomely mangled appearance.

"Pull back!" shouted Reynier, but the growling and yelling drowned out his words.

Linden reached for her sword, pulling it from her scabbard and wielding it with both hands. Green hieroglyphs pulsed along its blade, the hieroglyphs glowing brighter in the presence of Fallow magic. Two Glenbarran troopers charged, Linden and Reynier blocking thrust after thrust, sparks flying as metal blades clashed. The trooper nearest Linden lunged at her, the tip of his blade scraping against her chainmail.

"Oh no you don't!" she shouted, swinging her sword upward and stabbing her attacker's shoulder. The soldier shrieked and fell backward.

Glancing around her, she saw Reynier finishing off the second trooper. Farther down the line, Hemma lay on the ground, two of her warriors dragging her back from the fray. Orlaf and Serai battled a couple of grihms waving axes in the air.

Linden spun toward the sound of snapping jaws as a

grihm leapt in the air, intent on attacking her. As Linden twisted out of the grihm's way, Kal flew above the creature's head, clicking his beak. The grihm tried swiping at Kal with his ax, and Linden barreled toward the grihm, screaming and slicing through the air with her green blade. The grihm dropped his ax and ran. Several other grihms loped away behind the first one.

"Well done!" shouted Haydahn, who'd dispatched another grihm nearby.

"But it's strange," yelled Linden. "They don't normally retreat like this." They heard a high-pitched whistle, and the grihms who moments before had been running away, howled in pain. Turning around in their tracks, three grihms charged toward them. Kal clicked his beak and swooped, attempting to distract the pack bearing down on Linden and Haydahn.

Linden held her sword in front of her, waiting until the grihms were within striking distance, and lunged toward the nearest grihm. He swung his ax sideways, and as Linden twisted out of his way, the ax blade sliced her upper arm. Linden hissed at the searing pain but kept moving. She heard one of the other grihms yelp and fall nearby. *Good*, she thought, *Haydahn's evened the odds*.

Focusing on the drooling grihm who'd injured her, she held her sword steady, ignoring the pain in her wounded arm. He charged her again, this time on all fours, his wolfishness overtaking any memory of his once having been human. Waiting for the right moment, she shouted, brandishing the glowing blade of her sword until it met the soft flesh of the creature's neck. Yipping, the grihm rolled over and lay still.

Breathless, her legs trembling with exhaustion, Linden put her hand up to her head and pulled it away, bloodied.

She heard Kal squawking overhead, Haydahn yelling for her to duck, and a whirring noise that confused her. Haydahn tackled Linden, knocking her down, as a volley of arrows pelted the air and ground.

Linden tried to shift under Haydahn's bulk; he'd fallen face up and lay sprawled on top of her. "Haydahn, are you alright?" she croaked, the weight of his body squeezing the air from her lungs. She heard metal clanking against metal around her, and the whine of arrows flying from all directions. She hoped that meant Faynwood archers had recuperated sufficiently from their headaches to give their side a fighting chance.

"Can you move?" she wheezed, dizzy from blood loss and lack of oxygen. The sounds of fighting dimmed, growing fainter. She heard Kal flapping his wings, clicking his beak furiously, and boots hitting the ground near her head. Panting, her breath came in short gasps.

"Father!" cried Corbahn. "Father," he repeated more softly.

Reynier shouted, "He's fallen on Linden! We need to shift him."

Several pairs of hands lifted Haydahn and set him down on the hard-packed earth nearby. Reynier's face leaned over her, his brow rutted with worry. "Haydahn?" she gasped, coughing as her lungs inflated. Reynier shook his head. Kal flew in tight circles above their heads, missing some feathers but otherwise unscathed.

She looked past Reynier to where they'd laid Haydahn, half a dozen arrows protruding from his chest and stomach. Corbahn knelt on the ground beside his father's limp form, tears streaming down his bloodied face. Closing his father's eyes, he whispered the words to a benediction often recited at mages' funerals. "May you find peace in the realms of the dead, having followed Serving magic until the end of your days. This is the true path."

Linden echoed hoarsely, "This is the true path." She added, her voice a raspy whisper, "Your father took those arrows for me." Corbahn crossed the ground between them and dropped to his knees beside her. She reached toward him with her uninjured arm, and he gripped her hand firmly in his. "He saved my life."

Nodding, Corbahn's broad chest heaved. "He told me we had to protect you at all costs. Arrowood could never allow another Liege to lose her life in these woods."

"You should be proud of him."

"I am," he said, his voice breaking.

Linden gave his hand a squeeze, wanting to comfort him but knowing no words could ease his pain at that moment. He cradled her hand against his chest and wept.

CHAPTER 10

Toz ran over to Linden towing a makeshift litter, tree branches stripped of their leaves, held together with pieces of cloth and fashioned into a stretcher. Reynier and Corbahn gently transferred her to the litter, Linden moaning with each movement. As Corbahn brushed a lock of hair out of her eyes, she whispered, "The Glenbarrans, have they left Arrowood?"

"For now, my Liege," he said, stepping aside as Toz and Reynier lifted the litter to carry her back to the triage tents. Linden watched as Corbahn returned to his father's side, guarding his body until a servant brought the horses around. The smoldering, charred remains of oaks, sequoias, maples, and cedars, once the pride of Arrowood, stood like wounded sentries behind him.

Far too many Faymon mages and warriors lay on the ground where they'd fallen, a mere yard or two away from dead or dying grihms and Glenbarran soldiers. As Linden turned away from the massive graveyard, Toz said, "It's Valerra all over again. The Glenbarrans set the traps, and we walk right into them."

"But we couldn't let Arrowood burn," said Reynier.

"True," said Toz, "but we could have brought twice as many soldiers and cast protection charms before we went in to fight the fires. A small delay at the front end might have cost a few more trees but saved countless lives."

Linden tried listening but kept drifting off. She hurt all over: her upper arm where the ax sliced through, her thigh where one of the Glenbarran arrows struck her, and her head, still bleeding from a cut. She opened her eyes long enough to say, "Toz is right. They've outwitted us at every turn."

Reynier grunted, "Their Fallow magic shouldn't be able to defeat Serving magic, but so far, it's winning."

"Then we need to figure out why," said Toz.

Linden woke with a start when she heard Jayna exclaim, "Oh Linden!" Jayna surveyed the damage, cataloguing Linden's injuries for her assistant. "Deep gash to the left arm, below the shoulder. Two-inch cut above her left eye. Arrow embedded in the right thigh. Let's start with that arrow. I don't like the discoloration around the wound." Jayna sent her assistant scurrying for supplies.

Mara ran over to Linden's side and muttered, "Not again. You're a mess." Once the meanest girl in school and Linden's harshest critic, Mara had become her fiercest friend during the past year.

"Um, thanks?" Linden whispered. "So can someone start fixing me?"

Jayna sighed, which told Linden all she needed to know about the extent of her injuries. Reynier asked, "When can we transport her back to the stronghold?"

"I'll let you know," said Jayna, shooing Reynier and Toz out of the tent.

As Jayna cut away the fabric on her leg, Mara offered

Linden a drink of something bitter, an herbal concoction that made her gag.

"That tastes awful. Don't you have any honey?"

"This is a battlefield, not the still room back at Delavan Manor," grumbled Mara. The mention of Delavan Manor, where Linden had lived with her grandmother, reminded her yet again of how far she and her friends had traveled, emotionally and physically, since the start of the war with Glenbarra.

Linden found herself growing drowsy, the herbal drink containing sedatives as well as restoratives. She forced her eyes open long enough to ask, "The novices and juniors, how are they?"

"Better than you, that's for sure," said Mara, her bedside manner brusque, but her hands gentle as she helped Jayna dress Linden's wounds.

Jayna added, "They're recovered, for the most part. No lasting damage."

"That's something to be thankful for," mumbled Linden, yawning.

She slept during the trip back to the stronghold, strapped onto the litter and dragged by Ashir, arriving late morning. Linden woke up to wailing and weeping, as battered Faymon mages and warriors—those still able to ride—led the horses of their fallen and injured comrades into the compound. Family members swarmed around them, tearing their robes and crying.

Corbahn had wrapped his father in a blanket and laid him across his horse, the Arrowood banner-bearers riding ahead. He and his sister rode into the stronghold together, their father's horse between them. When their mother ran outside, she fell to her knees, weeping. Corbahn helped her up and guided her back into the longhouse, Carissa taking her little sister by the hand and comforting her. Servants gently removed the body of their clan chief and carried him inside, where they would prepare him for the funeral pyre that evening. Families from every clan had the same grim tasks that day; nurse the injured and prepare the dead.

As Jayna and Mara transferred her from the litter to her bed inside her tent, Linden said, "Whatever it takes, I need to attend the funeral rites tonight."

Jayna shook her head. "I knew you'd say that. Even though I don't think you should go, you'll go anyway, so I'll save my breath."

"That's good, much more efficient that way," mumbled Linden. "But I'm not up for riding Ashir, and I can't walk that far, so how will I get there?" Given the large number of dead Faymons to be honored that evening, the community funeral pyre would be in the clearing where they'd conducted the magic trials.

"We'll figure something out," said Mara. "Get some rest for now."

Linden didn't need any encouragement. She slept all day, until Garlan woke her to dress for the funeral. It took Garlan and another maidservant half an hour to get Linden into her undergarments and her darkest purple gown; she had to keep sitting down to rest, and she couldn't lift her left arm at all. Linden found Mara and Remy waiting for her when she limped out of her tent, every muscle screaming from the effort to remain vertical.

"What's the plan?" she asked, placing great faith in Mara's planning abilities, and much less so in Remy's.

Remy smiled and jogged around the corner. He returned with a sweet, docile donkey in tow. The animal had a strange contraption attached to his saddle. "What's that?" Linden pointed at the wooden saddle-thing on the donkey's back. It looked like Remy had taken apart and refashioned her litter into a seat that attached to the donkey's saddle.

"That's your ride," said Mara.

"*That?*" said Linden, wondering whether she should turn around and go back inside her tent. She couldn't imagine riding a donkey, however sweet, with a saddle-thing on its back, at least not in her current condition. She felt herself swaying, slightly feverish.

"Remy made that for you," Mara patted Remy's arm, which confused Linden even more. Mara and Remy argued all the time, about everything.

Linden didn't want to hurt Remy's feelings, and she could see storm clouds beginning to form in Mara's eyes, so she said the only thing she could. "Thank you, Remy. How does this work?"

Remy grinned and proceeded to explain that it worked like any other saddle, except this one had a backrest and safety harness to prevent Linden from falling. Linden had been right about one thing; Remy had repurposed the litter. "Are you ready?" Remy asked. "I'll lift you into the seat and Mara will secure your harness."

"I've brought a light throw to drape around the harness so no one will notice," said Mara. She added, "Well, they'll notice you're in a seat on top of a donkey, but they won't see the harness."

Since Linden wanted to attend the funeral rites to honor the fallen, especially Haydahn, she had no other choice. Besides, her friends had gone to a lot of trouble to fashion a custom seat for her. "Let's do this," she said, "and thanks."

After several tries, Linden crying out in pain with each attempt, they managed to get her into the saddle and secured her with the harness. Mara had been right, with the gold throw draped around her waist and legs, no one could see the straps holding her upright. And she could lean against the wooden backrest attached to the saddle, which Remy had thoughtfully cushioned with a small pillow.

Remy took the reins, leading Linden and the donkey into the clearing. Mara walked alongside Linden, periodically calling out orders to Remy, "Avoid that large group up ahead," "Turn to the left, it's less crowded there," and "I see Jayna and Toz standing with Reynier, over to the right. Let's head there." Each time, Remy redirected the donkey and Mara smiled happily.

Reynier raised an eyebrow at Linden sitting in the donkey seat and nodded his approval. "Ingenious," he said, adding, "I'm amazed you made it, my Liege."

"I wouldn't be here if you hadn't found me when you did," said Linden. She nodded at her friends. "I'd never have survived without all of you to help me."

The clans gathered in the center of the clearing, where servants had built five long, low platforms, one for each clan, each funeral bier able to accommodate dozens of the fallen. Below each platform they'd laid wood, kindling, and charcoal. Torches had been thrust into the ground at regular intervals, to provide light for the ceremony and fire for the final rites. Musicians blew on their ram horns, a rumbling series of solemn notes that reverberated across the plain.

Each clan brought forward their dead, the bodies wrapped in blankets and strewn with flowers, and laid them gently on the bier. Men and women keened at the loss of a parent, a spouse, a son, or daughter. One little girl from the Riverwood clan ran forward, screaming and sobbing as her mother was laid on the bier with the others from her clan. An old woman picked her up and carried her back to the clan, the child wailing, "Mama, mama."

The final bier was reserved for the Arrowood clan, the only clan to lose their chief during the battle. Each family stepped forward, laid their loved ones on the last platform, and prayed briefly before turning away, weeping. The entire gathering held its collective breath, waiting for the last body to be laid to rest. Silence descended across the field. Even the wind in the grasses stilled, as if paying its respects to Chief Haydahn Erewin of Arrowood.

Corbahn and another commander lifted Haydahn's body from his horse and carried him to the platform. Corbahn's mother walked behind them, gripping her daughters' hands and weeping. Linden focused on Corbahn, his forehead furrowed in grief, his eyes swollen. He'd become clan chief overnight, a role he'd never wanted and now had no choice but to accept. If he ceded his inheritance, the title and responsibilities would pass to his sister Carissa. While she might become clan chief one day, if Corbahn died without an heir, Linden was convinced he'd never lay such a heavy burden on a girl of sixteen.

Gently laying his father down with the others who'd fought beside their clan chief, Corbahn paused. Placing his hands on the blanket covering Haydahn's body, he cried out, "Arrowood's finest, gone! Faynwood's brightest and best, fallen, but never forgotten!" He turned away, his face streaked with tears, as he guided his mother and sisters back to their place with the clan.

Linden brought her hand to her chest, her eyes overflowing. She cried for all the clans, for every fresh loss, but especially for Corbahn, his grief so visceral, his pain so raw, she wanted to reach out and touch him. Strapped down as she was, barely able to walk on her own, she could only sit and weep in sympathy.

Young men and women from the five clans, each carrying torches, stepped up to the platforms. A lone musician blew one long, mournful note through his horn, and the torchbearers touched the kindling beneath the biers. As the fire took hold and spread, the crowd raised its voice, chanting as one. The chants continued until the pyre had consumed every last body, the flames reaching fiery fingers to the night sky above them.

Linden twisted a sodden handkerchief in her hands, sick at heart from the deaths wrought by the Glenbarrans and their Fallow magic. It was Valerra all over again. As she dabbed her eyes, she heard Corbahn's deep baritone. "My Liege, you look spent. Allow me to guide you back to your tent."

Linden looked into Corbahn's eyes, clouded with his own losses and worries. "But you have your family to condole with. I'll be fine."

"My sisters are with my mother. Besides, I can't sit in that house for one more minute, with the mourning and weeping and wailing. I need to walk, and I'd like to walk with you."

Linden nodded. "Of course. And you're right, I am worn out. If Mara hadn't strapped me into this thing, I'd have fallen out by now."

Corbahn picked up the reins and clicked his tongue to move the donkey forward. "I didn't expect you to attend. I saw the extent of your injuries."

"Jayna didn't want me to come, but I had to be here, to honor the fallen, especially your father." Linden felt fresh guilt, knowing Haydahn had sacrificed himself for her. "I'm sorry your father died in my place. I shouldn't have let it happen."

"Don't apologize. My father knew what he was doing, and he did it willingly. I'd have done the same."

Linden shook her head. "But it should have been me, not your father. I've always been a target."

Corbahn stopped abruptly. "What do you mean, you've always been a target?"

Linden didn't think this was the right time to talk about the bad blood, and there was a lot of it, between their two families. "I shouldn't have said anything. Let's forget it."

"If you're a target, then I want to know about it," said Corbahn, who stood rooted in place.

Linden brushed her hair away from her face. "Fine, but don't blame me if you don't like the story I'm about to tell you." Corbahn raised his eyebrows. When Linden pointed at the slack reins in his hand, he got the hint and started walking again.

Linden asked, "How much do you know about Mordahn's relationship with Liege Ayala's daughter, Nari Arlyss?"

Corbahn stopped walking again, and Linden sighed. She'd never get to her bed at this rate. "What relationship?"

Linden said, "Your great-uncle Mordahn and my grandmother Nari had been betrothed at an early age. Nari told me she was only fifteen, but she liked Mordahn well enough, and apparently, he was over the moon about her. Since the two families wanted to forge closer ties between our clans, they encouraged them to become engaged."

Corbahn picked up the reins and started walking, but slowly. "So when Mordahn's father assassinated Nari's parents, not only did it incite a civil war, but Mordahn lost the woman he loved."

Linden nodded. "Exactly. My grandmother held the funeral rites for her parents, and then sent word to Mordahn, breaking off her engagement. He wouldn't take no for an answer, pursuing Nari and her tutor across Faynwood until they managed to escape. My grandmother eventually wound up settling in Valerra."

Corbahn said, "I've heard that Mordahn turned against his father and renounced Fallow magic, at least when he was younger."

Linden repeated what Nari had told her. Mordahn eventually married a clanswoman and had a daughter whom he doted on. For a while, he managed to live a quiet, uneventful life, until he lost both his wife and daughter during a raid led by Tanglewood's clan chief, one of Nari's uncles.

"So Mordahn blames the Tanglewood clan, and your family in particular, for his losses?" asked Corbahn.

Linden said, "Aye, but there's one more reason why he's targeted me."

Corbahn slowed down even more, so Linden hurried to explain. "He's a revelator and has visions, same as me. I suspect he's had a vision of the future in which Serving magic defeats Fallow magic, and somehow, he perceives that I'm involved. He believes I'm a threat to him."

Corbahn shook his head. "I don't think that's why Mordahn's been targeting you, or at least, not entirely."

"Why not?"

Corbahn hesitated. "Maybe we should continue this conversation another time. We're almost to your tent."

Frowning, Linden said, "If you know something about Mordahn's motivations that I don't, please tell me. I need to know."

Patting the donkey's neck, Corbahn asked, "You're

familiar with the prophecies about yourself, the new Liege who would be crowned after a long period of war between the clans?"

Linden had learned about the prophecies from Mage Mother Pawllah, who'd explained that Faynwood had been without a Liege since Ayala was killed. According to the seers, the next Liege would be her great-granddaughter— the Faymons would need to wait until the third generation. Linden thought the only thing more difficult than becoming a clan chief at sixteen was becoming Liege at seventeen. She'd never have made it this far without the help and support of Reynier and her friends.

When she nodded, Corbahn continued. "According to the prophecies, the new Liege would help unite the Faymon clans. Without unity, we have no hope of overcoming Fallow magic." They were thirty feet from her tent, within hailing distance of the Tanglewood guards posted in front. Corbahn didn't seem to want to continue, either the conversation or the forward momentum.

"Do the prophecies reveal anything else?" she asked, anxious to climb off the donkey and into her bed. What Corbahn had shared she'd heard before, first from Pawllah and later from Reynier, who loved to discuss Faymon prophecies with Pryl.

"The new Liege also would heal the rift between the Tanglewood and Arrowood clans," said Corbahn.

Linden could tell he was holding back a crucial piece of information. He refused to meet her eyes and kept winding and unwinding the donkey's reins around his left hand. "How would she heal the rift?"

"Through the rites of binding," he said. Faymons sometimes used really old-fashioned terms. Rites of binding were what Valerrans called a wedding ceremony.

Linden hoped he wasn't talking about an arranged marriage. Some Faymons still practiced that tradition. As a girl raised in Valerra, where love-matches were the norm, she couldn't imagine marrying someone for any reason other than love. Certainly not because of some old prophecy.

"Rites of binding between?" she asked, stifling a yawn.

Corbahn stroked behind the donkey's ears. "Between the Liege from Tanglewood and the Chief from Arrowood."

CHAPTER 11

"We should speak about these things some other time," said Linden, hoping she never had to talk about this particular prophecy again. Not that she didn't find Corbahn attractive, everything from his muscular physique to his gruff, no-nonsense attitude commanded attention, but she'd just broken up with Stryker, she hurt all over, and the clans had a war to run.

Corbahn cleared his throat. "Aye, that is if you want to discuss it, but we don't have to mention this again. I didn't mean to embarrass you, only to offer another explanation why the Glenbarrans might be targeting you. They place great stock in the prophecies," said Corbahn.

"Linden?" called Jayna, coming up behind them with Reynier. Linden had never been more relieved to hear Jayna's voice. "We need to get you off that donkey and back into your tent." Turning to Corbahn, Jayna added, "We're so sorry for your loss. We're all going to miss your father. Please give your mother and sisters our deepest condolences. Now if you'll excuse us, I'll take Linden the rest of the way." Jayna held out her hand for the reins, taking them from Corbahn.

"Of course," said Corbahn. Reynier clapped a hand on Corbahn's shoulder and insisted on accompanying him back to his campsite.

Jayna led the donkey away, calling out to two of the guards for help. They struggled with the harness straps, eventually extracting Linden, who groaned as they lifted her off the donkey and carried her inside. Jayna and Garlan helped her undress, each movement excruciating. Linden shivered, despite the warm summer evening, and Jayna put a hand on her forehead. "Fever. I knew it. You never should have attended tonight, and I never should have let you out of my sight. I don't know what Commander, or Chief Corbahn was doing, but if he'd walked with you any slower, he'd have been moving backward."

Linden said through her chattering teeth, "You were right. I should have stayed in bed."

Jayna paused in the middle of changing one of Linden's dressings. "You really must be ill, if you're telling me I was right."

Linden leaned back on her pillow. "I don't think I'll be getting up tomorrow."

"You need complete bed rest for the next few days," said Jayna sternly.

Linden gave a slight head nod, her eyes already closed. "Whatever you say."

LINDEN'S DREAMS took on an other-worldly quality. Whenever she woke, someone—Jayna, Mara, or Garlan—mopped her brow and gave her bitter herbs to drink. She heard them speaking about her with Reynier, but she couldn't concentrate well enough to make sense of phrases such as, "Running too high," "Poisoned arrow," or "Leech it out."

A few times she thought she heard Corbahn's voice inside her tent, or maybe inside her head. He told her she had to live, that Faynwood needed her. He might have even said he needed her, but that also made no sense. Much later, she dreamt she was strapped onto a table, with probes and tubes attached to her arms and legs. Jolts of electrical energy coursed through her body, her back arching as pain wracked every fiber, muscle, and sinew. She heard someone say she'd be a pretty little doe soon enough, perfect prey for the panther next to her. In her dream, Linden turned her head. A crossbreed with Corbahn's face and chest, but the body of a panther, prowled around the table where she lay. When he bared his teeth at her, she screamed.

"Linden, wake up!" Jayna shook her good arm. "It's just a dream."

Linden opened her eyes, the scream dying on her lips. Her mouth felt as if she'd swallowed a wad of cotton. "Not just a dream," she croaked. Jayna brought a mug to her lips, but Linden stayed her hand. "No more herbs. Need water."

Jayna nodded and came back a moment later with a mug of fresh water. Linden drank thirstily and said, "More, please."

After she downed a second mug of water, Jayna asked, "What did you mean, 'not just a dream?'"

Linden brought her hand up to her head and patted her face. All her parts were still there, in all the right places. Jayna felt her forehead and said, "Your fever's finally broken. Why are you patting your face?"

"I dreamt I was being tortured and turned into a crossbreed, a doe-woman, so that a man-panther could attack me." Linden didn't want to mention the other crossbreed had been Corbahn.

"Sounds like a bad dream, the kind you have when your fever breaks," said Jayna.

Linden didn't want to argue, but something about that dream felt more like precognition. She also wondered whether she might have gained insight into the mechanics of crossbreeding, which was illegal in Valerra and Faynwood, but not in Glenbarra, at least not under its current regime.

Linden asked, "How long have I been out?"

"Three days."

"That long? What did I miss?"

Jayna said, "Let's see...we held Corbahn's formal chieftain ceremony two days ago. I think every mother with an eligible daughter showed up to congratulate him."

"I'm sure he enjoyed the attention."

"Actually, I think the attention made him acutely uncomfortable. He frowned throughout the whole ceremony, and promptly disappeared as soon as it was over."

The fact that Corbahn disappeared in the presence of all that female attention gave Linden the tiniest bubble of satisfaction. She asked, "Then what happened?"

"Then yesterday Pryl popped in, from wherever he lives the rest of the time, and really stirred the pot. I noticed that he waited a polite interval, until we'd buried our dead and installed Corbahn as the new Chief of Arrowood, before coming around. Why is that do you think?"

Linden shrugged. "Probably because Faymon customs and ceremonies remind him we're ninety-eight parts human and only two parts fay. Nari always used to tell me it's a minor miracle the fays bother with us at all." Linden didn't want to get sidetracked talking about fay customs. "So how did Pryl stir the pot?"

Jayna sat on Linden's basket seat and twirled it around to face her. "He waited until all the clan chiefs and commanders had gathered together, debating when to attack Glenbarra. Reynier, of course, reminded them that their first duty was to protect Serving magic, but they continued to argue. Corbahn was the loudest of all, demanding immediate action to avenge the deaths of so many Faymons, including his father.

"Pryl emerged from a cloud of mist looking like he'd just eaten a cobra. Reynier told me later that Pryl practically spat venom at the group. 'Stop talking about vengeance and focus! We have one goal—to stop the spread of Fallow magic. If we don't, none of us will be here twelve months from now. No more births, no more weddings, just destruction and death. Fallowness will spread over Faynwood like the plague it is.'"

"I wish I could have seen Pryl lose his temper. I didn't think he had it in him."

Reynier entered the tent and heard Linden's last remark. After asking about her health, he said, "Be thankful you were spared that ordeal. When Pryl yells, he sounds like a hissing snake, except much louder. A few of the chiefs complained of earaches afterward."

"So what's the plan?"

Reynier sighed. "We're still formulating one. As usual, Tanglewood, Shorewood, and Ridgewood want to proceed with caution, fortify the border with troops and protection charms. We want to know what we're up against before we go charging into Glenbarra."

"Makes sense," said Linden. "What about Arrowood and Riverwood?"

"Corbahn wants to cross over the border and conduct a series of lightning raids in Glenbarra, to demonstrate that we're too ornery to attack, that it'll be too costly a war. And you know that Riverwood will follow Arrowood's lead," said Reynier.

Linden recalled her father and his retired marine friends debating various military tactics. "It's not a bad strategy for a normal border dispute, but it won't work here. King Roi doesn't care about cost. He'll just throw more grihms into the war." Linden had lived through one war with Glenbarra already, and since her uncle had been Prime Minister of Valerra, she'd heard every argument and counterargument about King Roi, Commander Mordahn, and their Fallow ways. She hadn't expected to have to fight Mordahn again, not after killing him once onboard Captain Raff's ship, but that was Fallow magic for you, unpredictably evil.

"Exactly," said Reynier. "However, Corbahn is stubborn. We're leaving in the morning to fortify the border with more troops, but Corbahn won't stop at the border. He plans to cross over."

Linden leaned forward too quickly and winced. "He's what?"

"You heard me."

"But he'll be putting himself and his clan at risk for nothing; we'll gain absolutely nothing." Linden shook her head. "Reynier, could you please let Chief Corbahn know I'd like to see him in an hour?"

Reynier's eyebrows rose almost to his hairline. "Are you sure? You look like—"

Linden held up her hand. "I can only imagine what I

look like. Jayna, could you and Mara make me presentable somehow?"

Jayna put her hands on her hips. "I'm not letting you leave this tent until you're completely recovered, which you're not."

"Then let's ask Chief Corbahn to come here."

Jayna frowned. "I'm not sure how much we'll be able to do in an hour."

"Do your best," said Linden. "Too many lives are at stake!"

"In that case, we're going to need two hours," said Jayna. Reynier nodded in agreement. He and Jayna seemed of one accord about everything lately, and he left to call on Corbahn.

WITH GARLAN'S HELP, Mara and Jayna managed to get Linden bathed and dressed in a pale-yellow summer dress. Linden only yelped a few times, when the water touched her wounds, and when Garlan lifted her injured arm a little too high while they were dressing her. They left her long, dark waves loose, since her hair was still slightly damp from its shampooing, and they helped her onto the floor cushion behind the low table in her tent.

Mara draped a fringed shawl in shades of magenta and gold around Linden's shoulders and applied a touch of rouge to her lips and cheeks. When Linden objected to wearing a little makeup, Mara claimed she looked as if a necromancer had just raised her from the dead. Linden gave in and let Mara have her way.

"My Liege, I was relieved to hear you were awake. I stopped by a few times, but Mage Jayna said you were too ill for visitors." Corbahn stood in the entrance to the tent, his wide shoulders framed by the sunlight streaming in around him. Linden invited him to join her at the table, and he sat down on a cushion across from her. Lowering his eyebrows, he added, "You look better than I expected, given your injuries, but you're still too pale. How are you feeling?" Linden made a mental note to thank Mara for applying a bit of rouge.

"I'm much better now, thank you." Linden needed to phrase this next sentence carefully; Corbahn had just become clan chief because the Glenbarrans had killed his father. His grief was raw, his emotions ragged. "I understand from Reynier that you're leaving in the morning, and that you intend to cross the border to conduct lightning strikes in Glenbarra. Is that still your plan?"

Corbahn narrowed his eyes. "Aye. And why are you asking about my plans? As clan chief, I have autonomy over my land and clan. I don't need anyone's permission, not the Elder's and not the Liege's."

Undeterred by his reaction, Linden answered him tactfully. "I wasn't suggesting anything otherwise. But I wonder if you'll allow me to tell you a story?"

Corbahn frowned. "What kind of a story?"

"A story about another war with Glenbarra, about another clan and nation, and their battle plans and tactics."

"You're talking about Valerra, aren't you? Valerra lost its war. I don't intend to lose mine."

Linden smiled sadly. "My uncle used to say the same thing."

"Who was your uncle?"

"The Prime Minister of Valerra, sort of like Reynier, a clan chief and elder all in one. He was also Liege Ayala's grandson."

Corbahn waved his hand impatiently. "Fine. Go ahead and tell me your story. But don't expect me to change my mind, or my plans."

Linden wanted to describe Valerra's downfall in such a way that Corbahn learned its valuable lessons without having to experience the destruction firsthand. She thought about the best storyteller she'd ever known, her father, a retired Royal Marine colonel. Ric Arlyss could weave a tale so rich and full of personal details that he had his audience on the edges of their seats.

Taking a deep breath, Linden began by describing the first daytime raid Glenbarra had conducted more than a year earlier. They attacked her home and her school in Quorne, a Valerran border town. During the school raid, Linden had tried to make it to the gym before the teachers cast a defensive shield and locked it down. But she stopped to help a five-year-old who'd become lost, neither one of them making it to the gym in time. The two of them hid in a closet inside the school, Linden casting a veil of drabness around them as a grihm snapped his jaws on the other side of the door. Linden noticed Corbahn leaning forward as she told the story.

She said, "I almost yelped out loud when I looked through the crack where the closet door didn't quite meet the wall. Staring back at me was a grihm, his snout sniffing around the door, his canines bared, snapping and snarling. My heart seized up in my chest. I was sure he'd discovered us."

"How could you have escaped from a grihm just on the other side of the door?" asked Corbahn.

"The veil of drabness I'd cast hid us from sight, and from his superior sense of smell."

"Remarkable," said Corbahn, shaking his head. "What

about your house? You mentioned it had been damaged as well?"

Linden described dashing home after the raid to look for her parents. She'd reached the house before they did, and when she walked inside, she almost ran right back out. The Glenbarrans had targeted her home for destruction, and they'd cut her picture out of its frame and taken it with them. That had probably scared her even more than staring at the grihm's wolfish snout.

"Wait a minute," said Corbahn. "Glenbarran raiders stole an image of you?" When Linden nodded, he asked, "How old were you then?"

"I had just turned sixteen and a half."

Corbahn ran a hand through his hair. "That proves Mordahn and his Fallow friends have been tracking your whereabouts for quite some time. They knew a mage with your abilities would begin to manifest around age sixteen."

Linden said, "I sure did manifest some crazy talents. I started fires, blew up things, and saw visions. It was a difficult, confusing time for me."

"What did your parents do after the raid?"

"They sent me to the opposite end of the country, as far away from the border as possible. That's when I went to live with my grandmother Nari, who tutored me in Serving magic, and Alban, her son. Uncle Alban was my father's older brother."

"Is that when the war heated up?"

Linden shook her head. "The Glenbarrans took their time, almost toying with us. They conducted occasional border raids, but never in the same place, to test our weak spots. Meanwhile life went on pretty much normally, until news arrived the Glenbarrans had overrun the borderlands in multiple areas, killing large numbers of marines and residents.

"Meanwhile, our best mages couldn't overcome their Fallow spells. Our equipment malfunctioned, our defensive shields failed, and in the end, the Glenbarrans marched all the way across Valerra, laying siege to our capital, Bellaryss."

"Where were you living during that time?" asked Corbahn, who'd been following every word of Linden's narrative.

"In the capital. I helped the other mages cast shields of impenetrable fog along the city walls. But the Glenbarrans kept coming, their Fallow sorcery wearing us down. We finally pulled back into the Valerran Museum and waited until they stormed the building."

Corbahn's eyes grew wide. "How did you manage to escape, surrounded as you were?"

"The mages, including my uncle, had mapped out various escape routes for us, drilling us in each route. They made the apprentices, Jayna, Mara, Toz, Remy and me, promise to run when the Glenbarrans broke through our defenses. Each of us carried an important fay or Valerran artifact out of that building with us." Despite the summer heat, Linden shivered, pulling the shawl more tightly around her shoulders. Recalling that final battle inside the museum, where Glenbarran soldiers and grihms overwhelmed the last of the city's defenders, still gave her nightmares.

"What happened to your family?" Corbahn asked quietly.

Linden's mouth quivered and she closed her eyes, bringing up the faces of her loved ones, which became harder with the passage of time. "Nari was killed saving Toz and me at the start of the siege. My uncle and many others died in the museum, buying us precious time to escape. When the border fell, my parents sent word they planned to travel to the colonies, on the other side of the barrens. I don't know whether they ever made it. Matteo, my brother, was at the border with the Royal Marines when the Glenbarrans invaded. I know he suffered severe injuries, but I don't know anything more."

Linden added, "My story is no different than any of my friends. Every one of us has lost our families and our homes, all victims of Fallow sorcery and Glenbarran thuggery."

Corbahn reached across the table to take Linden's hand, his grip warm and firm. "I'm sorry for you, for all of you. Your losses are even worse than I'd imagined, worse even than what we've inflicted on ourselves during our civil war. I don't understand how these Fallow hacks can devise spells that outperform Serving mages. There's no historical basis for this either. I've spoken with Pryl, and he agrees. Fallow magic has never been as powerful as it is right now."

"What's changed? How can Fallow magic have become practically unbeatable?" asked Linden.

Corbahn squared his jaw. "I don't know, but I aim to find out."

Linden nodded. "We need to infiltrate Glenbarra, figure out the secret behind Fallow magic."

Gripping her hand harder, Corbahn's voice rose. "We? Who said anything about you coming along?"

"Ouch," said Linden pointedly, withdrawing her hand from his.

"Oh, sorry," he said, "but you're in no condition for a military campaign. I'll bet you can't even stand without assistance, can you?"

Linden ignored his question. "Now that the poison from that arrow is out of my system, I'll heal quickly. Give me one week, and I'll be ready."

"A whole week? Those thugs who killed my father will be long gone by then!"

If Linden could have stood up unassisted at that point, she would have stormed out of her own tent; Corbahn infuriated her, missing the whole point of her story. She slapped her hand on the table, her voice rising. "Just listen to yourself. You're making this about Haydahn, about vengeance, about you! If that's your strategy, then we've already lost."

Corbahn shouted, "My warriors can take on five Glenbarrans for every one of us! Arrowood will demolish their best swordfighters and archers."

One of the guards posted outside Linden's tent ran through the doorway, his hand on the hilt of his sword. "Is everything alright?" he asked nervously.

Linden and Corbahn both answered with a snappy "Aye!" Linden added more quietly, "Thank you, but we're fine." The guard nodded and quickly retreated.

Linden folded her arms. "How will killing Glenbarran soldiers help us solve the puzzle of their Fallow magic?"

Corbahn's fighting spirit seemed to have fizzled out. He rubbed his forehead and muttered, "I don't know."

Realizing she'd scored a point, she waited a few beats before saying, "Neither do I. But I have a feeling Pryl might have some ideas."

"If he has some ideas, why hasn't he said anything up until now?"

"He's had other priorities," Linden said. "He knew he had to stop the Faymon civil war once and for all. Pryl brought your father and Chief Orlaf to my crowning ceremony to urge reconciliation. He also encouraged us to resume the magic trials to help promote unity between the clans. And it was Pryl's scout who tipped us off about Mordahn and the necromancer, which means that scout has informants inside King Roi's court."

Corbahn said, "Let's discuss this when I get back."

"How long will you be gone?" Linden gripped the edge of the table, waiting for his answer, wondering whether her story had made any difference.

"A few days, maybe longer. We need to reinforce our defenses all along the perimeter."

Maybe he'd listened after all. At least Corbahn wasn't talking about invading Glenbarra in the next few days. Linden said, "I'll speak to Pryl while you're gone. It's time we learned what the Glenbarrans have already figured out, the secret behind the rise of Fallow magic."

CHAPTER 12

Corbahn rose from the floor cushion, preparing to leave. He waited, and when Linden remained seated at the table, he said, "You really can't stand up without assistance, can you?" Not waiting for her reply, Corbahn walked around the table and dropped on one knee beside her. "Put your arms around my neck."

Linden's pride warred with her practical nature for a few moments, but common sense won. She reached up to Corbahn, wrapping her arms around his neck as he scooped her up. Instead of feeling awkward when she leaned her head against his chest, a deep calm washed over her. She inhaled his scent, of wood smoke and leather. An image of her standing near the Pale Sea with Corbahn, watching as the waves rolled in, came to her. Linden heard the surf as it pounded the shoreline, and it sounded like the steady beat of Corbahn's heart.

He repeated his question, "My Liege, where would you like to go?"

Snapping her attention back to the present, Linden

said, "If you could deposit me in that basket seat on the other side of the curtain, I'll be fine until Jayna returns."

Corbahn gently set her down in the seat, Linden biting her lip to keep from crying out. "Thanks for the lift," she said quietly. Then addressing him formally, Faymon Liege to Arrowood Chief, she added, "Travel safely, Chief Corbahn Erewin, and rely on Serving magic to protect you. This is the true path."

"Aye, my Liege. This is the true path." Corbahn repeated the phrase, used by fays and Faymons to acknowledge the Serving way. He walked to the filmy curtain separating Linden's private quarters from the public space and paused. Turning partly around, his face in silhouette, he said, "We will defeat this thing, this Fallowness, that's claimed too many lives already. And then perhaps we could travel to the other side of Faynwood. I'd like to see that Pale Sea of yours one day."

Linden started at his words. Long after Corbahn had left the tent, she pondered the image of her and Corbahn standing together by the Pale Sea. She wondered whether she could have transferred that mental picture to Corbahn, or whether it had come to him unbidden. She closed her eyes and dreamt of sunshine reflecting off the sea, rolling green waves dappled with white light, extending from the water's edge to where the sea met the sky.

◞

SINCE REYNIER always contacted Pryl on her behalf, Linden was clueless how the communication channels worked between Faymons and fays, except that fays were masters of anticipation. Either that, or fays had figured out how to be in two places at the same time, which Linden didn't think was possible. About the time Linden had given up trying to reach Pryl, he appeared at the door of her tent, one of the guards announcing his arrival.

Linden found it easier to sit in her basket seat than on a floor cushion while she was healing, sometimes leaving the privacy curtain open to make it easier to greet visitors from her seat. When Pryl entered her tent, she started to rise, intending to walk over to the table with him, but he waved her back into her seat. "Please sit, my Liege. I'm in a pacing mood."

Linden thanked him and sat back down. Kal and the small black cat, whose name Linden still didn't know, greeted Pryl. Kal clicked his beak and walked around Pryl in circles, while the cat planted herself in front of Pryl, purring loudly. Pryl spoke in his buzzing fay language to Kal, who flapped his wings once and returned to his spot on the floor near Linden with a satisfied sigh. Pryl picked up the cat, scratched behind her ears, and handed her to Linden. "Zeena and Kal seem to be getting along."

"So that's her name!" said Linden, tickling Zeena under her chin. "I kept forgetting to ask Corbahn and Carissa, and then after their father died, there was never an appropriate time."

Pryl shook his head. "Haydahn's passing is a heavy blow, not only to his family and clan, but to me personally. I'd been his mentor from an early age."

"How does that work," asked Linden. "A fay mentoring a human?"

Pryl shrugged, "Much the same as any mentoring relationship. There must be a match, of personality and passion, and over time, a deep bond forms." Pryl added, "Haydahn begged me to take on Corbahn, and I'm doing my best, but he's much more headstrong than his father."

"Try storytelling."

"Storytelling?" Pryl gave her a puzzled look.

Linden explained how she'd told Corbahn a few of her stories from the Valerran war, and he seemed to have listened.

Pryl said, "Well done. Although I expect you may have more influence over him than the rest of us."

"How so?" asked Linden, who didn't think she had any influence whatsoever, with Corbahn or any of the other clan chiefs, including her own cousin. They politely listened to her opinions, and then did what they wanted to do anyway. Since Serai and Hemma were women, she didn't think being female was the issue. She figured it had more to do with her being young and only half Faymon, despite the fact she was a direct descendant of Liege Ayala.

As if reading her thoughts, Pryl said, "You're young, beautiful, and the Liege of all Faynwood. Of course you're going to have influence with Corbahn."

Linden shifted in her seat, hoping Pryl wouldn't bring up anything related to the rites of binding. Pryl stopped walking around the tent to face her. "You've heard about the prophecies surrounding you and the Chief of Arrowood?"

Linden held up her hand. "Aye. But I wish I hadn't, and no number of predictions or prophecies will be able to make me marry someone I don't love."

"Of course not," said Pryl, "prophecies are open to interpretation, much as any vision or foresight. Each of us must live in the moment, shaped by our history, informed by our knowledge. I believe in letting the future take care of itself."

"You really believe that?" asked Linden. "I thought fays were all about studying the prophecies and helping to shape the future accordingly."

Pryl shrugged. "That's true for the major prophecies, such as when and where our new Liege would arrive in Faynwood. But otherwise, we try not to interfere."

Linden stroked Zeena's soft coat. "What do the prophecies say about Fallow magic? Why is it so powerful? How do we defeat it?"

Pryl stopped pacing and stood in front of her, his gray eyes clouded. "The prophecies seem to diverge at the precise point that you, our new Liege, entered Faynwood. There are multiple threads and much disagreement."

"What does that mean?"

"It means the fays don't have any more answers than the Faymons. We must live in the present moment and muddle through this difficult time together."

Linden tilted her head, trying to decipher Pryl's words. She felt certain the truth must be hidden among the various prophetic threads he mentioned. "Can you tell me about those multiple threads? Which ones do you think are more likely to come to pass?"

Pryl put his hands behind his back and resumed his pacing. "While there are many possible outcomes, most of us agree on the likeliest." Pryl stopped in front of Linden. She thought perhaps she might not want to hear what Pryl was about to tell her.

She said, "We lose Faynwood to Fallow magic, don't we?"

Pryl's lips were compressed in a thin line. "That's what most of the seers believe."

"But not you?"

Pryl raised his shoulders in a half-shrug. "I'm a wee more optimistic than most fay folk. I have more faith in the power of Serving magic and my Faymon friends."

"Do any of the seers agree?"

"One seer predicted that Fallowness would spread across the continent, nearly swallowing us up, but that we'd be able to push back against it in the end."

"What did this seer foresee that the others did not?"

"That a small band of Serving mages would disrupt the Fallow places of power, restoring balance between the two magical systems."

"I've never heard of these places of power. What are they?"

Pryl said, "They're locations where the effects of magic are amplified. Think of them as sort of echo chambers, but for magic instead of sound."

"Where do we find these echo chambers?"

"They're not marked on any map. Many seers believe there is more myth than magic to them."

Linden knew Pryl deployed his scouts across the continent, a personal network of fay spies reporting back to him on a regular basis. "Are scouts such as Wreyn seeking information on these places of power?"

Pryl nodded. "I've asked my scouts to watch closely for any unusual spikes in Fallow magic. That's how Wreyn discovered necromantic activity, Mordahn returned from the dead, and rumors about a place of power that can amplify magical energy."

"Where is it? And can it be destroyed?" asked Linden.

Pryl waved his hand in a westerly direction. "Deep inside Glenbarra. And I believe so, but I've never encountered any incantations on how to destroy such places."

"So we need to travel undetected through Glenbarra, locate this place of power, and improvise an incantation to destroy it? And then find any other places of power and do the same?"

Pryl blew out a puff of air. "I know it must sound like a fool's errand."

"The odds are no worse than escaping from a museum swarming with Glenbarrans and grihms during the siege of Bellaryss."

"With an equally low probability of success," said Pryl.

"How do we even begin to plan for an operation like this?" asked Linden.

"We start with you and your friends. You've done the impossible once before. Let's learn from your experiences."

Pryl stayed for dinner, joined by Mara and Jayna, who'd spent their days since the forest fire and subsequent battle caring for Linden and the other injured patients in their camp. Toz and Remy had ridden out with the clan chiefs to help cast defensive spells along the border.

Pryl questioned Linden and her friends closely about the siege of Bellaryss, going over the same ground more than once to help him understand the Glenbarrans' battle tactics and use of Fallow magic.

"Each of you acquired weapons at the Valerran Museum, ancient fay weapons, by the sound of them. And you say these weapons 'chose' you?" Pryl asked. When the three women nodded, he asked to see Linden's sword.

Mara rose from the floor cushion and said to Linden, "I'll bring it to you. I know enough not to unsheathe it."

As Mara disappeared behind the tent's privacy curtain, Pryl asked, "Why can't Mara unsheathe your sword?"

Linden explained, "When we told you that the weapons chose us, we weren't exaggerating. If Mara tried using my sword, it might flip out of her hand or even cut her, not seriously, but enough to let her know she wasn't the sword's rightful owner."

Mara returned with the sword. Handing it to Linden,

she said, "And the hieroglyphs won't glow green for anyone other than Linden."

Linden laid the sword, encased in its burgundy scabbard, on the table. She gripped the hilt, withdrawing the sword slowly from its casing, the green hieroglyphs coming alive along the blade. When she'd pulled her sword halfway out, she paused and said to Pryl, "It's safe for you to touch the sword hilt, but don't pick up the sword."

Pryl reached out his hand cautiously, touching the hilt with his forefinger. The hieroglyphs immediately went from luminescent green to dull gray. "Amazing. I've heard of these weapons, forged by my ancestors more than a millennia ago, a perfect blending of fay technology and Serving magic. And you say they were part of a collection of weapons within the Valerran Museum? Hidden in plain sight." Pryl shook his head. "Who among you still retains these weapons?"

Jayna said, "The three of us, plus Toz and Remy."

"No one else?"

"We're the only ones who managed to escape that day," said Linden.

Pryl scratched his beard, deep in thought. Linden and the others waited as he closed his eyes and began whispering in his own language. Linden assumed he was talking to himself and not some invisible fay advisor. He swayed on his cushion, his voice rising and falling in a buzzing rhythm not unlike a swarm of bumblebees.

Nodding decisively, Pryl opened his eyes to explain. "Years ago, I memorized a scroll written by the one seer who believed we would have a fighting chance against Fallow magic. I've consulted its contents because our conversation jogged a memory. She predicted a small band of Serving mages, comprised of fays, Faymons, and Valerrans, would overcome Fallow magic and its hold over our entire continent, including the places of power. And there's more."

Pryl sipped from his wine goblet before continuing. "The seer predicted three events would herald the rise of Fallowness and formation of our band of mages: the fall of Valerra, the crowning of a new Liege, and the reunification of the five clans."

Linden's eyes widened. "Does she say anything else, give us any other clues?"

Pryl said, "She claimed four Valerrans would wield ancient swords imbued with Serving magic. They would be led by three Faymons and three fays. I'm assuming we will need to destroy the places of power, at least, that's strongly implied in the scroll."

"Four Valerrans? But there are five of us," said Mara.

"You're counting Linden, because she's your Valerran friend, but to us, she is the Faymon Liege," explained Pryl.

"Which other Faymons will join us?" asked Jayna.

Pryl lowered his eyebrows, considering the possibilities. After some deliberation, he said, "The Faymon Elder and the Arrowood Chief. That still leaves three other clan chiefs to lead Faynwood in their absence."

"Are you planning to come with us?" Linden hoped he would say yes; Pryl would be a steadying influence and could help mediate any disagreements between Corbahn and the others.

Pryl nodded. "Aye. As Chief of the Fay Nation, I must be part of the group. I'll bring my two best scouts, Wreyn and Efram."

"When do we leave?" asked Linden.

"As soon as you're well enough to travel, and the rest of our band of Serving mages returns from the border."

CHAPTER 13

TEN DAYS LATER, THE FIVE CLAN CHIEFS, PRYL AND HIS TWO scouts, and Linden and her friends, gathered around the table in her tent for their final war council meeting. When Pryl had first broached the plan, neither Corbahn nor Reynier thought Linden should go with them, despite the fact she grew stronger every day.

Reynier's reasoning was that it was risky to send both the Faymon Liege and Faymon Elder on such a dangerous mission inside Glenbarra. He would go willingly, but he wanted Linden to remain behind. Corbahn agreed with Reynier, but Pryl told them the Liege, the Elder, and the Chief of Arrowood had to work together to bring down Fallow magic and the places of power.

In the meantime, the three remaining clan chiefs, Orlaf, Serai, and Hemma, would be charged with protecting all of Faynwood from any further Glenbarran incursions. The three chiefs raised their goblets of wine in a toast to Reynier, Corbahn, Linden, and the others who would be departing in the morning, and to the success of their mission. The war council officially over, most of the group headed for their tents, until just Reynier, Jayna, Pryl, and Corbahn remained seated around Linden's table, discussing a few final details.

"Are you sure you will be able to transport us and our horses beyond the Glenbarran's border alarms undetected? Seems like a heavy load to me," said Corbahn. The Glenbarrans had stationed Fallow mages along their entire perimeter to establish one continuous border shield, making it nearly impossible to cross into Glenbarra without setting off magical alarms.

Pryl said, "Each fay can take one additional horse and rider at a time into the traveling mists. It'll be fine; we'll transport you in stages." Since fays could only translocate short distances using their traveling mists, and the heavier the load the shorter the distance, Linden hoped they would be able to clear the Glenbarran border without drawing attention.

"What I don't understand is how fays can use traveling mists without detection by Fallow mages. It's still magic, isn't it?" ask Jayna.

Linden felt a lecture coming, but she was just as curious as her friend. Pryl steepled his fingers together and said, "That's an excellent question. When fays use traveling mists to translocate, we tap into elemental magic—air, earth, and water—which effectively masks our Serving magic. Fallow mages can't detect elemental magic, which is ancient and exists outside of either magical system. The only way to detect elemental magic is to become part of it, for example, when you and your horse will travel on the mists with one of my scouts."

Jayna furrowed her brow. "Oh, I guess I understand."

Pryl smiled. "Magic, like many things in life, is best understood when experienced."

"On that note, I'll take my leave," said Corbahn, rising. "I promised my mother I'd stop in at the longhouse to say goodbye. I'll meet you back here at dawn." Turning to Linden, he added, "I may as well take Zeena with me now." Hearing her name, the cat raised her head from Linden's lap and meowed.

Linden kissed the top of Zeena's head before handing her to Corbahn. "Please thank Carissa for taking care of Zeena while we're gone." Lowering her voice, she added, "And for helping Garlan to look after Kal." Kal had been moping around the tent for the past few days. Not only were miniature griffins extremely rare, but they were also highly intuitive. Kal had already figured out Linden would be taking a trip without him. When she tried explaining to him that she couldn't very well sneak around Glenbarra with a pet griffin flying overhead, he flapped his wings and squawked at her.

Pryl and Reynier rose from the table, said goodnight, and followed Corbahn outside. After they left, Jayna reached down to pet Kal, who clicked his beak half-heart-edly. "This may be the craziest thing we've ever done, and we've done some pretty crazy things," she said.

"Which part?" asked Linden. "Sneaking across the border, disguising ourselves as Glenbarrans, or trying to bring down the Fallow places of power?"

"All of the above."

"I know," said Linden. She stared down at the table, still covered with half-consumed platters of food and several unopened bottles of wine. The servants waited until every last guest left the tent before clearing away the table, a custom instituted by Reynier to ensure no one accidentally or intentionally eavesdropped on privileged conversations.

"I'm uneasy about this operation. There are far too many unknowns."

"Have you had any more visions?" asked Jayna.

"Not since the nightmares I told you about," said Linden. "But this prophecy that we're using as the basis for our mission is awfully vague. And something Pryl said bothers me."

"Pryl says a lot of strange things. What did he say that's unsettling you?"

"Remember when we told him about the weapons we'd discovered in the Valerran Museum, and he said all five of us would need to carry those weapons with us to defeat the Fallowness that's spreading across our continent?"

Jayna said, "I remember. So?"

"Then why did he say that according to the prophecy, four Valerrans would wield ancient swords imbued with Serving magic? I don't like going from five to four," said Linden, crossing her arms.

"But Pryl explained that you're counted with the Faymons. The four Valerrans are Mara, Remy, Toz, and me."

Linden shrugged. "I know, but I'm half-Valerran, and I have one of those special swords."

A line creased Jayna's brow. "You think one of us isn't going to make it, don't you?"

"I don't know what to think, but I'm going to worry the entire time."

After Jayna left, Linden picked up *Timely Spells*, paging through it while the servants cleared the table. Pryl told her to leave her spell book behind. He explained they had to leave behind all personal items, anything that could connect them to Faynwood or Serving magic, except for their weapons from Valerra. She reviewed all the familiar spells, hoping to find a new spell written across the parchment, one that would explain the steps needed to destroy a Fallow place of power.

Finding no new spells, she closed the book and got on the floor beside Kal to scratch behind his wings, one of his favorite spots. He stretched out next to her with a contented sigh, his way of telling her, "You're forgiven for not taking me along."

Linden rose before sunrise the next morning, tidied her living space inside the tent, and dressed in the garb of a Fallow mage: black pants and tunic, topped with a black, hooded robe lined in red satin. She cinched the robe at her waist with a red sash. Linden had no idea where Pryl had secured the mages' clothes, and she didn't want to know.

Garlan brought Linden a cup of tea and a chunk of fresh bread, a last meal to savor in the privacy and security of her tent. Before she withdrew, Garlan said, "If ye don't mind me saying, my Liege, I wish ye weren't going. I don't like yer odds."

Linden looked at Garlan's kind face, her gray eyebrows drawn together, and smiled. "I appreciate your concern, Garlan, and I can't say you're wrong. Although our odds of protecting Serving magic by doing nothing are just as poor. I'm of the mind that taking action is an improvement over sitting on my hands."

Garlan nodded. "Aye, mum, I take yer meaning. I just wish there were another way, without sacrificing the lot of ye." Garlan pressed her lips together, as if to stem the tide of her own frankness. "Will that be all, mum?"

Linden gave the old servant a hug. "Aye, thank you. I have all that I need at the moment." Garlan bowed and left the tent.

Linden sipped her tea and tore off small chunks of bread, chewing slowly. She wondered when she would feel this safe again, probably not until after she'd returned from Glenbarra, if she made it back at all. Shaking off the gloomy thoughts, she gave Kal a final hug, slipped on a black chainmail vest, and belted on her sword and matching dagger, also from the Valerran Museum.

She stepped out of the tent as the first yellow bands of light peeked above the horizon. One of the servants brought her horse around, handing her the reins. Ashir bore no identifying colors, no ribbons or adornments, just a plain leather saddle and two saddlebags. Each traveler carried his or her own supplies: extra tunic and pants, small pup tent, sleeping roll, water skins, and basic food supply, consisting of jerky, fruit, nuts, and oats. They would need to supplement their food supplies by hunting for fresh meat and finding additional water sources along the way.

Toz arrived before the others, dressed as a Glenbarran trooper: bronzed chainmail layered over dark-gray tunic and pants, his sword from the Valerran Museum strapped to his side. As he dismounted, his chainmail reflected the rising sun, lighting up in a flash of white and then winking out again. "Can you imagine what my father would say about this get-up?" Toz grinned. "And he thought I'd never amount to anything!" Toz's father had been a cranky, difficult man, someone so completely the opposite of his son that Linden often wondered how they could have been related.

"It feels strange to be walking around in these clothes," she agreed.

Toz kicked the ground with the toe of his boot. "Honestly, it's all felt strange to me, the war, our escape, living here in Faynwood for the past few months. Some days I feel like I'm wandering around in limbo, trying to find my way home."

Toz's words sent a shiver down Linden's spine. She'd never known him to be moody, or gloomy, or even all that self-reflective. "How long have you been feeling this way?"

"Ever since your grandmother died saving my life."

Linden tried not to think about that moment, Nari stepping in front of Toz, the sword coming down on her neck instead of his, Linden screaming and dropping to her knees in front of her grandmother's still form.

Linden didn't know how to reassure Toz. She could understand his feelings of estrangement from everything familiar since she often shared them. Sometimes she'd wake up in the middle of the night and call out to her father. Then she'd remember that he'd fled Valerra with her mother, same as Linden, only they'd wound up heading in opposite directions.

Reynier and Jayna arrived, followed by the rest of their group. Corbahn seemed preoccupied. He barely uttered a greeting, and Linden caught him glaring at Toz standing next to her. Pryl introduced Efram, who appeared to be in his mid-twenties, with curly hair, brown skin, and an air of quiet confidence that Linden found calming.

The fay chief had instructed everyone with blue hair—the fays and Faymons in the group—to mask the color with dye. While they could have magically altered their appearance, Pryl insisted they had to avoid even the simplest of spells while they were undercover in Glenbarra. Linden's hair was still midnight black, but with copper streaks masking her blue. Corbahn and Reynier both wound up with bronze highlights running through their brown hair. The fays must have overdone the dye, because they all had dull black hair, as if they'd dipped their heads in boot polish. Linden hoped none of the Glenbarran guards examined them too closely.

Pryl inspected each of them, adjusting Efram's red sash, reminding Remy to tuck his pants into his boots. Finally nodding his approval, Pryl said, "We'll travel in three groups: Mage Toz, Mage Remy, and Mage Mara in the first group; Mage Jayna and Elder Reynier in the second; Chief Corbahn and Liege Linden in the final group."

Corbahn said, "I think we should dispense with using titles, first names only from here on out. Otherwise we might slip up at the wrong time."

Pryl nodded, "Aye, good idea."

"Alright then, are we ready to begin our trip across the Glenbarran border, into Fallow territory?" asked Reynier. Linden's stomach tightened into anxious knots, but she nodded along with the others.

"We'll attempt to do this as quickly as possible, so everyone, please mount your horses and be prepared to enter the mists on our cue," said Pryl. Climbing onto his horse, he came alongside Mara and her palomino. Wreyn and Efram trotted over to Toz and Remy.

Corbahn brought his champagne-colored stallion next to Linden and Ashir. Glancing at his horse, she said, "He's beautiful. What's his name?"

Corbahn patted his horse's neck fondly. "Chestir, a gift from my father a few years back." Corbahn's chest heaved as he took a deep breath.

Linden could tell he was trying to keep his emotions in check. She understood the rawness of his grief and wanted to say something encouraging, but no words came to her. She said simply, "Your father chose well."

"Aye, he did at that."

They watched the first group depart. Recalling a Valerran blessing for safe travels her mother used to recite before every trip, Linden repeated it silently as her friends prepared to enter Glenbarra. "May you travel in peace, arrive in safety, and rest in the hope of tomorrow."

Pryl uttered a buzzing command, and a thick white mist rose from the ground, enveloping Pryl, Mara, and their horses. As Wreyn and Efram each repeated the command, foggy wisps swirled around Toz, Remy, the two fays, and their horses. The misty tendrils reached upward, separate smoky puffs combining to form one massive cloud that swallowed up six horses and their riders. When Linden could no longer distinguish between Toz, Remy, Mara, and the fays, the cloud shuddered and then collapsed, the riders and their horses vanishing in a blink.

No one said anything for a few beats. Reynier broke the silence. "I've been watching Pryl come and go like that for years, but it still fascinates me."

"How far does he think he'll be able to transport us?" asked Jayna.

Reynier shrugged. "Definitely beyond the border and the shields. Wreyn scouted an area she believes offers low risk of detection."

Linden detected a note of uncertainty in Reynier's voice. "But it may be too far away to make it in one jump through the mists?"

Reynier nodded. "When loaded down with horses and supplies, the jumps are less precise."

Corbahn shook his head. "I knew it. I should have insisted we travel with more fay escorts, but Pryl based all of his calculations on this single, problematic prophecy, including who should and shouldn't cross into Glenbarra."

"Do you think fays are more superstitious than we are?" asked Jayna.

Reynier said, "Definitely, but I think Corbahn's right. Pryl is meticulously following every letter of the prophecy.

Let's hope the seer was equally meticulous in recording the vision."

Linden heard a horse neighing nearby, but none of their horses had made the sound. Scanning the area, she spotted Pryl emerging from the traveling mist about twenty yards away, his horse snorting as his hoofs landed on the ground. Pryl's hood was pulled down low over his forehead, and he seemed more distracted than usual. "Where's Wreyn?" she asked.

Pryl said, "She's coming. We ran into a spot of trouble with Efram's jump—he landed too close to the border and set off an alarm—but everyone's safe."

Wreyn emerged from the mist and said, "We need to move quickly!"

After Reynier and Jayna rode up to them, disappearing into the mists with Pryl and Wreyn, Corbahn said, "I think we should travel with one hand on our sword hilts and the other holding tight to our reins."

Nodding, Linden agreed. "I'll feel better when we're far away from the border shields. It should be easier to blend in when we don't have a Glenbarran patrol breathing down our necks."

"That's true, at least until we reach a place of power, where I expect we'll run into plenty of Glenbarran guards. In the meantime, none of us will be casting any Fallow spells, even to protect our cover. It's too risky," said Corbahn. Fallow magic and Serving magic were incompatible, the risk of contaminating a Serving mage too great to even consider it. Although dressed as Fallow mages, Linden and the fays would never attempt an actual Fallow spell.

Linden remembered a classmate a few years back, a precocious boy who'd managed to smuggle a book of Fallow spells into their magic-handling lab. When he attempted one of the basic spells in class, as a joke to draw attention to himself, he turned pale as a ghost, collapsing in a heap on the floor. The boy was rushed to the best healer in town, who declared she couldn't reverse the contamination. By trying the Fallow spell, he'd leached out every vestige of Serving magic within himself. Since he didn't want to become a Fallow mage, the boy had transferred to a different school to learn one of the trades.

Linden and Corbahn both started at the sound of hooves hitting the ground, as Pryl and Wreyn emerged from the mists. "Quick! We've no time to waste." shouted Pryl, waving his hand at Corbahn.

Wreyn trotted over to Linden and said, "Be ready to run!"

Linden shifted uneasily in her saddle. Wreyn's words brought back painful memories of the last time she'd been told to be ready to run. It had been during the siege of Bellaryss, right before Valerra fell to Glenbarra, when her uncle and many others fought against unbeatable odds to give her and her friends time to escape. Linden gripped the handle of her sword in her right hand and wrapped Ashir's reins more firmly around her left. "Ready!" she shouted as the mists rose up around them.

CHAPTER 14

ENSHROUDED BY MIST, LINDEN SAW ONLY THE SHADOWS OF THINGS whipping past—trees, the river, more trees. But she heard a crash of sounds, men shouting, horses neighing, grihms growling, and a woman whispering in her ear. Linden strained to hear the woman's words above the din. Then Ashir's hooves hit solid ground, and it was Wreyn's voice she heard, urging her to gallop straight ahead.

Since fleeing seemed the more pressing need, Linden gripped the reins with both hands and left her sword in its scabbard. She leaned forward for speed, following directly behind Wreyn's fast little pinto. Pryl and Corbahn landed behind them, Pryl shouting, "Heads down, and follow the ladies!"

A pack of grihms, yapping and snarling, pursued them, but Linden kept her eyes focused on Wreyn. Crouching even lower in her saddle, she clicked her tongue and flicked the reins. Ashir strained at his leads, putting more distance between them and the grihms. As the growling and howling grew fainter, tendrils of fog curled around them, and they were making another jump through the mists.

This time they landed on a rocky hillside overlooking the Windrun River, which separated Glenbarra from its neighbors to the east, Faynwood and Valerra. Wreyn slowed down and called behind her, "Watch your footing here!" Linden heard running water nearby, a stream or tributary feeding the Windrun River below. She guided Ashir around boulders and past rock outcroppings, the sound of rushing water growing louder.

Wreyn stopped in front of a cave entrance and shouted, "Dismount and follow me. Stay close to the wall." Linden, Pryl, and Corbahn led their horses into the cave, the din of water crashing nearby nearly deafening now. Points of light punctuated the cave, and Linden could see glimpses of sky above them. Wreyn rounded a bend, and Linden gasped. A gushing waterfall blocked their path, the water tumbling into a foamy pool a hundred feet below them.

Wreyn rounded another corner, and this time Linden found herself staring at a limestone ledge running behind the frothing waterfall. The roar of water was so loud that Wreyn pointed in front of her to indicate they'd be walking underneath the curtain of water. Wreyn's small pinto seemed unfazed, having made this trip several times already that morning, but Ashir flared his nostrils and snorted. Linden patted his neck and led him slowly across the ledge, hugging the damp rock face until they passed beyond the falling water.

After Corbahn led Chestir off the ledge, he said, "Good thinking, Wreyn. The running water makes it much more difficult for the grihms to track us."

Nodding, Wreyn added, "And running water distorts magical energy. A Fallow mage would have a more difficult time detecting us here and hitting us with a spell."

"Where is everyone else?" asked Linden.

"Waiting for you to arrive so we could have breakfast," said Remy. He carried two torches, and handing one to Corbahn, pointed to a passageway behind him. "We're down this way."

They followed Remy's point of light bouncing ahead of them, through a damp tunnel, and into a drier space with boulders of various sizes scattered about. Guiding them to an alcove where the rest of the horses were already munching on oats, he said, "Grab your meal kits from your saddle bags and leave your horses here."

Remy led them to the far side of the cave, where everyone else gathered around a fire pit, the smoke rising up toward an opening in the rock face twenty feet above them. Linden perked up at the scent of cinnamon-infused porridge cooking over the open flame and sat down on a low boulder next to Toz.

Nodding at the flame, she asked Remy, "What are you using to keep the fire going?" While Remy could magically start a fire without any fuel, simply by snapping his fingers, the fire had to physically consume something to continue to burn.

He pointed to a pile of dark rocks behind her. "They burn nicely."

"We're in a coal seam. Very convenient place to hole up," explained Toz, spooning some porridge into Linden's tin bowl before serving himself.

"Thanks," she said, stirring the hot mixture. Corbahn sat on Linden's other side and helped himself to the porridge.

"Glad to see you made it in one piece," said Toz, nodding at Corbahn.

"I prefer to travel with my horse's hooves on the ground rather than in the mists," grumbled Corbahn.

"I rather enjoyed it," said Toz. "Especially with a group of grihms nipping at my heels. I like to imagine the looks on their faces when we vanished from sight."

Corbahn shook his head. "You prefer flight over fight? No wonder Valerra fell so quickly to the Glenbarrans."

Toz lowered his eyebrows. "I choose to live to fight another day. And I'd not be so smug about the Glenbarrans if I were you. They're just getting started."

"You call that fire in Arrowood—and my father's death —just getting started?" Corbahn thrusted his chin forward, his eyes flashing.

"Aye, I'm sorry to say," said Toz. "If you don't believe me, ask Linden. She's seen far worse and suffered for it." Corbahn grunted but didn't answer, taking a bite of his porridge and scowling into the fire.

Linden worried that prolonged exposure to Corbahn's gruffness would antagonize just about everyone, including easygoing Toz. She intervened before things escalated. "Let's focus on next steps. Where are we? How far from a place of power?"

Pryl said, "Efram, tell everyone what you stumbled across."

Efram set his bowl down on the ground beside him. "I found a prison camp about half a day's ride from here. According to the conversation I overheard between two of the guards, the prison itself was built around a place of power."

"Who's housed inside the prison?" asked Toz.

"Men and women, as well as a large number of wolves."

Corbahn frowned. "That sounds like a crossbreeding hotspot." A collective gasp met Corbahn's statement, followed by horrified looks on the face of every fay, Faymon, and Valerran gathered around the fire.

146

Linden placed her half-eaten bowl of porridge on the ground, her appetite gone. Her crossbreeding nightmare came back to her, more real than any dream. She was strapped to a table with wires and tubes stuck to her body, screaming in agony. Linden shuddered. "I can't imagine what horrors those poor prisoners—and those captured wolves—must endure during the process."

Corbahn squared his jaw. "We need to destroy both the place of power and the prison. We have to prevent Fallow mages from turning any more people into grihms."

"You can't be serious," said Toz.

"Of course I'm serious," replied Corbahn. "The process of turning a human into a crossbreed is quite painful."

"But destroying both the prison and the place of power would kill a lot of innocent people. We can't do that," pointed out Toz.

Corbahn waved his hand in the air. "No one wants innocents to perish. If we can save any of them, of course we will. However, many will lose their lives, whether in the prison camp or elsewhere. They'll be casualties of war, same as my father and all the others we've lost in battle."

Toz shook his head. "I didn't sign on to kill civilians. If we don't plan to evacuate the prison first, then I refuse to go in."

"I guess it's flight over fight again, isn't it?" asked Corbahn. Linden drew her brows together, frustrated by the way he was deliberately provoking Toz, who was being perfectly reasonable. She couldn't understand it.

Toz stood up. "I need to get some fresh air." Noticing Linden's concerned look, he added, "I won't wander far."

Linden rose to her feet. "I'll join you. The smoke is bothering my eyes."

"Don't pass beyond the waterfall!" called Wreyn.

Linden nodded and followed Toz out of the large cavern, past the horses, and onto the narrow ledge. They stood close together to be heard above the surge of water tumbling past their ledge and crashing into the pool below.

"Try not to let Corbahn get to you. He's gruff with everyone," said Linden.

Toz snorted. "Not everyone."

"What's that supposed to mean?"

"It's pretty obvious that he's falling for you, and he seems to think I'm a threat."

Linden gaped at him and shook her head. "Impossible."

"Which part? Him liking you or me liking you?" Toz waited a beat and then gave her his most mischievous smile, dimples and all. "We do have some history, you and me."

Linden rolled her eyes. "We were twelve years old."

"He doesn't know that," shrugged Toz.

Linden didn't want to give Corbahn, or anyone else, the wrong ideas about her and Toz. He was her oldest friend, and when they were younger, she thought they could be something more. Although their relationship hadn't evolved that way, they'd remained good friends. She didn't believe for a minute Corbahn liked her in that way. Then she recalled his mention of the old prophecy about the rites of binding between the Chief from Arrowood and the Liege from Tanglewood.

Rubbing her forehead, she said, "I hope you're wrong, but in case you're not, I better not linger out here with you for too long."

Toz said, "Go on ahead. I'll stay out here a while longer before rejoining our happy little group inside."

When Linden returned to the cavern, she found Reynier, Pryl, and Corbahn leaning against a large boulder, watching as Efram and Wreyn sketched various routes in the dirt of the cave floor. Linden joined Mara and Jayna, perched on a long, low boulder nearby. "Where's Remy?" she asked.

Mara pointed behind them to a bedroll and a still form snoring softly. "How can he sleep like that? It's still morning," said Linden.

Mara shrugged. "Don't you remember how Remy used to fall asleep in class? I think he sleeps almost as much as my old kitty."

Linden smiled at the memory of their school days, not so long ago. They'd traveled a great distance since then, in mileage and circumstance. Jayna whispered, "How's Toz? He seemed upset."

Linden nodded. "He's fine. Fortunately, he's not easily riled up."

Jayna lowered her voice. "After you left, Reynier said that Toz is right. Everyone else agreed as well. We have to find a way to save the people in that prison camp before we destroy the place of power inside."

"I'm glad to hear it. How did Corbahn react?"

"He agreed we should attempt to rescue the prisoners," said Mara. "But at the same time, he's concerned it will jeopardize our primary mission."

Linden tilted her head to one side. "So how do we rescue the prisoners without letting ourselves be discovered?"

"That's an excellent question," said Corbahn, who'd wandered over to where they were sitting. "We're still tossing around ideas, none of them foolproof."

"What are the best of the worst?" asked Linden.

Corbahn ran through the ideas and variations, all of which involved having part of their group sneak into the prison, find a way to disarm the guards, free the prisoners, and destroy the place of power, all while remaining unde-tected. Meanwhile, the rest of their group would be waiting for a signal to help the freed prisoners escape and provide any assistance needed with the rest of the plan.

Linden shook her head. "I don't like any of those ideas."

"Neither do I," said Corbahn. "Can you come up with anything better?"

Linden had been thinking about it since she first heard about the prison camp. "For one thing, I don't think we can sneak into that prison. We need to walk in."

Corbahn stared at her. "Walk into the prison? You'll make the guards' day. They'll get to throw all of us in into a cell."

"That's the general idea—although not all of us—but a few of us, definitely," said Linden.

"I'm not following."

Linden said, "You and some of the others disguised as Glenbarran soldiers will escort several men and women, the rest of us, to the prison. We'll be thrown into cells with other prisoners, where we can gather intelligence, while you mingle with some of the guards. Your job will be to learn more about the prison and how to break everyone out of there before we destroy it. Simple."

Corbahn scratched his beard. "It's far from simple, but maybe there's something we can work with."

Wreyn and the others had joined them part way through the conversation. She said, "We'd need to dress like merchants or farmers and ditch these mages' robes."

"Why do we need to change our disguises?" asked Pryl. When Linden and Corbahn described the new approach, walking in instead of breaking in, he nodded slowly. "With a lot of planning and rehearsing, it could work."

"Are you suggesting we allow ourselves to be taken into custody by the Glenbarrans? Completely at their mercy?" asked Reynier, his eyebrows almost to his hairline. When Linden nodded, Reynier paced back and forth inside the cave, waving his hands. "That's a terrible idea. We're going to waltz inside a Glenbarran prison with the Liege of Faynwood in disguise? What will you think of next? Infiltrating the prison population?"

"Something like that, aye," said Linden quietly. She'd learned from Jayna that the best way to deal with Reynier's over-protectiveness was to stay calm and use logic to advance her ideas.

This time she didn't have to win over Reynier, since Corbahn ran through all of their arguments and counterarguments, concluding with, "This is the best option we have at the moment."

Pryl added, "Wreyn and Efram will return to Faynwood on the mists. They can secure new clothes to replace these mages' robes. In the meantime, I suggest we carefully script our roles and practice our parts."

Reynier heaved a loud sigh. "I don't like it, but I can't think of a better alternative."

Since Toz and Remy had been class clowns in school, they had no trouble rehearsing their parts of being junior soldiers under the command of their "captain," played by Corbahn, who had the military bearing to pull it off. However, he was so assertively awkward that Pryl asked Linden to coach him so he wouldn't blow their cover.

"Stop glaring when you say your lines. You look as if you want to lop off someone's head with your sword," said Linden.

Corbahn threw up his hands in disgust. "This won't work. We've been practicing for hours and I'm terrible at play-acting. Maybe we should have Reynier be the captain."

Linden said, "He's doing just fine as the sergeant. Besides, you're too much of a commander to play someone else's foot soldier." She paused and added, "I think we've given you too many lines. We need to use your gruffness to our advantage."

Corbahn thrust out his bottom lip. "I'm not so gruff as all that."

"Actually, you are. It's pretty much part of your personality."

Corbahn kicked the ground with the toe of his boot. "I didn't realize..."

Linden found it hard to believe she may have hurt Corbahn's feelings, but he cast his eyes down and kept kicking the ground with his boot. She decided to soften her message. After all, if he couldn't pull this off, then the rest of their plan went up in smoke. "It's only natural that someone with your responsibilities will speak in a more authoritative tone."

"But sometimes I take it too far?"

Linden couldn't argue with the truth, and she figured a bit of self-awareness might help Corbahn become an even better leader, that is, if they survived and returned to Fayn-wood. "Sometimes."

Nodding, Corbahn said, "I don't mean to be so grouchy. I know I was hard on Toz earlier. He's so bubbly all the time, and yet he has a depth I can appreciate as well. I can see why you like him."

Linden said, "Toz and I have known each other since we were toddlers. He's my oldest friend." Toz's earlier warning rang in her head. Although she owed Corbahn no explanations, she decided to clarify. "And nothing more."

Corbahn raised his eyes and squinted at the far wall of the cave. Shrugging, he said, "Let's run through my lines again."

Linden smiled. "I'm going to cut out some of these words. That way you can deliver them with more punch."

"That sounds more like my style." Corbahn gave her a half-smile in return. Her heart responded with the tiniest of flip-flops, which she chose to ignore.

CHAPTER 15

Pryl, dressed as a wealthy merchant in colorful robes and tall pointed hat, led them out of the cavern at dusk. They'd burned their mage disguises and erased all evidence of their presence in the cave. Linden preferred her new garb, a striped robe in various shades of blue and yellow layered over a dark blue tunic and leggings. She'd felt almost polluted wearing the robes of a Fallow mage. Now she could pretend to be Pryl's niece, with Efram and Wreyn playing the parts of his son and daughter.

Their story was that Pryl had been caught trying to bribe the captain of the guard, played by Corbahn, and now he and his family would have to pay the price. Before they left, Linden handed over her weapons to Toz, who strapped her sword and dagger onto his belt.

They rode through the night, relying on their horses' night sight and the faint glimmer from the new moon to guide them. After they'd cleared the rocky terrain around the caves and waterfalls, the ground leveled off. They avoided the main roads, traveling on paths that criss-crossed through woods and orchards.

"How much longer?" asked Remy, after they'd ridden for most of the night. "I'm getting hungry." Linden wondered how much longer Corbahn would be able to tolerate Remy's complaints without snapping, since Remy asked the same question about an hour earlier, and again two hours before that.

"We're not stopping," barked Corbahn. "Eat some of your jerky." Linden had her answer; Corbahn's patience with Remy's constant hunger complaints lasted about as long as Mara's used to last, before she decided Remy had other, more endearing qualities.

"Here, take some of mine," Mara offered, as she rode up next to Remy.

Remy thanked her and took a bite of Mara's jerky. "You still didn't answer my question. How much longer before we're at the prison?"

Corbahn muttered something about traveling with youngsters under his breath, which was technically true, since Corbahn was older than Linden and her friends by about four or five years. He answered cordially enough, "We'll be able to spot the prison camp after we climb that hill over there." Efram had drawn detailed maps for them in the sandy soil near the cave's entrance, which everyone but Remy had committed to memory.

Since the hill itself was an hour or more away, and then they still had to climb it, Remy sighed, "Oh, that far, huh?" and returned to chewing his jerky.

"I think he's nervous," said Linden quietly to Corbahn riding beside her.

"It's understandable. I think everyone, myself included, is on edge."

"You'll do fine as the captain of the guard. When the

time comes, your adrenaline will give you the extra push you need to deliver your lines," said Linden.

"Are you speaking from experience?" he asked. As a student, Linden had never been good at public speaking and mumbled her way through presentations at school. But later, during the Faymon ceremony when she was "crowned" the Liege—her crown consisting of a circlet of leaves, flowers, and berries, since Faynwood was no ordinary land, and she was no royal princess—she'd been able to deliver a speech without faltering. Even her mother, a provincial governor before the war, would have been proud of her at that moment.

Linden told Corbahn about the speech she delivered during her crowning, and how studiously she'd rehearsed beforehand. Since Arrowood and Tanglewood had been enemies then, Corbahn hadn't attended, but his father, Haydahn, had watched the ceremony in secret. Linden had pleaded for unity across all of Faynwood during her speech. Afterward, Haydahn was the first to seek reconciliation. True to his word, Haydahn had been a loyal friend to Linden from that moment until his death.

Corbahn said, "My father told me about your speech. He said your words spoke to his heart. He'd already been mulling over peace and unification for some time in his head. I hope I can perform half as well in a few hours. Everything hinges on it."

"You will do exactly what you need to do in that moment."

Corbahn arched an eyebrow. "Spoken like a true Serving mage. My father used to say, 'Strength comes to those who use it, not to those who wish it.'"

"Your father would have liked Nari. My grandmother had a quote for just about everything," said Linden. She fell silent, thinking about the strong bonds that connected their families, about the good blood and bad running between and through the Arrowood and Tanglewood clans, coloring decisions made and words spoken even to the present day. If she were a better seer, she might be able to tie everything up with a neat bow, see how the past, present, and future all linked together, but her visions only provided her with the barest glimpses of what might come to pass. Her grandmother had told her that with enough practice and maturity, someday she might be able to accurately predict the future about half the time. Until then, she'd have to rely on her visions and her instincts to determine possible and probable outcomes. Most of the time, she thought her visions were more hindrance than help.

"It's remarkable how interconnected our families are, and the strength of our relationships, for good or ill, impacts all of Faynwood," said Corbahn.

Linden sighed. "Sometimes I still dream that I'm back home, before the war, before I knew anything about Faynwood, except the old myths. When my only responsibilities were caring for Kal, who's pretty self-sufficient, and doing my homework."

"I've never known anything but war, civil war until a few months ago, and now war with Glenbarra. But I know what you mean. I long for my father's steady hand, for his guidance right now."

"What would your father say, if he were here?" asked Linden.

"He'd remind me the time to worry about the details of a plan is beforehand. Once we've committed to a course of action, he'd say to stop worrying and start executing the plan."

"That's wise advice."

"My father was a wise man," Corbahn said. Squinting at the lightening sky, the dark blue horizon fading into bands of gold, he added in a low voice, "If the worst happens, remember the last, hardest part of our plan."

Linden nodded. "Understood." They'd all agreed, even Toz, that if they couldn't find a way to escape from the prison, they'd destroy it from within, sacrificing themselves and the prisoners, if needed. "But I don't intend to let the worst happen."

"Neither do I."

All conversation stopped as they climbed the hill, single file, following a worn path barely wide enough for a horse and rider. As the path wound around the hill's crest, the sun emerged from behind a cloud, casting a dull beam of light over the valley and the prison camp far below. Linden's heart sank at the sight of wooden fences topped with sharp pikes and barbed wire, encircling a gray mass of a building that seemed to have been molded from dirt and rocks and misery. She rubbed her side, a sharp spike of pain in her lung reminding her they were deep in Fallow territory. Sorcery and cruelty ruled inside those prison walls.

When they reached the bottom of the hill, Corbahn repositioned the group, so Pryl, Linden, Efram, and Wreyn were in the center, surrounded by the soldiers in disguise. He handcuffed each of them, pausing as he placed the manacles on Linden's wrists. "I hate this part of the plan most of all," he said, "I'll not rest until you're free again."

"I suspect none of us will be resting anytime soon."

Corbahn rode in front, tall and erect in his saddle, a Glenbarran officer by all appearances. When they were within hailing distance, a horn blasted from the prison's guard tower, and the gates opened. A small contingent of Glenbarran guards rode toward them, swords drawn. Their leader, a heavyset man with a pair of gold front teeth, shouted, "State yer name and yer business!"

Corbahn took a deep breath and delivered his lines flawlessly. "I am Captain Yael with the Fourth Battalion, delivering four prisoners into your custody." Goldie asked for their paperwork. Linden held her breath. Corbahn dismounted, handed over the forged identification papers for her and the fays, and waited while the man examined the documents. Goldie grunted a few times and finally said, "You'll need to come inside to sign the formal charges, which are?"

"Bribery of a senior officer. Show me the way, I'll sign whatever you need," said Corbahn.

Goldie barked out a series of commands, and the guards ran up to Linden, Pryl, and the other fays, yelling at them to dismount. As soon as Linden's feet touched solid ground, several of the guards shoved her roughly toward the prison gates. One of them, his rank breath hot on her face, whispered that he'd find her later and would be bringing some of his friends. He cackled, sending a frisson of fear down Linden's spine. Averting her eyes, she resisted the urge to use magic on the man, tempted by the thought of casting the smallest of spells. Perhaps he might trip suddenly or run into a doorjamb, but even the faintest whiff of Serving magic would blow their cover.

Corbahn held up the keys to the manacles. "Shall I unlock them now, since the prisoners have been delivered into your capable hands?"

Goldie puffed out his chest. "Let's wait until we're inside and you've signed the charges."

"Very well." He handed the reins of his horse to Jayna. She and Reynier led the horses to a small grove of trees about a hundred yards away. They would be the final fail-safe team; if none of the others emerged from the building by moonrise, Reynier and Jayna would deploy Serving magic to destroy the prison camp and everything, and everyone, inside. Meanwhile, they'd observe the prison and learn as much as possible from outside its walls.

Toz, Mara, and Remy fell into place behind Corbahn. Goldie flicked his eyes over Mara's statuesque figure and grunted, "Perhaps yer soldiers would like refreshments?"

Corbahn said, "Aye, thank you." Inclining his head at Toz, he added, "This trooper here needs to see a healer." Their plan called for Toz to peel away from the rest of the group and use his gift of gab to gain intelligence from the prison staff, starting with the healers on duty.

Goldie ordered one of the guards to accompany Toz inside the compound. Up close, the dilapidated wooden fence surrounding the camp looked like a strong breeze would topple it. The squat, square prison building was constructed of uneven gray stones molded together by weeping mortar. When the guard pulled open the pockmarked gate leading into the camp, the door squealed on rusty hinges.

Toz glanced back at Linden and gave her a ghost of a smile, his dimples barely visible. Then he was gone. Her heart caught in her throat, worried that Toz would be too friendly and gregarious, and wind up getting himself imprisoned or worse.

A jumble of men's and women's voices, some shouting, others grumbling, grew louder as Linden approached the gate, as did the baying of wolves penned up somewhere out of sight. She heard something else: screeching and yowling noises that made her want to clap her hands over her ears. As she entered the prison compound, she realized the screeching and yowling came from grihms, very unhappy grihms. Linden suppressed a shudder.

Once everyone entered the compound, Goldie grunted, "Captain, go ahead and unlock them cuffs now, then follow me. My boys will take it from here." One of the guards prodded Linden and the fays into a semblance of a line and told them to extend their wrists.

Corbahn pulled out his keys. Beginning with Pryl, he went down the line and unlocked the manacles encircling each pair of wrists. When he reached Linden, his hands grazed hers as he wiggled the key into the lock. Linden heard the click of the lock opening, the manacles falling away from her wrists. Corbahn gave her hands a firm squeeze, as if trying to endow her with extra strength. She glanced up, her stomach tightening when she looked into his sea-green eyes. Corbahn stepped back, turned to Goldie, and said, "They're all yours, sergeant."

The guards hustled Linden and the others down a dark passageway, the only light coming from a narrow slit of a window at the opposite end. Thick wooden cell doors, with small, barred windows at the top, lined both sides of the passage. Prisoners reached their hands through the bars of their doors, hurling slurs at the guards as they passed by. One man threatened to return as a grihm so he could tear the guards limb from limb. The stench of urine and unwashed bodies assaulted Linden's nostrils and her stomach heaved. She swallowed hard against the bile rising in her throat.

The guard with the putrid breath paused in front of one of the cells. He opened the padlocked door, and a couple of guards shoved Linden and Wreyn inside. Three miserable-looking women huddled against one wall. The youngest woman rose from the floor, screaming and shaking her fists.

The guards slammed the door shut, pushing Pryl and Efram farther down the passage. The young woman fell back to the ground with a sob. An older woman spoke to her in soothing tones, rubbing her back. Linden thought they were probably mother and daughter. The third woman, the eldest, pushed a shank of gray hair out of her face. Squinting at Linden and Wreyn through rheumy eyes, she pointed to a couple of mats on the floor. "Welcome to Hotel Zabor. If the guards don't kill you, the mages will. You'd best pray it's the guards."

Linden and Wreyn sat on the tattered mats indicated by the old woman, wrapping their robes carefully around their legs to avoid coming into contact with the filthy floor. Linden realized they were behaving like the spoiled heirs of a well-to-do merchant. Since that was the goal of their playacting, she didn't care if they came across as overindulged; she had no intention of letting the maggots squirming on the floor get into her clothes.

"Why should we pray it's the guards?" asked Wreyn.

The old woman, probably the grandmother of the trio, shrugged her bony shoulders. "Your suffering is short-lived."

"What could the mages do to us that's any worse than what the guards inflict?" Linden tried not to think about Smelly Breath's threat to visit her later.

The middle-aged woman glanced up and said, "How can you not have heard of Zabor Prison?"

Wreyn said, "We've heard this is a staging area for prisoners who are transferred elsewhere."

The grandmother snorted. "Prisoners aren't transferred out of here. Transformed, more like."

"Transformed?" Although Linden had a good idea what was happening at Zabor Prison, she wanted to hear it from the old woman herself. "Are they crossbreeding right here? Using prisoners?"

The young woman, her voice shaking, answered, "They start with the men—my father and fiancé were taken weeks ago—we're certain they're grihms by now."

"If they survived the crossbreeding process," replied the grandmother grimly.

"What about the women?"

"The guards have their way with us first," said the mother, as her daughter stifled another sob. "Sometimes they kill us afterward, other times they send us to the mages to be crossbred."

Linden compressed her lips together firmly. Corbahn had been right all along. They couldn't permit the prison camp to continue turning men and women into grihms. They'd have to find a way to destroy Zabor Prison and the place of power inside it, although Linden was more determined than ever to save as many innocent lives as possible.

CHAPTER 16

THE GUARDS CAME FOR THEM IN THE MIDDLE OF THE AFTERNOON. Their three cellmates stared at the ground, refusing to make eye contact, as Linden and Wreyn were half-dragged from the cell. Although Linden's stomach growled—she'd had a crust of stale bread and a sip of water for lunch—she would have thrown up if she'd eaten an actual meal. The guards shoved them down the dim passageway toward the sliver of light at the end. Linden wondered which cell housed Pryl and Efram, and whether Toz or Corbahn had learned anything useful.

They turned a corner and ran into Smelly Breath, holding open a door, a leer plastered on his pimply face. The guards pushed them into a small room, not much larger than a storage closet, with thick gray wads of material tacked onto the walls and ceiling. It took Linden a moment to realize they were standing in a soundproofed cell. Even the barred window at the top of the door had been padded over. She sensed Wreyn quivering next to her, whether with indignation or anger, she couldn't tell. Since fays were known to have terrible tempers, she hoped

Wreyn didn't blow their cover prematurely. On the other hand, she wouldn't be letting Smelly Breath get too carried away; she wanted to hold out just long enough to learn something useful.

Smelly Breath flicked his wrist, and two of the guards advanced on Linden, pinning her against one of the padded walls. The remaining two guards restrained Wreyn. Smelly Breath sauntered over to Linden and reached one beefy paw toward her face. Linden turned away. Cackling gleefully, he gripped a handful of her hair. Twisting her head painfully, he forced Linden to face him. He leaned in, his breath hot on her skin. "Such a fine young lady, so proper-like. Don't worry, lovey, I'll take my time with ye."

In one rapid movement, he gripped the neck of Linden's tunic and ripped it open. Linden screamed and struggled. Her arms held fast by the guards, she managed to kick Smelly Breath in his shin with the toe of her boot. Howling, he wrapped his hands around her throat and squeezed. Linden gasped for air as tendrils of vapor wrapped around her legs.

"What the—" muttered Smelly Breath. The rest of his words disappeared in garbled shouting as Linden and Wreyn vanished into the traveling mist. They landed in a different passage, dank and gloomy, lit by a few flickering torches. Linden stumbled into Wreyn, who reached out an arm to steady her. Wreyn dug into one of her pockets and handed Linden a pair of hair barrettes.

"Here, use these to patch up your tunic," whispered Wreyn. "We don't have much time."

"Where are we?" asked Linden, clipping together the top of her tunic with Wreyn's barrettes. They could cast a spell to repair the tunic, but that would attract too much attention and reveal their location. The guards would be on their trail soon enough, since Wreyn had just used fay traveling mists right under their noses. Not that Linden minded. If Wreyn hadn't transported them, Linden would have pommeled Smelly Breath with magical darts, that is, if he didn't choke her to death first. Unlike fays, who were magical beings through and through, Linden had to meticulously cast her incantations, either verbally aloud or silently in her mind. Casting a spell while in a chokehold, with Smelly Breath's hands wrapped around her throat, would have proved challenging. If Reynier or Corbahn found out, she'd never hear the end of it.

"Efram figured the place of power had to be underneath the prison."

"So we're in the basement. Makes sense they'd build over a place of power to camouflage it," said Linden. She felt the floor vibrating beneath her feet. "Do you feel that?"

Wreyn said, "You mean that vibration? There's probably some sort of steam-powered engine running nearby."

"But how can their mechanical equipment operate around so much magic? It doesn't make any sense."

Wreyn nodded. "I wondered the same thing, until I found out the Glenbarrans build their engines with twisted steel. It's costly, and they use it sparingly, but it works." Linden recalled how Valerran equipment failed during the war with Glenbarra. The Glenbarrans had figured out how to use twisted steel machine parts to ensure their equipment functioned, regardless of the amount of magical energy within range.

"I wish my uncle had known that during the war with Glenbarra. No one could figure out why their equipment kept working in the presence of so much magic." Linden peered down the passageway to her right, then to her left, uncertain which way would yield the most information the quickest. A few closed doors dotted either side of the hall. She was tempted to start opening random doors to get her bearings. Linden jumped as an ear-splitting scream rent the air, followed by another and another, wave upon wave of agonizing cries. Somewhere off to the left, a pack of wolves howled in response. Linden's nerves ratcheted up another notch.

"This way!" said Linden, jogging toward the screams, Wreyn fast on her heels. As they approached the source of the engine whines, the loud screams gave way to soft whimpers that chilled Linden's heart. She sensed the Fallowness of the place, the magic dark and sorcerous, and hissed through her teeth as fresh pain stabbed her injured lung. Turning humans into grihms, creating a slave army of crossbreeds, was as forbidden as necromancy, and yet the Glenbarran government relied on both to fuel its war machine.

Someone throttled the engine back to idle and called out, "Take him to the recovery pen. Make sure he has plenty of water in his bowl and a chunk of fresh meat when he wakens." Wreyn yanked Linden behind a stack of empty cages, stored in an alcove, as two men carried a grihm past them on a stretcher. Linden's head swirled with everything that needed to be done: freeing the prisoners, smashing the crossbreeding equipment, destroying the place of power, and doing something with the grihms who'd been bred against their will. She wished her grandmother were with her right then, to provide her with some direction. She closed her eyes, concentrating. *What would Nari do first?*

An image came to her. She was sitting in one of Nari's stuffed chairs in her study, sipping a cup of tea and listening intently. Nari explained about the places of power, which could be used for good or ill, depending on the intentions of the magic handlers. Linden realized they'd misunderstood the magical energy fueling a place of power, an energy source that could be misused or misdirected, but never destroyed. She knew what they had to do first. "We have to find the place of power and neutralize it," whispered Linden.

"Neutralize it? I thought we were going to destroy it," hissed Wreyn.

"A place of power can't be created or destroyed, but it can be neutralized," said Linden. "At least, I think that's what Nari told me during one of my magic lessons."

Wreyn frowned. "If we can neutralize it, then maybe someday it can be reconsecrated and used by Serving mages once again. It's worth a try. But how?"

"You might have just come up with the answer. If we reconsecrate the place of power, then we've probably neutralized it, at least I think so."

"You are correct," said Pryl, who walked out of the traveling mists next to the cages, with Efram, Toz, and Corbahn following in his wake. Startled, Linden nearly knocked over the cages, exposing their position to every guard stationed in the lower level.

"Where's Mara and Remy?" whispered Linden, concerned her friends had been captured or worse.

"I sent them outside with the excuse of bringing food to Reynier and Jayna," said Corbahn. "They also brought a message from me to stand down until we signal for them. I didn't want Reynier and Jayna to attempt to destroy anything if we're not out by moonrise."

"Why the change in plan?"

"Because of what Pryl told me about places of power," said Corbahn.

Pryl cleared his throat. "Aye, well, I've been giving this a great deal of thought while entrapped with four miserable men, all terrified out of their minds at the prospect of being crossbred. Not that I blame them, of course; it is a horrifying thing to contemplate. Anyway, the more I thought about it, the more I came to the same conclusion as Linden. A place of power is, at its core, a magical mystery. Not only would it be sacrilege to destroy it, but I also don't believe it's possible. The best we can hope for is to neutralize it."

Pryl's mini lectures always put Linden into a bit of a stupor. The sound of hobnailed boots, lots of them, striking against the stone floor, roused her. "They know we're here, which means we need to move fast!"

Pryl said, "Quick, hold hands; I'll lead the way through the mists." The mists swirled around their legs, tendrils reaching up to their chins, and with a soft whoosh they left the alcove behind them. Linden held tightly to Pryl's hand and Corbahn's, followed by Wreyn, Toz, and Efram. Linden felt a downdraft, the air growing chilly and humid as they descended. She landed on the ground with a thud. Pryl tugged her hand and she followed, glancing around at what seemed to be an underground burial site. A couple of torches rimmed the edge of the site; otherwise she'd not be able to see even her own hand in front of her face. Limestone sarcophagi, covered in fay hieroglyphs faded with age, were stacked in columns six coffins high, six deep, and arranged, row upon row. The elaborate lineup of sarcophagi formed a semi-circle around a sunken pool, the water source long since dried up.

Pryl put his finger to his lips, to indicate they shouldn't so much as whisper, and he positioned them around the edge of the pool. Pryl silently cast a defensive shield around them, the sunken pool, and the rows of sarcophagi. The air around the shield shimmered slightly, the shield itself invisible to the naked eye. Instructing them to hold hands once more, he said softly, "Let's begin the incantations to reconsecrate the place of power. I'll incant first in the fay tongue, and then I'll translate each incantation. Repeat everything I say and do, as precisely as possible."

Wreyn asked, "What if we're interrupted?"

"Under no circumstances can we stop once we've begun. We must complete the incantations through to the end." Pryl threw his head back and shouted in the buzzing language of the fays, his voice echoing around the burial chamber. He translated the opening phrase, "In harmony and enmity, in peace and war, in remembrance of what's past and readiness for what's to come, we dedicate this place to the preservation of Serving magic, in time and out of time, the hope of the ages."

Linden and the others repeated each phrase of the incantation, careful to mimic Pryl's words, pauses, and hand motions, raising and lowering their hands in a rhythmic pattern discernible only to the fay chief. Linden noticed a white dot in the center of the sunken pool she hadn't seen earlier. As she focused on the dot, it grew larger and began pulsating. Before long, the white dot transformed into a bolt of lightning that repeatedly struck the pool's center, scattering sparks of bright white light all around the burial chamber, until every sarcophagus was bathed in the glow from the sparks.

The reconsecration ceremony continued, Pryl's incantations increasing in volume and pace. Linden heard hobnailed boots approaching the burial chamber, guards shouting as they ran toward them. Tempted to glance behind her, she turned her head slightly. Corbahn gave her hand a firm squeeze, a reminder to maintain her concentration. She returned her attention to Pryl, the incantations and hand movements coming faster now.

Although the shield vibrated from the impact of the guards' fists and swords attempting to break through, it held fast, a testament to Serving magic and fay power. Linden wondered if all reconsecration ceremonies lasted this long, or if Pryl tacked on his own special binding spell. Focusing on Pryl's words and gestures, she frowned. The defensive shield seemed to be melting, as several dozen dark splotches, inkblot-like, dotted its surface. The splotches spread, oozing streams of inky blackness down the sides of the shield.

As the darkness stretched across the shield, Linden heard a raspy, breathless cackle. Something about the cackle made Linden's scalp tingle. She'd heard that sound before, on Captain Raff's ship months earlier, off the coast of Faynwood. Mordahn had laughed at her even as he lay dying—or so she thought at the time—she'd never factored in necromancy. Still, she found it hard to believe he'd been wandering around the prison camp, waiting for them to show up.

Linden wondered whether she was the only one who heard his irritating cackle inside the shield. She grimaced, as the pain in her lung spiked again. Pryl wavered and then shouted his incantations even louder, so Linden knew he heard Mordahn too. The cackling grew in strength, vying with Pryl's voice for dominance. Beads of sweat broke on out on Pryl's brow, and he sputtered. Linden squeezed his hand, and Pryl carried on, choking out the final incantation of the ceremony, which Linden and the others repeated.

The ceremony over, Linden expected something to happen. Silence filled the shield, which had become a dark void, without so much as a pinprick of light. Pryl blew out a puff of air, the tiny air current visible as a ribbon of sparkles leaving his lips. The sparkles danced across the void, providing small globes of light by which to see.

Linden whispered, "What now?" The guards pounded the outside of the shield, hurling threats and insults at them. Inside, the group held hands, unwilling to break their bond. Mordahn's crazy cackling continued, loud and raspy, a constant irritant on Linden's nerves. *Why does he keep laughing, without saying anything?*

"We wait," said Pryl, who added, "Don't let that laughter fool you. Mordahn isn't really here, but the Fallow spell that he cast around this place of power is active and is gradually unwinding itself. You'll hear the laughter begin slowing down soon enough."

"So the darkness and laughter are from a spell Mordahn cast to discourage anyone from performing the ceremony we just completed?" asked Corbahn.

"Precisely," said Pryl.

Mordahn's cackling spell devolved into something closer to giggling, breathless and annoying, but no longer earsplitting. Light from the torches began permeating the dark void, creating stripes and splotches of flickering yellow inside the shield. Linden exhaled in relief, the pain in her lung easing somewhat as Mordahn's spell unwound. She'd found the darkness oppressive and lonely, especially after Pryl and Corbahn dropped their hands, breaking the intimate connection.

"How much longer?" asked Efram.

"Anytime now," said Pryl.

"Anytime for what?" grumbled Corbahn. Linden sensed his restlessness beside her. He practically quivered with pent-up energy, every muscle poised for action.

A howling roar filled the room, followed by the sound of

paws scrabbling for purchase on the worn stone floor. The guards stopped pounding on the shield and turned around, swords up, as a pack of grihms loped into the chamber. With three or four grihms to every guard, the grihms quickly overwhelmed them. Linden looked away, refusing to watch the bloodbath unfold, the guards' screams giving way to cries, then whimpers, and finally silence. When she turned back, the guards lay on the ground, dead or dying, their weapons scattered about them.

The leader of the pack, a powerful grihm with intense black eyes, glanced at Pryl, who brought his hands together in front of him and bowed. Nodding his head in return, the leader turned, barking orders at his pack. The grihms gathered up the discarded swords and carried away the guards' bodies. They removed all evidence of the battle, other than the bloodstains on the floor. Pryl clapped his hands once, dissolving the shield. Clapping again, the bloodstains disappeared, the chamber cleansed of every vestige of Fallowness.

"What just happened here?" Toz scratched the stubble on his chin. "Did I just see a pack of grihms helping us out?"

Corbahn said, "If I didn't see it with my own eyes, I'd never believe it. But it sure looked that way to me."

Pryl nodded. "Efram and I explained our mission to the four men imprisoned with us, and they were eager to help. After we unlocked the cell door, they took care of the rest."

"What did the men do?" asked Wreyn.

"We brought them down to where the grihms were penned up, and they explained what we needed the pack to do," said Efram.

"But you can't talk to a grihm," said Corbahn, folding his arms.

"Oh, but you can, especially if that grihm is your father

or brother or sister. Grihms know their family members and will fight for their pack, both wolf and human," said Pryl.

Linden nodded. "It makes sense to me."

"How so?" asked Corbahn.

"Nari used to say 'nothing, not even death, can break the bonds of love.' She swore love was stronger than hate or envy or greed. We've just proven that love defies Fallow crossbreeding programs, and that makes it pretty strong in my book."

Toz shrugged. "Perhaps the grihms simply smelled their human family, maybe their superior sense of smell motivated them, and it had nothing at all to do with love."

Linden rolled her eyes. "Fine, you can go with sense of smell. I'll go with love."

Chuckling, Corbahn said, "I think I'm with Toz on this one."

Toz grinned. "Finally, we agree on something!"

"What about the rest of our plan? Even though we neutralized the place of power, there are still a lot of innocent people trapped inside this prison camp," said Wreyn.

Pryl said, "Not anymore."

Wreyn looked at her fay chief and nodding slowly, she said, "When you set those four men free, you liberated the rest, didn't you?"

"We cast an unlocking spell. Every door in the prison opened up about thirty minutes ago," said Pryl.

Efram smiled. "My guess is that most of the guards are pretty well occupied at this point."

Corbahn said, "Let's not assume anything. I made the rounds this morning, and I can tell you, these guards are well trained and equipped."

"Good point," said Toz, unbuckling his belt to remove

Linden's sword and dagger. Handing them over to her, he added, "I'll be happy when we're out of here. I'm not a fan of prisons or dungeons or anything that locks me inside."

Linden nodded, remembering what happened the last time Toz thought he was going to be locked away in a prison cell. He'd lost his head and nearly gotten them both killed, until Nari had stepped in front of them, taking the killing blow herself. Linden looked into Toz's blue eyes, usually full of mischief and good humor, but she saw something else this time, a grim determination to see their mission through to the end, whatever the cost. She thought, *your father would be proud of the man you've become.* She wanted to tell him so, but not with Corbahn and the fays listening to her every word. Instead, she silently strapped the weapons onto her waist.

Wreyn put out her palm and conjured her sword. Glancing at Pryl and Efram, their swords hanging from their belts, she said, "It looks like we're ready."

The traveling mists wrapped around their legs and arms and Linden felt an upward air draft. They emerged in the same alcove as before, down the hall from the cross-breeding equipment. As he landed, Toz knocked over several of the empty cages, announcing their arrival with a loud clatter.

Toz gave Linden a dimpled grin and mouthed "Sorry!" He stepped into the passageway to retrieve one of the cages that had tumbled out of reach. A guard, bleeding from a gash on his forehead, jumped at the sound. He charged, running Toz through with his sword.

CHAPTER 17

Toz clutched his chest, a red bloom seeping between his fingers. He crumbled to the floor as Linden screamed, "Toz! Don't you dare die!" Corbahn leapt over the fallen cages and sprinted after the guard. Linden didn't need to watch what happened next. She knew Corbahn would dispatch the guard.

Dropping to her knees beside Toz, she pressed her hands on top of his, trying to stem the flow of blood from his chest. Linden's breath caught in her throat as she looked at his still face, the sprinkle of freckles across his nose a stark contrast to his pasty complexion. The three fays silently surrounded Toz and Linden, swords up in a defensive posture.

Toz shook his head. "I'm sorry, my love," he whispered. "I wanted to be around to see you do great things." Toz exhaled in one long sigh, his bright blue eyes clouding over.

Linden's heart cracked inside her chest, tears streaming down her face. "Oh no, Toz, no," she sobbed, brushing his hair with her fingers. Memories of the two of them, playing tag as children, sharing a first kiss, dancing on her seventeenth birthday, flitted through her head, each memory bringing a fresh bout of tears. Not only was Toz her oldest friend, but he'd also loved her unselfishly, always putting her needs before his own, and never demanding anything from her in return.

Wreyn leaned over and gently closed Toz's eyes, which made Linden cry even harder. As she wept, Linden indwelled some of his passing sparks of magic before they dissipated, her way of honoring Toz as her friend and fellow mage. Even though he was gone, Toz's magical energy would remain, strengthening her in times of stress.

Placing a hand on Linden's shoulder, Wreyn said, "He's gone, there's nothing more you can do for him now."

Her face streaked with tears, Linden rose to her feet. "I can't just leave him lying here like this," she said, her voice as unsteady as her legs.

Pryl cleared his throat. "Efram will take Toz back to Faynwood, where he will receive a hero's funeral rites." Pryl and Efram conferred in their buzzing language. When they finished, Efram's mists curled around Toz like a foggy shroud, and they were gone.

Corbahn returned, grim-faced, to the alcove. He took one look at Linden and wrapped her in a bear hug. She sagged against the hard wall of his chest, weeping softly. Somewhere down the passageway came the sounds of swords clanging and men yelling. He said, "We need to keep moving. There's fighting happening in pockets all around us and above us." Corbahn pulled Linden gently away from his chest. Reaching into his pocket, he removed a handkerchief and wiped the blood from her hands, as if she were a small child.

"What about the equipment? Shouldn't we destroy it while we're here?" asked Wreyn.

"Aye, but we need the rest of our group to help us," said Corbahn.

Something stirred in the back of Linden's mind, and she struggled to identify it. Her head felt woolen, her heart shattered. She said, "The ensorcelled swords from Valerra. We need them to break down the twisted steel and destroy the crossbreeding equipment, don't we?"

Pryl said, "Aye, at least, I think so."

"But now there are only four of us who can wield the swords. Do we need four or five?" she asked.

Pryl sighed. "I don't know. The prophecy was unclear. I retrieved Toz's sword before Efram left, just in case. But I'm not sure whether it's of any use to us."

Another memory came to Linden, so vivid she felt as if she were back home, during the siege of Bellaryss. She was standing in the Weapons Room in the Valerran Museum. She and her friends, Toz among them, walked slowly around a stash of ancient fay-spelled weapons, picking up various swords, daggers, and sabers, and discovering that the weapons actually chose their new owners. With Toz now gone, would the sword choose someone else?

Linden swayed slightly, and Corbahn reached out a steadying hand, gripping her shoulder. She said to him, "Please take Toz's sword from Pryl."

Corbahn retrieved the sword, holding it gingerly between his fingers. Linden said, "Now grip it as if for battle."

Corbahn raised an eyebrow but complied, gripping the hilt firmly in his calloused palm. The sword's blade came to life, gold sparks lighting up the hieroglyphs along its surface. "What the—"

"How did you know?" asked Wreyn.

"I didn't, not really," said Linden. Turning to Corbahn,

she said, "You need to start using this sword. I know it may seem strange at first, but it's chosen you and will only respond to your hand on the hilt."

Corbahn nodded, fastening the sword and sheath onto his belt. "I'm honored to use Toz's sword. I'll guard it well." They heard a commotion on the floor above them and he added, "That's probably Reynier and the others. I asked them to create a diversion right about now. I'll find them and bring them down here."

"Why don't you clear out anyone in our path on the way to the crossbreeding room," said Linden. "And I'll go fetch them." She didn't want Corbahn to become overconfident with his fay-ensorcelled sword and fight his way to the main floor. He tended to be overconfident anyway, and a sword that glowed might lead him to believe he was invincible.

"I don't hear anything down that side of the passageway, so I doubt there's much to clear out. Most of the fighting is in the other direction and on the floors above." Corbahn drew his eyebrows together. "Besides, that's not a good idea in your present state." Linden folded her arms across her chest, ready to argue about her present state, but the traveling mists curled around Pryl, distracting her.

"I prefer to preserve my energy for fighting, not running up and down the stairs. I'll go," Pryl said, as he vanished into the mists.

Wreyn shrugged. "I guess we should head toward the equipment room and barricade ourselves inside."

"That's a happy thought," muttered Corbahn. "I can't imagine a worse fate than being strapped to one of those tables." Linden shuddered but said nothing. His words brought to mind one of her nightmares involving Corbahn, herself, and a pair of crossbreeding tables.

Corbahn took point, Linden and Wreyn behind him. They slithered along the dimly lit hall, swords drawn and ready. Linden heard men shouting and swords clanging, but some distance behind them in the opposite direction. Corbahn had been right; the way forward seemed eerily quiet. *Did no one think the crossbreeding equipment needed protecting?*

Corbahn arrived at the horror chamber where the cross-breeding occurred. He pushed the door open and stepped back quickly, flat against the wall, waiting for guards to pour out of the room. When nothing happened, he peeked inside, and then motioned for Linden and Wreyn to follow him. The three of them split up, scouring every nook and cranny in the huge, creepy crossbreeding suite before they were satisfied the place was empty. Linden locked the door, Corbahn pushing a tall cabinet in front of it for good measure. Wreyn circled the room's perimeter, stopping at each wall sconce to light the candles.

"Does anyone have an idea how this equipment works?" asked Corbahn. "I want to make sure once we break this thing, it's unfixable."

Linden walked around the contraption, examining it from every angle. She had no idea how accurate her dream was, but the two tables, covered with straps and pulleys, looked identical to what she remembered. The tables were connected to each other and to five box-like machines with twisted cords of wires. Dials and knobs dotted the fronts of the machines, with one large lever in the middle machine that probably initiated the crossbreeding process. Two beakers, one clear and one stained red, sat on top of each machine. Ropes of tubing connected the beakers and ran around the edges of each of the tables.

Linden ran her hands along the table on her left,

deciding the wolf would be strapped there. The man would be lying on the table to her right. She tried visualizing its operation, following the lines of tubing that twisted around the tables and up to the various beakers, but soon gave up. Instead, she removed her dagger and began poking each of the machines, sparks flying from the twisted steel exteriors.

Linden examined the intricate swirls etched into the steel for clues, tracing the pattern with her fingers. The pattern ended and started again. Frowning, she realized the pattern seemed broken in various places on the machines. Using the tip of her dagger, she managed to loosen one of the twisted steel plates. Turning back to Corbahn and Wreyn, she said, "These machines aren't made from twisted steel!"

"That looks like twisted steel to me," said Corbahn. "And if it's not, how can they operate around so much magic?"

Wreyn wandered over to where Linden had pried loose one of the steel plates and poked around inside. "She's right —take a look. This machine has a twisted steel engine at its core, but all of its other parts are made from wood. Then the whole thing is covered over with a veneer of twisted steel. Brilliant engineering—just enough twisted steel to enable the machine to function around magic, and just enough wood to absorb the magical energy expended during crossbreeding."

"Brilliantly wicked," said Linden. "But does this make it any easier to destroy?"

"It would take a long time to pry off all of these steel plates," said Corbahn, running his hands over the machine closest to the door. "I'm not sure we have that much time."

"I'm not sure we have much choice," said Wreyn. "Even an ensorcelled sword can't cut through this steel."

Linden raised her sword at the sound of boots hitting the stone floor. She resheathed it when she saw Reynier emerging from the mists with Pryl, followed by Jayna, Remy, and Mara. "What took so long? I was beginning to worry," said Linden.

Jayna's dark hair had gone all wild and curly, which usually happened in extreme humidity or when she'd been exercising. "We had to fend off a dozen or so guards long enough to escape."

"It won't take them long to figure out what we're up to," said Reynier.

Remy glanced around the room and asked, "Where's Toz?"

Linden's heart constricted at the thought of having to deliver the bad news to Remy, who'd been Toz's friend and sidekick since kinder-class. "We've lost him, Remy. He's gone," said Linden, her voice cracking. "I'm so sorry." Jayna's eyes welled with tears. She threw her arms around Linden, who bit her bottom lip, which had started to wobble. Linden couldn't afford to start crying again; if she did, she'd come undone.

Mara brought her hands to her mouth to stifle a sob, as Remy said, "No, you're wrong. It can't be. Not Toz."

"Efram's taken him back to Faynwood for his funeral rites," Wreyn said softly.

Remy shook his head. Pinching the bridge of his nose, he kept repeating, "No, not Toz. It can't be." Mara rubbed his back, trying to comfort him.

Reynier turned to Corbahn and said, "I'm deeply sorry to hear about Toz. Unfortunately, we haven't much time. Have you learned anything that can help us?"

Corbahn waved his hand at the machines. "We discovered the machines are made of wood, with twisted steel engines and veneers. We're not sure whether that makes them any easier to destroy."

Rubbing his beard thoughtfully, Pryl stared at the loose steel plate. He asked Corbahn to use his new sword to strike the steel plating. Just as before, when Linden had struck the steel, sparks flew but the steel remained intact. Then he asked Corbahn to try scoring the steel to damage its swirly pattern. Corbahn held his sword in both hands and dragged the sword across the etched plating. He leaned over to examine the steel. Not a scratch marred its surface.

Corbahn shook his head. "Even with this sword, I'm not making a dent."

Linden walked over next to Corbahn. Withdrawing her sword, she said, "Let's try using two swords on the same steel plate and see what happens."

They each struck the center of a steel plate, stabbing it several times. Corbahn leaned in and said, "Alright, some progress. We've dented it here and here," using his finger to point out a couple of dents.

Linden went over to Remy, his face a crumpled mess. "Remy, I really need your help. Can you help me?"

Remy swiped his eyes with the back of his hand and nodded. "What do you need?"

"We need to use all five ensorcelled swords to strike the same machine, over and over, until the steel plating cracks off."

Remy walked over to the machine and took a shaky breath. "Let's do this." Mara and Jayna joined them, the five of them forming a semi-circle around the middle machine, swords drawn.

Corbahn said, "Now!" All five swords struck at once. An explosion of sparks—green, gold, purple, blue, and red— flew from the steel plating. As they continued striking the machine, the twisted steel began to glow, turning to burnished silver.

Remy hesitated, but Linden said, "Keep going. It's started to melt."

Beads of sweat, from the heat of the metal and the exertion, formed on Linden's brow. She focused on striking the hot steel, over and over, funneling her pain and anger into every blow. Finally Corbahn shouted, "Step back!" and pulled her away from the machine, which had turned into a hot mess of molten steel and splintered wood.

The molten steel spread out toward the neighboring machines, where Linden noticed the steel plates beginning to warp from the heat. "Maybe we should concentrate on the two outer machines next. Hopefully, the whole thing will melt down," she said.

"Whatever you do, do it fast," said Wreyn, who'd vanished into the mists and quickly returned. "There are about twenty guards heading our way."

"What about the prisoners?" asked Pryl. "Or the grihms? Any chance they can slow down those guards?"

"They're trying."

"Can't we cast a defensive shield?" asked Mara.

Wreyn shook her head. "That's a lot of twisted steel on those machines. We'll have too much interference to be able to maintain a proper shield."

Corbahn and Linden decided to work on the machine farthest from the door, figuring that when and if the whole thing gave way, they'd want to be on the other side of the equipment. Jayna, Mara, and Remy joined them, each of them focused on smashing through the steel plates. Linden wondered if they'd be able to accelerate the melting process, but it seemed to take the same number of blows from all five swords before the steel began to melt.

Linden's legs and arms ached from the exertion, and her right palm sported fresh blisters. She removed her striped merchant's robe, now stained and tattered, and used it to wipe her brow before tossing it aside. She could move much more freely in the navy tunic and leggings. "Take a look. The steel on the second machine is melting now on both sides. It's working!"

"Let's do this last machine and get out of here," said Corbahn.

As they lined up, swords drawn, ready to strike at the final machine, Linden heard pounding on the other side of the door. "Go!" she shouted. As they began their assault on the last machine, the molten steel from the first three machines puddled on the floor. Pryl and Reynier knocked over one of the tables, laying it on its side to keep the hot metal from spreading over their feet while they worked on the fifth machine.

Reynier, Pryl, and Wreyn took up positions in front of the door, which the guards rammed repeatedly, while Linden and the others worked on smashing the last machine. "How much longer?" shouted Reynier. "They're almost through!"

Before Linden could reply, two things happened. The hot metal on the fifth machine gave way, and the guards broke down the door, crashing into the tall cabinet that blocked the entrance. The cabinet toppled onto Wreyn, knocking her unconscious and preventing the guards from rushing into the room. Reynier lifted one end of the cabinet so Pryl could shift Wreyn's crumbled form. The fay chief shouted, "She needs a fay healer," before vanishing into the mists with her. Linden knew he'd be back, but she wasn't sure any of them would be left standing when he returned.

The heat from the melting steel turned the room into a

furnace, as the scalding flow burned through the over-turned table, joining up with the puddle from the last machine. "We're trapped," said Remy, staring at the molten river behind him and the guards at the door.

"Then we fight!" yelled Corbahn. He leapt onto the overturned cabinet, pulling Linden up alongside him. Reynier helped Jayna and Mara climb up next to Linden. When he realized there wasn't enough room for both Remy and him, he pushed Remy toward the cabinet. Reynier sprinted around it, a sword in his right hand and dagger in his left, ready to face the guards edging through the door.

"Reynier!" screamed Jayna, "Get back here!"

Corbahn jumped down from the cabinet to stand next to Reynier, a sword in each hand, the fay-spelled sword from the Valerran Museum pulsing with gold hieroglyphs. Linden thought of Toz, the pain so sharp she wanted to drop her sword and be done with it all. She couldn't bear the thought of losing anyone else. Pressing her lips together firmly, she pointed her sword at the guards swarming the door and hallway, the hieroglyphs lighting up a fiery green all along the blade. Linden summoned every ounce of magical energy left, pulsing with the latent power of Toz's magic, and Nari's, and so many other mages lost alongside her in Valerra, all joined with hers.

Leaping off the cabinet, Linden brandished her sword and shouted an ancient fay war cry, "Evakunouz!" She ran headlong into the nearest guards, who backed away, star-tled. Corbahn came alongside her, guarding her left flank. They pushed their way into the hall outside the cross-breeding suite, their friends following behind them. Corbahn and Linden fought as a unit in the passageway, at times back-to-back, other times side-to-side, Linden's green sword and Corbahn's gold sword clashing against

Glenbarran blades, the sound of metal-on-metal ringing in their ears. In the haze of the battle, she noticed Jayna and Reynier backed against a wall by several of the guards. She was too far away to help, but Remy arrived, followed by Mara, their swords blazing red and blue.

The guards kept coming at them, an endless supply, Smelly Breath among them. When he recognized Linden, he barreled toward her right flank, his eyes full of loathing. Linden parried his first blow and riposted, nicking Smelly Breath's arm. He charged once again, pointing his sword at her chest. She brought her green blade up with both hands and batted away his sword. Counterattacking, Linden jabbed Smelly Breath in the side. He yelped, gripping his abdomen and considering his next move, when the pack of grihms who'd come to their aid earlier scrabbled into the passageway. Two of them zeroed in on Smelly Breath with particular zeal, knocking him to the ground.

When one of the grihms clamped his jaws around the man's throat, Corbahn pulled her away. "Let's leave this battle to the grihms!" Linden nodded and turned around, looking for her friends. She spotted Reynier on the floor, Jayna bending over him as Mara and Remy took up defensive postures. Linden weaved around the grihms and guards, locked in various death matches, until she reached them. Dropping to her knees, she gripped Reynier's hand. "Let's get you out of here." She glanced at his leg, which Jayna had wrapped in a piece of Remy's tunic to form a tourniquet, the blood seeping through the makeshift bandage. They had to get him somewhere safe, where his leg could be properly looked after, and soon.

Where was a fay with a good traveling mist when you really needed one?

Reynier shook his head. "No, you need to leave me. I can't walk, and I'll slow you all down."

"We're not leaving you," said Jayna fiercely, blinking back tears.

"She's right. We leave together or not at all," said Corbahn, who joined Mara and Remy, standing guard alongside them.

Linden stood up, trying to figure out how they were going to carry Reynier out of there without causing the wound on his leg to bleed out. Squinting, she shook her head, confused by what she saw coming down the passage toward her. The three women she'd been imprisoned with that morning were hugging two grihms, who yipped and rubbed up against them. Linden called out to the daughter of the trio. "Are they your relatives?"

The woman nodded, pointing to an average-sized grihm, "My dad," and to a huge grihm, "And my fiancé. They just changed him yesterday. He's still a little disoriented, but at least we're escaping together."

Linden asked the craziest question she'd ever thought to ask. "Do you think your dad and fiancé can carry our friend here? He's severely injured."

"But he looks like a Glenbarran soldier," the woman objected. Looking at the others, still in uniform, she added, "They all do."

"It's a disguise. These are my friends who broke open the prison."

Nodding, the young woman quickly explained to the two grihms. They clambered over to Reynier, who raised his eyebrows but was in too much pain to object. The grihms reached underneath Reynier and hoisted him off the ground, Reynier moaning with each movement. Standing on their hind legs, the grihms picked their way around the battle scene and ascended the steps, Corbahn and Linden in front, swords poised, and Remy and Mara taking up the rear, behind the grihms' family members. Jayna jogged alongside Reynier, gripping his hand.

They reached the first floor and sprinted toward the entrance of the prison. They passed injured prisoners and grihms, limping along the hallway past the open cell doors, climbing over dead or dying guards. One guard leapt up from the floor, half in a stupor, but Corbahn used the hilt of his sword to knock him out again.

As they reached the main door, Corbahn said, "Hold on a sec, let's make sure there's not a garrison of soldiers on the other side."

The huge grihm grunted and paused. Linden and Corbahn crept up to the door, which was slightly ajar. Corbahn nodded at Linden, who pulled the door open. He gripped both swords firmly, poised for a fight, and exited through the doorway. Linden followed him, scanning the grounds. She found nothing more threatening than escaped prisoners and grihms, leaving the prison camp in pairs and groups. She signaled to the large grihm that it was safe and grunting again, he and the other grihm carried Reynier back to their horses, waiting under the trees where they'd left them that morning.

"Thank you," said Linden, as the two grihms laid Reynier gently down on the ground. They dropped to all fours and loped back to their family. The old grandmother insisted on leading the way, the granddaughter running her hand along the smooth back of the huge grihm, who leaned protectively against her legs.

"How is he?" she asked Jayna, who'd grabbed her healer's kit and dropped to the ground next to Reynier. As she applied a fresh tourniquet to his leg and treated a gash on his shoulder, he groaned and thrashed but didn't come fully awake.

"He needs to be back home. He's feverish, and I can't properly treat his injured leg out here in the open." Jayna smoothed the hair back from Reynier's forehead.

"Who's injured?" asked Efram, emerging from the mists. Glancing around nervously, he asked, "Where's Pryl? And Wreyn?"

"Wreyn was knocked unconscious, and Pryl took her to a fay healer," said Corbahn. "I'm sure Wreyn will be fine. In the meantime, we need your help transporting Reynier back to Faynwood."

"Of course," said Efram, a worried look crossing his brow. "But what about the rest of you? I feel bad leaving you here in the middle of Glenbarra."

Linden shook her head. "Don't feel bad. Our work here isn't finished." As the mists curled around his legs, Efram promised to return after he transported Reynier. Jayna quickly leaned over and kissed Reynier on the lips before stepping out of the way.

Linden put her hand on Jayna's shoulder. She felt for her friend, who was torn between Reynier's needs and the mission itself. While Faynwood had many skilled healers who could see to Reynier's injuries, no one else could wield Jayna's ensorcelled sword. Jayna must have realized that as well because she stayed behind in Glenbarra with Linden.

Remy waited until Efram and Reynier had vanished into the mists before asking, "How come our work here isn't finished?"

"We set out to find the places of power inside Glenbarra, and prevent Fallow mages from using them again," she reminded him.

"But we've done that," pointed out Remy.

"Since we haven't found Mordahn, and he's sure to be somewhere near a place of power, we can't be done yet," said Linden.

Corbahn agreed. "I learned at least one useful piece of information inside that prison today. I found out there's one more place of power inside Glenbarra."

"Where is it?" asked Linden.

"In the worst possible location."

"How can it be any worse than that prison camp?" asked Mara

Shaking his head, Corbahn replied, "There's one location that's even more heavily guarded. We have to break into Glendin Palace, King Roi's private residence, to neutralize the other place of power."

CHAPTER 18

"You can't be serious. It was hard enough breaking into a prison camp, where we lost Toz." Remy's voice wavered. Mara slipped her hand into his, and he paused to compose himself. "How are we supposed to pull off something like that?"

Linden shared Remy's concerns, but she wasn't about to give into his pessimism. "We'll figure it out as we go, but first we need to find a safe place to rest for the night." Turning to Corbahn, she asked, "Any ideas?"

Nodding, Corbahn pointed behind them. "I noticed a good spot tucked between those hills. It's well hidden, with a good view of the valley."

"That works for me. What about the rest of you?" asked Linden, waiting to see if anyone, especially Remy, had objections. Everyone was more than ready to leave the prison camp. Although they altered their course a few times as they crossed the valley, in case they were being followed, they managed to reach the hills by nightfall. Corbahn guided them to a grassy, flat area partway up one of the hills, where they set up camp.

Linden unsaddled Ashir and brushed him down, taking extra care with his mane. She caught herself looking around for Toz's horse before realizing Efram had transported the horse back to Faynwood, along with Toz. Shaking her head, she moved to Hoff, Reynier's horse. Corbahn came over to help her brush Hoff's chestnut coat. "How are you holding up?" he asked in a low voice.

Linden flicked a chunk of black hair out of her eyes and resumed brushing Hoff. She'd learned last year during the fall of Valerra that if she kept busy, she could cope more easily with her losses. It's when she stopped moving or ran out of useful activities that all of it, her grief, her pain, crashed in on her. "I'm still in shock that Toz is gone. I can't even grieve for him properly, at least not yet. And I'm really worried about Reynier's leg, and Wreyn. I thought she had a concussion, but with no sign of Pryl, I'm concerned it's more serious."

Corbahn paused, holding the brush in his hand. "Pryl has been gone overlong, but there could be a hundred reasons that have nothing to do with Wreyn. Have you noticed how fays have a different sense of time?"

"You mean sometimes they're super prompt and other times they're really, really late?"

"Exactly. Pryl may be taking care of fay business while Wreyn is being treated by their healers and simply lost track of time."

Linden shook her head. "But he left in the middle of a battle. Don't you think he'd have some sense of urgency about returning?"

Corbahn resumed brushing Hoff. "He has a sense of urgency about our mission, but he could be chasing down an old scroll or consulting with a seer, trying to learn something that will help us."

"Pryl doesn't even know we survived that battle inside the prison," said Linden.

"Oh, he definitely knows. Don't ask me how, but fays have ears and eyes everywhere, in the present, the past, and the future."

As if on cue, Pryl's horse landed in the middle of the grassy area. He dismounted and removed his horse's saddle before joining Corbahn and Linden. Linden waved her hand. "How do you do that? I was just wondering out loud when you'd return and suddenly you're here."

"I brought my personal healer to Faynwood to help with Reynier's treatment. She's certain we'll be able to save his leg."

Jayna overheard and ran over to Pryl. Grasping his hand, she said, "I can't thank you enough for looking after Reynier. He doesn't take good enough care of himself."

Pryl patted her hand. "I am glad to help. Reynier is my friend, besides being the Elder of Faynwood. I want to see him walking again."

"How is Wreyn doing?" asked Linden.

"She has a concussion but is recovering. The healer will not permit her to travel, by horse or by mist, for a couple of days at least."

"I'm glad to hear both Reynier and Wreyn are doing better," said Linden.

"Aye," said Corbahn, adding, "Now tell us what you've learned while you've been gone."

Pryl wandered over to a small campfire Mara had started and sat down. He was no longer dressed as a traveling merchant, but as a fay chief in a dark blue robe, various runes embroidered in gold thread at his cuffs and hem. Pushing back his hood, he ran his fingers through his thinning hair. "I'd long suspected that places of power were synonymous with ancient fay burial sites, which we confirmed today. That's both good news and bad news. Good news because we know what they are and how to neutralize them. Bad news because there are literally hundreds of such sites scattered over Faynwood, Glenbarra, and Valerra."

"Why would there be so many, and spread out so far?" asked Mara, handing Pryl a mug of hot tea.

Pryl took a swallow before continuing. "They probably didn't teach fay history in your magic-handling classes, did they?" When Mara shook her head, Pryl said, "I'm not surprised. I suppose only fays still study the fay classics, and even our younger generation seems less interested in learning from the past."

"My grandmother owned several fay history books," said Linden. "I remember reading that fays once populated our entire continent. I guess that would explain the large number of fay burial sites."

Pryl nodded. "That's right. At one time, when Faynwood was ruled by fay kings and queens, its borders extended beyond all of modern-day Glenbarra and Valerra."

"What happened to all the fays?" asked Jayna.

"My ancestors looked for excuses to fight over nearly everything, the fastest horse, the best wine, and even, according to legend, the longest beard, until we became almost extinct. The few surviving fays withdrew to the north, to the thick forests of present-day Faynwood, where they lived in isolation for generations before the first group of men arrived on our shores. Men and women kept coming, building communities over the old fay burial grounds, which had been all but forgotten during the intervening years."

"But someone discovered a few of the ancient burial

sites and figured out how to harness their latent power," said Linden.

"Please don't say it was Mordahn," said Corbahn. "My father always told me he wasn't very smart, cagey perhaps, but mostly just manipulative."

Pryl said, "Fallow mages have been around for as long as Serving mages. No one knows who first discovered how to use, or abuse, the magic within a fay burial site, creating a place of power. I'd guess it was a Fallow mage long before Mordahn. Fallow spells drain much more magical energy than Serving spells, so Fallow mages are always seeking a power boost."

"So where does that leave us?" asked Corbahn. "How can we possibly find and neutralize hundreds of old burial sites?"

"We don't have to find all of them. Most are inaccessible, buried beneath layers of sediment and slipped beyond all memory."

"Then how many do we have to find?"

"There's one beneath Glendin Palace," said Pryl. When everyone nodded, he added, "Which apparently you've already figured out. While that's going to be difficult to access, there's one other that is well-nigh impossible to reach, at least for now."

Linden drew her brows together, deep in thought. She used to spend hours at the Valerran Museum, one of her favorite places back home. The museum covered three city blocks, housing the largest collection of sculpture, art, books, maps, and scrolls anywhere in the world. The entire imposing structure practically hummed with magical energy. Fay hieroglyphs decorated much of the building, with wall murals depicting ancient fay history and prophecy, including, weirdly enough, predicting her crowning as the Liege of Faynwood. "The other place of power, it's under the Valerran Museum, isn't it?"

Pryl sighed. "I should have known sooner, before Mordahn and King Roi figured it out and marched across Valerra to secure the most potent place of power anywhere. Based on my study of the ancient scrolls and consultation with a fay elder, I believe the museum sits over a royal burial site, for fay kings and queens."

"There's no way we're going to be able to reach the Valerran Museum anytime soon," said Jayna. "Even if you could translocate all of us there with traveling mists, we'd be dodging Glenbarrans at every jump along the way."

"And even if we made it all the way—" Mara didn't finish her thought.

"It would be a one-way trip," said Remy grimly.

"What I don't understand is why the burial sites still retain so much magical power," said Corbahn. "We know magical energy dissipates at the moment of death unless another mage is near enough to absorb the sparks of energy. Why didn't that happen with the ancient fays?"

Pryl looked like he was about to launch into another lecture, so Linden hastily interjected her own theory. "Is it because the fays were, and are, magical beings? So even if some of their energy dissipates, most of the magic remains with their bodies, seeping into the locations where they've been laid to rest?"

Pryl nodded. "Aye, that's more or less correct. At least, that's Mage Mother Pawllah's theory, and I think it's the most likely."

"When did you see Pawllah?" Linden leaned forward, nearly spilling her tea. "How is she? What's the news from

Valerra? Has the scope picked up anything more about my brother's whereabouts?"

Pryl put up his hand to stop the flow of questions. "I traveled to Sanrellyss Island and spoke with Mage Mother about the places of power, before returning here. Pawllah sends her love along with this message, and I quote, 'We have consulted the electromagnetic insight scoping device. Fallow magic rules across Valerra, but insurgent groups are growing in strength and numbers. One rebel leader stands out from the rest, in both magical and military abilities. You must continue on to Glendin Palace and neutralize the place of power there. Most of all, do not lose hope, despite the loss of our dear Toz.'"

Linden's shoulders slumped. She felt even worse after hearing the Mage Mother's message, reminding her how much she missed Toz. Plus, she still had no news about her brother. Everyone looked at her expectantly. As the Liege, she had to rally, even though her muscles screamed from the strain of fighting her way out of the prison camp, and her head ached almost as much as her heart.

Linden recalled her days as an apprentice with her grandmother. Nari always emphasized the importance of good posture for young ladies, so their clothes fit properly, and for mages, so they could summon the energy needed to incant a spell. She pulled up her shoulders and straightened her back. Thanking Pryl for the message, she asked, "Do you have any thoughts on how we can get into Glendin Palace?"

Pryl said, "Not yet. Getting into a royal palace is quite a bit harder than getting into a prison camp."

"You've been inside the palace though, haven't you?" asked Corbahn.

"Aye, when King Roi's father ruled. The fays had good relations with old King Barre."

"Could you transport us into the palace undetected?" asked Jayna.

Pryl stroked his beard for a few moments, deep in thought, before he responded. "Fallowness has seeped into every nook and cranny of the palace. Traveling mists are unpredictable around so much Fallow magic. Even in Zabor Prison, my traveling mists were a bit less precise. The reason we could travel at all was because most of the Fallowness was concentrated in the crossbreeding suites on the lower level. It was human misery darkening the walls of that prison compound, more than Fallow sorcery. But at Glendin Palace, we could land ourselves right in King Roi's lap. We need to find another way in—a ruse of some sort that will give us enough time to act."

Linden brushed her hair out of her eyes, mulling over Pryl's comment about needing time to act. "I like the idea of landing in King Roi's lap, figuratively speaking, of course."

Remy shrugged. "I'm not following. Why would we want to get that close to King Roi himself?"

"Because Mordahn won't be far from his side," said Linden.

Corbahn nodded slowly. "True enough, but Pryl's mists won't be able to help us. What are you thinking?"

"Let's put on a royal show for the king," said Linden, who knew the Valerran queen had often enjoyed a rousing drama or silly comedy. Before she fled the Glenbarran invaders, the queen frequently invited playwrights and actors to the castle. "A special performance, from a renowned traveling troupe of actors."

"You want to perform for crazy King Roi?" Corbahn frowned.

"And his closest friends, Mordahn and the necro-mancers."

Remy rolled his eyes. "What will be our reward? A one-way visit to the fay burial ground? Or perhaps the cross-breeding room?"

Pryl said, "It's a long shot, but it could work as a means of getting us inside. Neutralizing the place of power is a different story. It takes uninterrupted time as you know, which will be at a premium, especially if Mordahn catches wind of it."

"Once we're inside, will your traveling mists work well enough to be able to get us outside again?" asked Jayna.

Pryl nodded slowly. "Aye, although I'll probably need to transport us one at a time, given the amount of Fallow magic that will surround us. We'll be as ungainly as if we're sitting on our horses, and we may even wobble a bit. Think of it this way: the Fallowness at the prison was like a roomful of bad magic; at the palace, it'll feel like a long-house full of wicked sorcery."

"How about the Valerran Museum?" asked Linden, thinking how her injured lung had become a barometer for Fallowness. Would she even be able to breathe if she returned to the museum?

Pryl blew out a puff of air. "The Valerran Museum will pulse with enough Fallow energy to fill an entire strong-hold. Casting Serving spells inside the museum will take tremendous concentration. I think we have enough to worry about at the moment, without trying to solve for the museum just yet. Let's focus on the palace."

Mara said, "I can't think of a better way to get into that palace than Linden's idea. We can wear disguises as part of a traveling troupe, and there's usually a dinner for the actors where we can gather more intelligence about what's going on inside."

"Will it be a real sit-down dinner with multiple courses?" asked Remy.

"Of course. It's hosted by the royal family."

"Good. I'll have a decent last meal before they figure out who we really are—and lop off our heads," grumbled Remy.

CHAPTER 19

Efram showed up as they were breaking camp the next morning. Pryl sent him back to Faynwood with Reynier's horse and a detailed list of supplies they needed to transform into a proper traveling troupe. The fay chief instructed Efram to find or conjure everything on the list and meet up with them by nightfall at their next stop. Pryl and Corbahn estimated they had a two-day ride ahead of them.

They avoided the main roads, traveling through the foothills and wooded plains of eastern Glenbarra. Corbahn and Linden alternately rode point, with Remy taking up the rear, offering periodic complaints about the lack of fresh meat and insufficient rest stops. At one point Corbahn muttered, "How can you stand his constant complaining? He's driving me up a tree."

Linden shrugged. "I hardly notice anymore. It's almost part of his charm. Besides, Remy was as close to Toz as I was. He's really hurting right now."

"Fine," said Corbahn, "I'll try to restrain myself from leaving him behind the next time we stop."

"You're going to need Remy and his sword if you want

to break down that crossbreeding equipment inside Glendin Palace," Linden reminded him.

Corbahn squinted at the horizon and then glanced over at her, his eyes troubled. "We're talking about the most fortified building in all of Glenbarra. Do you really believe we'll be able to destroy that equipment?"

Linden exhaled slowly, gathering her thoughts. She didn't want to succumb to despair about their mission, nor did she want to pretend it would be easy. In truth, she didn't think many of them would survive, which meant whatever horrors were happening inside Valerra would continue. That idea made her saddest of all. "I know this is a long shot. I doubt we'll be walking out of Glendin Palace in one piece. But if not us, then who? Who will do this? Even Mage Mother Pawllah said as much to Pryl."

Corbahn nodded, his forehead furrowed. "Aye. I just wish—"

Linden waited for Corbahn to complete the sentence, but he shook his head. "What do you wish?" she prompted.

"It's been a long time, not since I was a boy, that I started a sentence in that way. My father encouraged us to face reality head-on, no wishing it were different. It's not like me to start wishing about things now."

"But sometimes wishing is all we have left when the truth is too hard to process. I often wish I could turn back the clock, to before the Glenbarran invasion. Valerra was such a beautiful country, idyllic even," said Linden, "but if I spend too much time wishing, then I feel too sad to actually do anything that needs doing right now."

Corbahn ran a hand through his hair and seemed to make up his mind. "Then I'll say this one wish out loud and won't dwell on it. I wish the two of us could have more time together, away from our clans and responsibilities, away from battles and bad magic, just two people getting to know each other better. And if we both manage to survive this, I aim to make that wish a reality. So you're fore-warned." Corbahn's sea-green eyes bored into hers, the heat behind his gaze causing her to blush. He left Linden with no doubt about the nature of his wish or the object of his desire.

A flush of warmth spread throughout her body, surprising Linden almost as much as Corbahn's words. She hadn't realized how numb she'd been feeling inside, dead-ened to the possibility of loving again, after losing Stryker to his own foolish pride, after losing so many people she loved, including Toz. Something shifted for her in that moment. Numbness gave way to a small bubble of hope. Corbahn waited for Linden to say something. A ghost of a smile crossed her lips as she said, "Then let's make sure we survive, every last one of us."

Corbahn grinned. "Aye, let's do it."

They had a little over an hour of daylight left before night descended. Although Corbahn wanted to push ahead and travel another hour or two after sunset, Pryl insisted they make camp and post a careful watch. The fay chief didn't like traveling in Glenbarran territory and didn't want to be caught off guard.

Linden took first watch because she wasn't ready to turn in after their sparse dinner of roasted rabbit, split six ways, and some roots and berries Jayna had harvested during their rest stops. Too many scenes kept playing in her head, mostly of Toz, but also the family of women and their grihms, helping them carry Reynier to safety. She couldn't imagine the torment the men suffered during the cross-breeding, nor their family suffered when they realized what they'd become.

The sound of hooves hitting the ground nearby startled her. Linden put her hand on her sword and called out, "Who goes there? State your business!"

Efram said softly, "'Tis only me. But I could really use some help with these props."

Linden ran over to Efram's horse, whose saddlebags bulged with the paraphernalia of an itinerant theater company, as well as new clothes to replace the torn and stained disguises they'd worn at Zabor Prison. Jayna left her tent to join them and together they wrestled the heavy saddlebags off Efram's horse.

"Have you heard any more about Reynier?" Jayna asked.

"He's still in pain, but the healer says he's awake and asking a lot of questions, which is a good sign," said Efram, his eyes darting around the camp, looking for something or someone.

Jayna smiled. "That does sound like Reynier."

Efram jumped at every sound from the trees surrounding their campsite, squirrels scurrying, cicadas mating, owls hooting. Linden asked, "What's wrong? Do you have more news?"

Efram bowed. "With apologies, my Liege, but my report is for my chief's ears only."

"Of course," said Linden. Efram scurried over to Pryl's tent and called his name. As Pryl's head emerged from the tent flap, Efram dropped to the ground next to him. They spoke in soft tones until Pryl exploded in a series of loud buzzing that Linden could only assume were fay swear words.

"What's all that noise? Sounds like a fay council meeting," grumbled Corbahn. He scrambled out of his tent, his hair loose and flyaway around his wide shoulders. Linden tried not to notice that he slept bare-chested, his muscles rippling with every movement. She looked away, focusing on Pryl and Efram instead.

Pryl uttered an incantation that whisked away his tent and bags, stowing them neatly on his horse. He was dressed for travel in his traditional chieftain's robe, his beard quivering with indignation. "You're not far off. The fay council has voted, in my absence, to withdraw fay support of our mission to neutralize the places of power and stop the spread of Fallowness across the continent."

"What are they thinking? How is this even possible?" Corbahn waved his hands dismissively at the hidden fay council and their secret vote, his voice rising as the implications began to hit home.

"Many fays believe it's time to leave men and women to their own devices. There's been talk for half a millennia at least of withdrawing entirely from Faynwood."

Linden put her hands on her hips, her temper flaring. "Why would the fays do such a thing?"

"Because fays are tired, tired of humanity, of the factions and fighting and corruptions of Serving magic," said Pryl.

"But we're not all like that," replied Jayna. "Many of us are sworn to protect Serving magic."

"What will happen when the fays withdraw completely?" Mara had come out of her tent to join the conversation. Remy was the only one still sleeping. It seemed he could sleep through just about anything, even a discussion about the end of the world as they knew it.

"How will Serving magic survive if the fays leave?" asked Linden.

"How will we survive? If Serving magic fails, then every Serving mage will be hunted down and destroyed."

Corbahn folded his arms across his chest, his biceps bulging.

Can't that man go put on a shirt? Linden thought crossly. They were talking about matters of life and death, and she found his bare chest distracting. Linden redirected her attention to Pryl and said, "You told us the fay race was once more belligerent than we are. If fays can change over time, why can't we?"

Pryl put up his hand, palm outward, and sighed. "I can't disagree with any of your points. I've made the same arguments myself, many times. The ancient fays learned to solve their disagreements peacefully over two millennia ago. That's a long time to wait for humankind to follow suit. The fays have grown weary and want to leave people and their problems behind."

"Where are you going now?" asked Corbahn.

"To the fay council. I'm going to try to talk some sense into those stubborn, biased heads of theirs."

"But we're a day's ride from the palace. What are we supposed to do if you're not back in time?" Linden didn't relish the thought of facing Mordahn, King Roi, and the entire palace guard without the fay chief at her side. The odds were bad enough as it was.

"There's a deep lake high in the hills surrounding Glendin Palace. Ride into those hills and go to the western shore of that lake. You'll find a cave with fay symbols etched into its walls. Wait for me inside that cave. You'll be protected by the ambient fay magic within the walls. Don't venture out until I return," said Pryl. He and Efram mounted their horses and vanished into the mists.

CHAPTER 20

Corbahn glanced down at himself, seemed to notice he was shirtless, and said, "Oh, ah, be right back." He re-emerged from his tent a few moments later wearing a loose linen shirt. "I'm wide awake. I can take over the watch for you," he said to Linden.

"Thanks, but I'm not sleepy either." Linden's head swirled with questions about the fay council's decision to abandon Faynwood. She knew she'd be tossing and turning in her tent if she tried to sleep.

Jayna said, "Well, I'm turning in. I refuse to think about the end of the world until tomorrow morning at the earliest." Yawning, Mara agreed with her, and both stumbled back toward their tents.

Corbahn shook his head at Remy's soft snores. "He really can sleep through anything, can't he?"

"Pretty much," said Linden. Switching subjects, she asked, "Will the fay council listen to Pryl?"

Corbahn picked up a handful of small stones and heaved them, one by one, into the trees at the edge of their camp. When he reached for another handful, Linden said,

"Come sit down and tell me what you're thinking." She patted the flat boulder she'd been perching on before Efram's arrival.

Corbahn dropped down next to her, his shoulder brushing hers. She found his nearness almost as distracting as his bare chest and wished she hadn't invited him to sit next to her. Neither one of them could afford to be diverted from their mission, however attractive the diversion might be. Fingering the small stones in his hand, Corbahn said, "This is something my father always feared, that one day, the fays would decide to up and leave us, and over time, we'd lose all connection to Serving magic."

"I always believed that Serving magic would survive anything, until I saw what happened in Valerra. Fallow sorcery overwhelmed our best mages," said Linden.

"Without the fays to help us, I don't know how we'll be able to hold onto Faynwood," said Corbahn.

"Do you think Pryl can convince the fay council members to change their vote?"

Corbahn shook his head. "I doubt it. Pryl's been fighting a losing battle for a long time with the council. The most he'll be able to do is to get them to delay their decision."

"Delay for how long?"

"Let's hope long enough for us to restore the places of power to their proper Serving magic state," said Corbahn. He resumed tossing the remaining stones in his hand, Linden watching in silence as the stones pinged against the trees in the dark. She could sense his frustration building with every toss. When he finished, he brushed off his hands and rested them on his thighs with a long sigh. It took every ounce of willpower Linden possessed to not thread her fingers through his and draw him close for a kiss. Heat spread through her insides like a brush fire at the thought, and she hopped off the boulder, startling herself and Corbahn.

"I think I'll take you up on your offer to sit watch," said Linden. Her voice sounded high-pitched in her ears.

Corbahn stood up and faced her. He tucked a chunk of her hair behind her ear, his touch gentle, almost a caress. "Aye, sleep well, my Liege," he whispered, sending shivers down Linden's spine. She hurried to her tent and crawled inside her bedroll, willing herself to think about their mission and what was at stake.

Linden brought to mind all those lost to the Glenbarrans and their Fallow ways, from her grandmother and uncle, to countless neighbors and friends she'd grown up with, to Haydahn and finally Toz. She resolved to get her emotions under control, a tall order after losing Toz, and focus on the only thing that mattered at the moment: neutralizing the place of power inside Glendin Palace.

Mara volunteered to take point in the morning, alternating with Remy, who grew more sober with each hour they drew closer to the palace. He didn't even complain about their meager lunch of roots and berries, eaten in the saddle since Corbahn insisted they keep moving. Jayna rode alongside Linden in the afternoon. They crossed a plain covered in prairie grasses so tall not even the tips of Ashir's ears showed above the rolling waves of green. Linden inhaled the sweet air, the beautiful summer morning making her want to turn Ashir around and ride in any direction other than the palace.

"How are you holding up?" asked Jayna.

Linden shrugged. "Still numb, I guess. I can't believe

Toz is really gone, and I don't want to face the possibility of losing anyone else. I don't think I can bear it."

Jayna nodded. "I know. I'm actually relieved Reynier was injured. At least I won't have to worry about losing him when we face Mordahn again."

"Promise me that no matter what, if you have a chance to escape, you'll take it."

"And leave you behind?" Jayna's dark curls bounced in protest as she shook her head. "No way."

Linden knew Jayna would say that, and she also knew Jayna and Reynier needed each other. They completed each other in ways that Linden almost envied. She decided to appeal to Jayna's sense of duty. "If we're backed into a corner and only one of us can escape, I want it to be you. I don't want to leave Reynier all alone again. Not only would he have to rule Faynwood as the Elder, but he'd also have lost the woman he loves for the second time. I think it would break him completely."

Linden waited while Jayna processed her words. Jayna started to open her mouth a few times, looking as if she wanted to refute Linden's argument, but closed it again without uttering a word. Finally Jayna said, "I'll do it for Reynier, and for the greater good. Faynwood needs a strong leader, not a spent, bitter man. But it would break my heart to leave you behind. You know that."

Linden gave her friend a weak smile. "I know. And thank you."

Jayna glanced behind her at Corbahn and lowered her voice so Linden had to strain to hear her. "You and Corbahn seem to be getting along. If I didn't know better, I'd say there's an attraction there, a strong one, between you two."

"My only focus right now is our mission, same as Corbahn. I can't think about anything beyond the present."

Linden wasn't about to acknowledge to anyone, even Jayna, her attraction to Corbahn. Besides, her feelings at the moment were a tangled muddle.

"Uh-huh," said Jayna, "I have eyes."

Linden drew her brows together and shot her friend a look. Jayna grinned. "And I know when to seal my lips."

Linden chuckled softly, realizing she hadn't so much as smiled since the battle in the prison camp where they'd lost Toz. Taking a deep breath, she felt a stitch in her side. She blinked and tried breathing more shallowly, the pain in her lung intensifying. Linden called out ahead of her, to Mara and Remy, "Hold up! There's some serious Fallow magic about." Mara and Remy pulled up their horses and waited for Linden and the others to catch up.

"What's going on?" said Corbahn, waving his hand. "We're in the middle of a prairie and far too exposed. We need to keep moving."

Wincing, her hand on her side, Linden said, "This prairie is steeped in Fallowness. We need to cast a veil of drabness now!"

Corbahn scanned the horizon. "Are you sure? I'm not picking up anything."

Remy asked, "But won't that attract any Fallow mages in the area?"

Linden shook her head and said through gritted teeth, "Inactivating spells, like a veil of drabness, won't draw their attention. We'll be safe."

Beads of sweat broke out on Linden's forehead, and she struggled to breathe. As the pain intensified, she gasped out the incantation for a veil of drabness, Jayna, Mara, and Remy incanting along with her. Corbahn peered at Linden, obviously confused by her distress and insistence on pending danger. Linden gave him an encouraging nod.

Corbahn returned her nod to indicate he trusted her instincts. He joined the others, repeating the incantation until the veil snapped into place above their heads. Ashir's ears twitched as Linden leaned forward to catch her breath, clutching his mane as she pointed at a swarm of dark dots punctuating the white clouds overhead. Corbahn looked in the direction Linden pointed, his demeanor transforming from mildly curious to fully at attention in a single glance.

"Dorihms," he muttered, "I've heard stories of them but never encountered them."

"What are they?" Jayna asked, her voice an octave higher than usual.

"Part condor, part human, entirely Fallow," replied Corbahn as the dots grew larger and more numerous, spreading like ink above their heads and blotting out the blue sky. Linden could see them now: wicked-looking bird creatures, their wing spans twelve feet across, their claw-like hands open and ready to snatch or maim or kill.

"They're coming right at us!" said Mara. "Can they attack us through this veil?" Linden thought hard, bringing up pages of her *Timely Spells* book in her mind. She knew if they cast a defensive shield inside the veil, the dorihms would know their precise location.

"Aye, they can attack us through the veil, but they won't be able to see us or hear us if we're completely quiet and don't move a muscle," replied Linden. Then she thought of the horses, which couldn't possibly remain still while the dorihms circled overhead. "I'm going to immobilize our horses now. Don't worry, they won't feel a thing. After that, we'll need to continue to silently repeat the veil of drabness spell until they've moved on." The immobility spell was incredibly difficult, a spell that only a master mage could cast, and one that should only be used in extreme circumstances, and never, ever on another human. Linden took a shaky breath, focusing every ounce of her strength and concentration on the spell. She uttered the words to immobilize Ashir and the other horses, which locked down most of their joints and muscles, except for those needed for breathing and circulating their blood. Ashir snorted once, as if to scold her. Linden didn't blame him at all.

Remy said, "I suppose if those things discover us, we could cast a defensive shield at that point—"

"But we won't be able to hold it indefinitely, by ourselves, against so many," supplied Corbahn, his mouth set in a grim line.

"Show time," whispered Mara, nodding at the swarm of dorihms who'd slowed down over the large field of tall grasses and now swooped over the west end of the plain, dipping low to look for prey and then soaring back into the sky. The air hissed with the sound of their massive wings in flight.

Linden resumed the drabness incantation, continuously repeating the words of the spell and binding it in her head. She found she could breathe a bit easier now, almost as if the searing pain were a warning signal of a pending Fallow attack. She didn't know why it was so much more acute now than it had been in Faynwood during the fire, or even at the prison camp. Did the sharp pain have something to do with Mordahn's proximity? Or that she was traveling deeper into Fallow territory?

The dorihms broke into trios, three birdmen per formation, and scoured each section of the large prairie. Linden observed their pattern as she repeated the spell in her head. The lead dorihm flew in a circle, surveying the ground before diving down low to skim the surface of the grasses, and the other two dorihms flew on either side, effectively serving as the wingmen. They scanned their section of prairie thoroughly and then the lead dorihm would squawk once and soar into the sky, the wingmen following slightly behind.

Linden found herself impressed with their thoroughness and prayed the veil of drabness would hold up against their scrutiny. The dorihms were about fifty yards to the west and working their way, very methodically, toward them.

A trio of dorihms circled directly above their heads and then dived toward the ground, the steady hissing sound of their wings becoming a loud roar. Linden's heart lurched as she repeated the words of the spell in her head, wondering whether she ought to cast a defensive shield immediately, despite knowing it would only delay the inevitable. She thought back to her magic lessons, first with Nari and later with Pawllah, and concluded with a grim certainty that their only chance of survival was to stand rock-still and wait out the attack. Corbahn was right; they'd never be able to hold a defensive shield in place long enough to survive.

The dorihms skimmed the grasses, mere feet above them, zigzagging to cover every square foot of ground. Linden decided that dorihms looked scarier than grihms, with their hooded, birdlike black eyes, two slits for a nose, and beaky protrusion ending in a human mouth full of pointy teeth. Feathers covered their torso and wings, with two legs near the tail presumably for landing and two arms in the front. They had talons instead of fingers on their claw-like hands, which constantly opened and closed as they flew.

Linden spotted a pencil-thin mustache on the lead dorihm's upper lip and stopped herself from leaning forward to gape. *How ridiculously vain!* Something about the mustache, the facial features, and the dorihm's vanity stirred a memory. Forcing herself to repeat the veil of drabness spell in her head, she tried to steady her nerves, ignoring the rising tide of nausea in her stomach. She recognized the lead dorihm. He was Ellis Steehl, or what was left of him after being crossbred with a condor. A constant visitor to her uncle's home office in Valerra, Linden had often encountered the preening advisor to the queen. During the chaos following the Glenbarran invasion, Ellis Steehl showed his true colors by turning against his homeland and friends. His co-conspirator had been Linden's former magic instructor, Mage Rudlyn. Together, they schemed to join forces with Mordahn, killing anyone who got in their way, including Linden's grandmother.

Linden shifted her attention to the other dorihms flying in formation with Steehl. Sure enough, the dorihm on his right wing appeared to be Rudlyn, her lips pursed in concentration as she scanned the ground for intruders. After her grandmother's death, the authorities searched in vain for Steehl and Rudlyn, but they'd escaped. Linden had always assumed they'd managed to cross the battle lines and pledge their allegiance to Mordahn.

Linden sensed Rudlyn's piercing black eyes scanning the veil of drabness above her head. Linden furrowed her brow in concentration, gazing steadily at the back of Ashir's head rather than following the flight of the dorihms across the field. She didn't realize they'd moved on until she heard Corbahn say, "Linden, did you hear me? They're gone. We're safe, at least for now."

She exhaled a shaky breath and uttered the words to unbind the immobility spell and drop the veil of drabness. Ashir tossed his head back with a loud snort and pranced on his hooves, eager to flex his muscles. Smiling, Linden patted his mane, "You were a very brave horse. Even Kal would be proud of you!"

Corbahn took point and led them at a brisk pace across the field. They encountered no more dorihms as they entered the forest at the base of the Glendin foothills. If anything, the woods seemed unnaturally silent, no birds calling, no squirrels chattering, nothing but the sound of twigs snapping underfoot. As they headed deeper into the forest, the canopy of trees above them grew so thick it blocked the sun, casting everything in shadow. Linden shifted in her saddle uneasily. The darkness seemed to seep into her pores, filling her with uncertainty about their mission. The deeper into the woods they traveled, the greater her sense of dread. She wanted to turn tail and run. Was this Fallow magic, or simply her imagination playing tricks on her?

"How much longer 'til we're at the cave?" whined Remy. "I'm sick of these woods and feel like I've passed those trees over there before."

Linden glanced in the direction Remy pointed. Tilting her head, she said, "Actually, now that you mention it, those sequoias do look familiar."

Corbahn brought his horse up short and said, "Wait here." He rode over to the nearest sequoia, dismounted, and taking his dagger, etched a squiggly line into the trunk of the tree. Rejoining the group, he said in a low voice, "I agree, this entire section of forest looks familiar, and yet, I'm certain we haven't circled back."

Glancing up, Linden located the sun through the thick foliage overhead. "You're right, the sun has moved slightly in front of us. That means we're still heading in the right direction, toward the lake in the hills."

"Look!" said Mara, pointing at the sequoia. "The symbol you etched is gone."

"Alright," said Corbahn, "these woods are enchanted. We can't be sure of what we're seeing, but we keep moving west. So long as we can see the sun ahead of us, we should be fine." Almost as the words were out of his mouth, a cloud passed over the sun, casting the woods in even deeper shadow.

"I don't know about the rest of you, but I feel almost oppressed in these woods. I don't like my thoughts," said Jayna.

Linden knew enchantments were localized, low-grade spells that fed on negative energy. Which meant the more they expressed their fears, the stronger the enchantment grew. Ashir shifted uneasily and gave a whinny; even he was feeling the effects. Linden said, "I don't want to draw attention to ourselves, so we can't cast a counterspell. What we need to do is focus on something that makes us happy. Laughing out loud will help. And we need to keep going. The enchantment feeds on our fears."

"The only thing that would make me happy right now is a five-course meal," grumbled Remy.

"That's a good thought," said Corbahn, who was clearly trying to humor Remy. "Describe your ideal dinner to me. What's your favorite first course?"

"Herbed black truffles with garlic butter," said Remy. He and Corbahn debated the best way to prepare truffles as Corbahn took point again. The two of them moved onto the next course, soup, agreeing that white chowders were superior to tomato chowders. As they discussed their favorite fish, meat, side dishes, and dessert, Linden smiled. It was working. Her mood felt lighter, and the woods started to thin out. She noticed more variety, fewer sequoias and more maples and oaks. Even more encouraging, she spotted two squirrels skittering across their path and heard the chirping of birds again in the trees. The sun peeked out from the clouds, lighting their way as they began to ascend the closest hill in the Glendin range, which was comprised of brown, rocky hills dotted with scraggly trees.

Corbahn followed a travel-worn path that wound its way around the boulder-strewn hill. As they climbed Linden scanned the area, searching for signs of Fallowness, but the mountain air felt refreshing, no enchantments or dorihms to interfere with the sunny afternoon. She and Corbahn searched for the landmarks Pryl had described to them.

"Do you think that's the tree he was talking about?" asked Linden, indicating a silver maple, its trunk split in two, forming a perfect Y. "And those must be the twin boulders he mentioned."

Nodding, Corbahn said, "Let's wind our way to that outcropping of rock over there." They fell in behind Corbahn again, careful to guide their horses along the narrow, gravelly path. Their trail leveled off, and they rode onto a plateau overlooking a dark blue lake that sparkled like a sapphire in the sunshine. "It's beautiful," said Jayna, inhaling deeply. "And it smells so clean and fresh up here. If I didn't know better, I'd think we were back in Faynwood or Valerra."

Mara agreed. "Maybe the Fallowness just crawls along the ground and can't climb into the mountains."

"Maybe," said Linden, "or maybe Mordahn and his Fallow mages don't need to enchant these hills."

"But why not?" asked Remy, fear creeping back into his voice.

"Because whatever's on the other side of this range offers more than enough protection," replied Corbahn.

"Like what?" Remy whispered.

"Like grihms and dorihms," said Corbahn with a shrug.

Linden didn't want to scare Remy, but a darker form of Fallow magic worried her even more than crossbreeds. "Or necromancers and whatever they decide to raise from the dead."

CHAPTER 21

REMY PALED, TURNING THE COLOR OF A STARCHED COTTON SHIRT. Swallowing hard, he said, "Can we find that cave and get some food? I'm feeling peckish."

Linden appreciated how Remy was trying to stay focused on the here and now, without letting his overactive imagination run away with him. "Good idea. Do you want to take the lead?" She figured Remy needed the distraction, despite Corbahn lowering his brow and glaring at her.

Remy gave her a businesslike nod and rode to the front, Corbahn riding directly behind him. Linden took up the rear, with Jayna and Mara between them. The group traveled silently, concentrating on picking their way along a thin ribbon of trail that wound across a ridge. Linden's focus was on the path in front of her; one stumble, and she and Ashir would plunge over the side, a drop of several thousand feet.

They'd almost cleared the ridge when Ashir's right-rear hoof slipped on a stone. His leg started to slide out from under him, and Linden leaned as far over to his left side as she dared. "Come on, Ashir, you've got this!" she yelped.

Ashir grunted between his teeth as his leg found purchase on the flinty surface. He stepped off the ridge and onto a broad hillside, his body trembling and sweaty. Linden patted his neck and said soothingly, "You're a mage in your own right. That was amazing." Ashir flicked his ears forward at the praise and whinnied softly.

Corbahn climbed down from his horse, worry etched in the fine lines of his forehead. "I heard some rocks sliding off that ridge behind me. That was you and Ashir, wasn't it? You nearly went over."

Linden had dismounted by then, her hand running through Ashir's mane. She nodded. "But we didn't."

"Why didn't you cast a spell?"

"Because I would have saved my life but sacrificed the rest of you, and our mission."

"I hate the fact we can't use active magic to protect us as we move," said Corbahn, a stern expression on his face. "I'll say this, and I mean it, Linden. If that happens again, cast the spell, and we'll deal with the consequences later."

"Found it!" called Remy, who'd been scouting for the fay cave farther along the hillside. "And it's well stocked too."

Corbahn said to Linden, "To be continued." Linden inclined her head to prevent further debate, but she had no intention of doing anything to jeopardize her friends or their mission. Everyone knew what they'd volunteered for, more or less, although even she'd have to admit that breaking into King Roi's palace to neutralize the place of power and destroy his crossbreeding equipment was more than even she'd bargained for.

The cave entrance seemed too small to be promising, a narrow slit in the hillside barely wide enough for her to enter. Linden wondered whether Remy's enthusiasm had run away with him. Remy said, "Go on, it's bigger than it looks."

Shrugging, she slipped into the cave, passing by the intricate swirls of hieroglyphs covering the entrance. A sense of peace immediately washed over her; somehow, the cave felt like home. Remy was right, the cave was much bigger on the inside and split into three roomy interior chambers. She waited a minute to allow her eyes to adjust to the gloom, although narrow openings in the roof of the cave allowed for slants of light to enter. The large main chamber stretched as far back as she could see, its walls covered floor-to-ceiling in hieroglyphs painted by fay mages and infused with Serving magic.

A second chamber opened up to her right. This seemed to serve as a stable and grazing area for livestock, since half the floor was covered in layers of hay. Clumps of tall grasses grew in the other half of the room, the grasses receiving sufficient light from a wide opening in the roof above. Linden followed the drip-drop sound of water trickling inside and discovered a pool of water, fed from an underground spring, occupying the far corner of the stable area.

She re-entered the main chamber and nearly collided with Corbahn, gaping at the size of the cave. Heading to the opposite side she entered the third chamber, also covered in fay drawings, although these seemed to be more artistic, used to tell stories rather than infused with magic. She assumed this was the sleeping chamber. Returning to the main chamber, she followed Corbahn deeper into the cavern. Jars of sand used to store preserved vegetables lined one of the walls. A drying rack containing well-preserved meat stood next to the vegetable jars, and another underground spring gurgled along the rear wall. A fire pit completed the kitchen area, with a hole in the roof above for the smoke to escape. Linden decided this was the best-stocked cave she'd ever encountered, more of a home away from home than anything else. Perhaps this had served as a home for an ancient fay tribe at one time. More recently, she suspected that Wreyn, Efram, and other fay scouts used this as a secure hideaway while spying on Glenbarran activities.

"What do you think?" she asked Corbahn.

"It'll do," he said. "I guess this is what the fays consider 'roughing it.'"

"Let's bring in the others and get the horses settled." Linden stepped out of the cave long enough to retrieve Ashir and invite her friends to bring in their horses. They looked at her skeptically but then oohed and aahed once they entered the cave.

Smiling, Linden paused at the threshold and listened to their lighthearted banter. Patting Ashir's neck, she glanced at the deep blue lake down below and the surrounding hills. Clusters of wildflowers gathered at the base of the hills, the valley surprisingly peaceful given its proximity to Glendin Palace. The tranquility reconfirmed that King Roi would have plenty of defenders on the other side of the mountain range. Swallowing hard, she worried yet again how many of them would survive this mission.

Could we wait out our future right here in this cave, ignore the Fallowness spreading like a plague, and simply live? Linden shook her head. As tempting as the thought was, it wouldn't do. She and her friends had been called or chosen or whatever for this dangerous work, and so they'd go ahead with the plan. But she vowed that no one else was going to die on her watch. Somehow, they'd get in and get out without any more loss of life. An unrealistic wish perhaps, but she'd call on every shred of Serving magic she possessed to protect them when the time came.

Remy's mood improved considerably when he saw the preserved food. "I'll make dinner. My mother's famous stew recipe is tucked inside my head"—he tapped the side of his head for emphasis—"waiting for a moment such as this. I guarantee the stew is so mouthwatering it'll bring a tear to your eyes, even yours, Corbahn."

"Leave me and my eyes out of this," grumbled Corbahn good-naturedly. "It's dinner that I want, not weeping." He and Remy both laughed, probably their first bonding moment, and Remy got down to work.

True to his word, Remy concocted a delicious stew. Mara discovered the fays' stash of wine and passed around mugs to everyone. Corbahn took a sip and stared at the ruby liquid in his hand. "This is really, really good wine. How do the fays manage to keep wine this good hidden away in a cave in the middle of Glenbarra?"

Remy held his mug aloft, his expression turned serious. "Let's drink to Toz and Chief Haydahn."

"Aye," agreed Corbahn, "and my brother, Riordahn."

"And Nari and Uncle Alban," said Linden, "and Matteo and my parents, wherever they are." Everyone else began listing the names of relatives and friends missing or lost during the war with Glenbarra.

Corbahn started asking them questions about the final siege of Bellaryss and their narrow escape from the Valerran Museum. After hearing their stories, he shook his head. "All of us have survived unthinkable odds, and now we find ourselves in the Glendin hills, preparing to infiltrate the palace itself. Without a doubt, we are here on purpose, for a special purpose, to save Serving magic from the plague of

Fallowness. Regardless of the outcome, I'm proud to be here with you, my Valerran friends."

Tapping his mug against Corbahn's, Remy said, "I'll drink to that." Everyone else tapped their mugs together.

A thin line creased Jayna's brow. She asked, "How long do you think we'll need to wait for Pryl to return?"

Linden shrugged. "I have no idea how long fay council meetings last."

"Anywhere from five hours to five days," said Corbahn.

"Five days?" repeated Mara. "How could any meeting last that long?"

"You know how Pryl enjoys expanding on topics he's passionate about?"

When Mara nodded, Corbahn said, "All the fays on the council are like that."

"I can well believe it. Valerran politicians aren't all that different," said Linden, recalling her uncle working late, preparing for parliamentary votes.

"Nor Faymon clansmen, if the truth be told," said Corbahn.

Patting his stomach, Remy said, "I intend to enjoy the food, the wine, and the rest for as long as we're holed up here, whether five hours or five days!"

"Wreyn!" Linden hugged the fay woman, who emerged with Pryl and Efram from their traveling mists two days later, looking fit and healthy. Linden was relieved to see her fay friends again, and equally relieved their waiting period inside the cave was over. She'd become increasingly restless, and Corbahn had taken to pacing around each of the chambers, even the stable area, claiming his muscles weren't used to "lying dormant for so long."

"How are you feeling?"

"Much better." Wreyn smiled. "And glad to be here instead of drinking disgusting herbal broths and listening to bickering fays."

Pryl arched an eyebrow. "Those bickering fays are your elders."

"And thorns in your feet," replied Wreyn, adding, "I'm sorry Chief, but they've grown soft and lazy. The council has no understanding of what's at risk here." Wreyn sat cross-legged next to Linden, who wondered whether the fay scout was fully recovered. Linden had never heard her speak so openly.

Pryl found a spot where he could lean against the cave wall and sat down with a grunt. Pushing back the hood of his robe, he said, "The council has made a concession of sorts."

Efram sighed. "Chief, I heard some of the council members taking bets on whether we'll return."

"Fays love to gamble. It means nothing," said Pryl, waving his hand.

Corbahn asked Efram, "What are the odds?"

"When we left, they were 498 to 1 that we'd neutralize the place of power and make it back to the fay council alive."

"498 that we'd make it?" asked Remy hopefully. Efram shook his head and Remy slumped against the wall. "Thought so."

"Those are not terrible odds," said Mara, "considering."

"Even I think those are discouraging odds, and I'm the optimist here." Jayna shook her head. "But since I'm not a gambler, I'm going to ignore our odds, unless they improve dramatically."

Corbahn turned to Pryl. "You mentioned concessions. What are they?"

"The fay council has decided to view our mission as a test of sorts," said Pryl. "If we succeed in neutralizing the place of power and destroying the crossbreeding equipment within Glendin Palace, then the fay council will throw their support behind my plan to free Valerra from occupation."

Linden sat up straighter. "They will? That's good news, isn't it?"

"They only promised that because they don't think we'll get out of Glendin Palace alive," said Wreyn.

An image of another ancient fay burial site surfaced in Linden's mind. The underground mausoleum lay in ruins, with sarcophagi scattered haphazardly, the desiccated bones of their owners sprawled on the ground. Statues of long-gone fay elders, most lying on their sides, were smashed beyond recognition. A haze of smoke and thick dust hung about the site, making it difficult to see. As the vision faded, Linden glanced around for clues and spotted several Glenbarran guards running away from the burial chamber. Linden blinked rapidly as the image gave way to the faces of her friends staring at her. She massaged her temples to relieve the headache that always accompanied a vision.

"Are you alright?" asked Jayna. "You just *saw* something, didn't you?"

"What did you see?" Corbahn's eyes locked onto hers, searching for clues. "Anything useful for our strategy?"

Remy folded his arms across his chest. "If it's bad news I'd rather not know."

"It's good news, at least this version of our future, or probable future, that revealed itself to me," said Linden. After she described her vision, she added, "I didn't see how we did it, or where we were when the Glendin place of power was destroyed, but for what it's worth, I also didn't see any of us lying on the ground." She didn't add that the image was obscured by the smoke and dust.

"That's something, anyway," said Mara thoughtfully. "It seems our mission to neutralize the place of power may be successful. We'll have to assume we'll find a way to break down the crossbreeding equipment as well."

"And escape the palace with our heads intact," grunted Remy. "Let's assume that too."

Corbahn said, "So if all goes according to plan, the fays will help us retake Valerra. But in the end, the fays will still leave." He looked at Pryl for confirmation.

Pryl nodded. "True enough. However we will leave you better able to defend Serving magic on your own."

"How can that possibly be the case, since fays originated Serving magic in our world?" asked Jayna, her normally gentle disposition giving way to pure skepticism. Linden wondered whether her own prickly nature was finally rubbing off on her friend, or whether Jayna had become as weary of wars, factions, and political systems as everyone else.

Wreyn's mouth formed an *O* and Efram shook his head vigorously. Pryl steepled his fingers, which meant they were in for another lecture, but this was a lecture Linden longed to hear. Neither Nari nor Pawllah nor any other mage or teacher had ever been able to explain the origins of Serving magic. Linden had a lot of questions without answers.

"As you know, fays have lived here for as long as memory itself. We occupied this continent for many millennia before the first woman or man ever stepped onto our shores. And as far back as our most ancient scrolls have recorded, magic has been part of the fabric of our lives, of our very essence. We fays have always been preternaturally magical. However, we did not, and could not, originate Serving magic. How could we? It is far older even than our race, and as existential as any fay or human or other mortal creature. *Serving magic simply is.*

"Is what?" prompted Linden.

"Is itself, existing wholly on its own, without reference to anyone else," replied Pryl. "Serving magic neither begins nor ends, manifesting everywhere. Although it grows dim with the rise of Fallowness across our land, Serving magic will never cease. If we lose this battle, Serving magic will merely go dormant, waiting to be unleashed by a new generation of mages, under a new Liege, at the appointed hour."

Corbahn ran a hand through his unruly hair. "What are you saying? That we will lose this battle? That we are not those mages, and this is not the appointed hour?"

Linden recalled the mosaics on the walls of the Valerran Museum, depicting the history of Faynwood and its Lieges. The last mosaic in the series was of a young Liege leading fays, women, and men, in a grand battle. They won, containing and confining Fallowness until it became a small, dark blotch on the landscape. That same image, of a young Liege with long, dark, blue-streaked hair, had shown up three times for Linden while she was still living in Valerra.

Later, Mage Mother Pawllah had told Linden she was that Liege, the one who would lead Faynwood and help defeat Fallow magic. She'd never believed that was her true destiny; she felt more like an imposter at worst, a poor substitute for the true Liege at best. But sitting here in the cave, contemplating the destruction of everything she loved, Linden thought maybe, just maybe, *she was that Liege*. If so, she wasn't going to allow Fallow magic to win, not on her watch.

Pryl looked at Linden, as if he knew what she was thinking, and he nodded at her. Linden stood and walked a few paces away from the intimate circle of friends gathered together in the cave, their upturned faces awash in the orange glow of the firelight. She thought of her father, a retired Royal Marine officer, the bravest man she'd ever known. He used to say that battles were won or lost inside his soldiers' heads, well before they drew a sword or strung a bow.

Taking a deep breath, her voice shaking with emotion, she said, "We will save Faynwood, and Valerra, and yes, even Glenbarra, from the plague of Fallow magic—from its foul sorcerers and necromancers, grihms and dorihms— from forced crossbreeding, slavery, and outright cruelty. This is the appointed hour, and we are the mages who will do this thing. We will defeat Fallow magic. Call it our destiny, our purpose, our place in history, call it our worst nightmare, but we will do this. We must do this."

Linden stopped and waited, her temples throbbing. She'd never liked public speaking, and even a short speech before an audience of her friends caused her heart to race. Knowing her father would have done the same thing had boosted her confidence in the moment, but now she wondered whether she'd gone too far.

Silence filled the cave, wreaking havoc on Linden's already frayed nerves. She felt rooted in place, waiting for someone to say something to break the spell. Corbahn rose from the ground first and began to clap. Jayna and Mara leapt to their feet, applauding. Wreyn hopped up, followed by Efram, both of them whistling and cheering. Linden assumed it was the fay version of applause. Pryl, who was beyond the age of hopping, gathered his robes and stood to join the others. Remy was last. Shrugging, he rose slowly to his feet. Nodding in Linden's direction, Remy thumped his fist against his chest before bringing his hands together.

Pryl said briskly, "Well said, my Liege. Now let's get down to business. Each of us needs to assume a new identity, and we need to rehearse. Efram, where are those costumes you collected for us?" Everyone groaned, Corbahn the loudest. Linden started to laugh, relieved that her pulse was returning to normal, that they were all in this together. Corbahn arched an eyebrow at her and smiled. Jayna and Mara hugged her, laughing like schoolgirls, which they would have been if not for the war.

Wreyn, a mischievous glint in her eye, sighed. "It's too bad we don't have a lyre handy."

Linden noticed Pryl scowling at the younger fay and asked, "Why? Do one of you play?"

Wreyn waved her hand in Pryl's direction. "Chief plays and sings beautifully, although not so much anymore."

Pryl's mouth dragged down at the corners. "I will never sing again before the likes of Mordahn!"

Wreyn's mouth dropped open, and everyone stared at Pryl. Linden found her voice first. "Do you mean to say you've actually sang in front of Mordahn?"

Pryl glanced out toward the mouth of the cave, his eyes unfocused. "A lifetime ago, before the Faymon civil war. I performed a ballad around a campfire similar to this one. Mordahn was there, and so were Pawllah and Nari." He shook his head, as if to rid himself of a painful memory. "I rarely play the lyre these days."

Linden sat up straighter. "You knew my grandmother?"

Pryl gave her a wistful smile. "Aye, lass. But we have no time for reminiscing. We have much rehearsing to do, if we're to perform before the king." Linden wanted to hear more about Nari as a young woman, but she knew Pryl was right. They had a lot of work to do to transform into something approaching a traveling troupe.

The moon was high in the sky when Pryl decided to call it a night, declaring he couldn't perform any miracles, and went into the sleeping chamber. The others followed until just Linden and Corbahn remained, sitting near the fire. Corbahn got up to stir the embers and sat down again across from her.

Linden wondered how to thank Corbahn, deciding on the direct approach. "Thank you for helping me get past that awkward silence earlier."

"We needed to be inspired, and you knew exactly what to say in that moment. I'm proud to call you my Liege," said Corbahn, his eyes reflecting the soft glow of the smoldering embers. Linden's breath caught in her throat when she looked at him, his tousled hair brushing his broad shoulders, his muscular solidness a constant reminder of the man himself: brave, action-oriented, capable, true.

His voice dropped a decibel, growing husky. "As for the other names, the endearments, that I'd like to call you, they will have to wait, especially after your rousing war speech."

Linden's heart raced for the second time that evening. While her attraction to Corbahn had been growing in direct proportion to the amount of time she spent with him, she was in no position to commit, let alone respond. Corbahn saved her from having to say anything at all. Rising to his feet, he said, "Goodnight, my Liege," and headed into the sleeping chamber.

Rather than try sorting out her jumble of thoughts and feelings, Linden grabbed her bedroll. Stretching out in front of the dying fire, she yawned and fell, mercifully, asleep.

CHAPTER 22

Dawn came early, a clear day with not a single cloud to mar the sunrise. Linden wished she could stay one more day in that safe cave, perhaps sleep late and then take a dip in the crystal-clear lake down below. Pure fantasy, she knew. Every day she delayed was another day that Fallowness destroyed more lives, threatening everything and everyone she held dear.

Before leaving the cave, Linden gathered the ensorcelled swords from Corbahn and her friends. Placing her sword and dagger with the others, she carefully wrapped the weapons in a blanket. "Somehow this feels more final than anything else we've done. Burying our swords, I mean."

Corbahn used a small hand shovel to dig a shallow hole in the stable area of the cave. "Aye, but it's a wise precaution. We can't march into the king's palace with these swords, and we surely don't want them falling into the wrong hands, to be misused like the places of power."

"But I'm not sure how we're going to destroy that cross-breeding equipment without them."

Corbahn shook his head. "I don't know either, but our first priority is to neutralize the place of power inside the palace, and that doesn't take any weapons." Corbahn placed the bundle of swords inside the hole and covered it. Then he scuffed over the soil with the heel of his boot, sprinkling a layer of hay over the recently disturbed dirt. When he was finished, he rose, brushed his hands, and said more to himself than to Linden, "'Til we return."

The group decided Pryl should serve as the traveling troupe's leader and spokesman. As fay chief, Pryl possessed the fays' natural talents for subterfuge and misdirection, in addition to his sixth sense as a politician and negotiator. As they were preparing to leave, their packs stowed and horses saddled, Pryl paused at the threshold of the cave. He rested his hand on one of the fay hieroglyphs etched into the wall, as if to gather strength from the ancient magic, and said, "We are riding into the mouth of the lion, where dark arts and Fallow sorcery are the norm. We ride without wards or charms or protections of any kind, because even the whiff of a spell will destroy our cover. Once we cross over these hills, our real test begins. We will see and hear the stuff of nightmares on the road to the palace, but we must not stop. Ride on, heads down, as if your lives depend on it because they surely will."

Linden's stomach hardened with fear, and she wished she hadn't eaten porridge for breakfast. Her brave speech the night before seemed a distant memory, and she bit her bottom lip to keep it from trembling. She patted Ashir's neck and reminded herself she was the daughter of Colonel Ric Arlyss, the most decorated officer in the Royal Marines, and the great-granddaughter of Liege Ayala, who never flinched from battle.

They filed out of the cave a somber group of fays,

Faymons, and Valerrans. Pryl rode near the front, directly behind Efram, who volunteered to ride point. Corbahn rode in the back, to keep a sharp lookout for any sneak attacks, and he insisted Linden ride in the middle of their group. Given Linden's past encounter with Mordahn, he wanted her to fade into the background as much as possible. Pryl agreed, giving Linden a supporting role in the drama they planned to stage for the king, if they survived long enough to perform.

Linden couldn't argue with their logic. She'd chosen the plainest clothes she could find—a dark gray cape layered over a lighter gray dress—among the stash of outfits Efram had brought back from Faynwood. She had no idea where he found the clothes, costumes, and props for their traveling troupe, but she was impressed with his resourcefulness. She encouraged Mara, Jayna, and Wreyn to dress more flamboyantly, with their red, purple, and magenta capes, multi-colored gowns, and flowing veils edged in lace. Each of the girls wore thick tights under their gowns, despite the summer heat, so they could hike up their dresses when riding.

Efram guided them downhill from the cave and around the lake. Wildflowers stirred in the breeze as they passed by, waving gently, almost beckoning Linden to dismount and pick a fresh bouquet. Ashir seemed just as distracted by the summer morning; Linden had to steer him firmly past the grassy shoreline, perfect for grazing and lazing. She wondered whether the hills had been enchanted to encourage meandering and deter anyone from crossing to the other side.

The sun had drifted well past its zenith by the time Efram led them out of the hills and onto the palace road. The temperature dropped about twenty degrees in a matter of minutes, the air much cooler at the base of the mountain range than at the higher elevations. Linden grimaced as a sharp pain stabbed her side. She had no doubt now about their proximity to the palace and took shallower breaths to ease the throbbing.

The road they traveled had been cut through a dense forest. Towering trees blocked the sun, giving the impression it was well past dusk rather than the middle of the afternoon. As she rode along the path, an occasional tree branch brushed Linden's shoulder, causing her to flinch. She recalled the bedtime stories her father used to read to her, stories about bad things lurking in the middle of dark, unnatural forests, and about children who wandered into such forests and were never seen again. While Linden had no doubt these were tales dreamt up by adults to keep active children in check, the deeper they penetrated the forest, the more her scalp began to tingle, and her stomach tighten.

Linden heard twigs snapping and then a rumbling noise that seemed to rise from the ground itself. The rumbling intensified, separating into distinct sounds like the beat of a drum. This was no ordinary drum roll, but the steady thump of horses' hooves—scores of them—pounding the roadway on either side of them. Linden knew they couldn't be there, that this was a Fallow trick, but from the corner of her eye she saw them, nonetheless. The horses were skin and bones, more like bones knit together with spare bits of sinew and scraps of skin. Riders sat astride each horse, with rags for clothes hanging off their skeletal frames. The jackets of their moth-eaten uniforms flapped in the breeze, as the bones of their hands grasped imaginary reins.

The undead riders—for that's what they were, raised from whatever unholy grave the necromancers found them in—stared straight ahead, their eye sockets empty and their mouths hanging open, revealing nothing inside but the teeth they died with. The horses and their riders pressed closer to Linden and her friends, so close Linden could smell the odor of death on them. The nearer they came, the more the temperature fell, until frost gathered in Linden's hair and face, her fingers growing numb in the cold. Fear gripped Linden's insides, rattling her to the core, shaking her resolve to stay on that road to the palace. The undead riders and their horses pressed closer, a mere arm's length away on either side. Ashir trembled beneath her, but she leaned forward, urging him on as Efram picked up speed and they galloped ahead, the living and the undead.

Mara, riding directly in front of Linden, passed under a low tree branch and started flailing one of her arms. Before Linden could figure out why, she and Ashir rode under the same tree. Three furry brown spiders each the size of a fist dropped onto them. Linden screeched as one landed on her shoulder, a few inches from her face, and quickly brushed it away. A second arachnid, its pincers drawn, perched on Ashir's neck. Linden had no idea whether it was venomous and didn't wait to find out. She flicked the spider off Ashir with the back of her hand. It fell onto the road, where Ashir crushed it underfoot.

The last arachnid burrowed into Linden's hair. She screamed, reaching behind her head. Linden wrapped her fingers around its wriggling body. A burst of pain seared her hand as the spider bit into her flesh. Pulling the creature free from her hair, she tossed it at the nearest undead rider, who didn't flinch. The spider sailed through the rider's open chest cavity and landed somewhere on the other side with a crunch.

Linden began to shiver inside her thin cape, as frost

grew thicker on Ashir's mane and on her arms and legs. Her teeth chattered, her right hand and arm tingling with pain from the bite. The wind whipped up around them, tangling hair and tossing leaves from trees, as Linden struggled to grasp the reins with her frozen fingers.

An ear splitting roar pierced the air. The riders opened their ghastly mouths wider, the hinges of their jaws creaking as they screamed in reply. The forest came alive with a cacophony of shrieks and screeches, as if an evil headmaster scratched a giant piece of chalk across a blackboard. Linden wanted to cover her ears, to blot out the discordant noise, but she gritted her teeth and held on. Just when she thought she'd reached her breaking point, the squawking and shrieking subsided to a murmur, and then a whisper.

But the whisper seemed to curl around Linden's head, reaching inside her skull to sift through her memories. Linden recognized Mordahn's handiwork and focused her energy on blocking the insidious spell, imagining a golden door with swords crossed before it. Linden struggled to keep the golden door firmly shut. Panting with the effort, her temples ached as tears streamed down her face. The whisper wrung all the strength from her, until she leaned over onto Ashir's mane, barely able to sit in the saddle.

The murmuring in her head floated away on a gust of air. She let out a shuddering breath and winced as she pushed herself upright. The pain in Linden's side had subsided to a dull ache, a constant reminder of her battle with Mordahn.

Linden swiped at something wet above her lip. The back of her hand, swollen from the spider bite, came away smeared red from a nosebleed. She wiped her nose with the edge of her cape and blinked at the sudden silence all around her. She heard no more shrieking or screaming or whispering. The undead horses and their riders were gone, and patches of gray sky peeked from between the treetops.

Linden brushed a mass of hair out of her eyes and glanced around. Everyone looked as battered as she felt. Mara's hair was a tangle of wheat-colored knots, her red cape askew on her shoulders. Jayna's curly hair looked more like a swirly beehive on top of her head. Remy's cape was gone, his tunic hanging in shreds.

"What just happened back there?" asked Remy, his voice cracking. "And how much of it was real?"

"It was all quite real," said Pryl, pulling alongside Remy. "I'm sure your mother read you the old fay tales, about darkly enchanted woods and evil kingdoms, when you were a child?" Pryl waited for Remy's head nod. "Now you've been able to experience a fay bedtime story firsthand."

Remy shook his head. "I'd rather face a pack of grihms with axes than ride down that stretch of road again." Everybody chuckled, helping to lighten the mood, although Linden had to agree with Remy. She much preferred dealing with the living than the undead.

As the dense forest thinned, Efram slowed their pace from a full gallop to a steady trot. When Glendin Palace came into view, the group let out a collective gasp. The roof was a jumble of towers, turrets, and steeples, spiraling upward to the sky like jagged, pointy teeth. Bolts of lightning struck the palace repeatedly from dark clouds gathered above it. The building itself seemed constructed from solid onyx, shiny, black, and impossibly smooth. A muddy brown moat surrounded the entire structure, accessible only via a drawbridge. The bridge, currently drawn closed, receded into high walls made of the same onyx-like material. Linden couldn't imagine a less inviting stronghold.

As they approached, a dozen heavily armed soldiers, swords drawn, poured out of the guardhouse in front of the drawbridge. Linden and the others pulled up their horses, their raggedy procession coming to an immediate halt. The sergeant-at-arms, dressed in a black uniform with gray trim, shouted, "Who are ye, and what's yer business with His Imperial Majesty, the Highest Lord and Most Royal King Roi?" Linden refrained from rolling her eyes at the king's ludicrous title.

Pryl bowed. "My name is Samish," he said, sweeping his hands at the group, "and this is the finest traveling troupe in all of Glenbarra, come to entertain His Imperial Majesty, the Highest Lord and Most Royal King Roi and His Court."

The sergeant thrust out jaw and scanned the disheveled group. "Undead riders atop their horses? Or was it howling grihms chasing ye?"

"Could've been swarming dorihms too," offered the corporal.

"The undead riders," replied Pryl.

The sergeant nodded. "Thought so. Assuming yer the leader of this here troupe, follow me. Ye have a lot of paperwork to complete before I can ascertain if the king will see ye."

"And if the king won't see us?" prompted Pryl.

The man pointed to the road and forest behind them. "Then at least ye know the way back."

"Or ye can camp on these grounds and try again tomorrow," said the corporal.

The other guards sniggered. "And have their bones picked clean by morning, what with the grihms roaming these grounds and dorihms flying overhead."

Linden knew the guards were trying to scare them. And if Remy's pasty complexion was any indication, they were succeeding. Pryl cleared his throat. "That won't be necessary. I understand the king is a man of refinement and good taste. I'm certain he'll want to see us perform."

"Ye better hope His Highness is in the mood," muttered the sergeant as Pryl followed him into the shelter. The guards remained in position, pointing their swords at Linden and the others. A loud thunderclap rumbled overhead, followed by a lightning bolt. The thunderstorm produced a constant drizzle that coated the onyx walls and ramparts of the palace. Linden felt the mist on her face, but the road behind her was dry, the sky overcast but not raining.

"Why does it storm directly above the palace?" she asked the corporal.

Shrugging, he said, "'Tis the mages and 'mancers. Something to do with their experiments."

"What sort of experiments are the mages and necromancers running? I've never encountered stationary storms like these," said Linden.

"Ye will have to ask 'em yerself. But I'd recommend keeping yer mouth shut unless yer performing. Otherwise ye may wind up finding out the hard way, in one of their experiments." The corporal cackled at his own bad joke. Linden decided that King Roi hired the stupidest guards he could find. Perhaps he believed it was safer that way since the guards couldn't possibly give away any secrets. They lacked basic understanding and curiosity.

Pryl and the sergeant emerged from the guardhouse thirty minutes later, chuckling over something. Pryl returned to his horse while the sergeant pointed at one of the guards. The guard followed his sergeant to the moat, where they climbed into a skiff and took off across the murky water. While the guard rowed in quick, efficient strokes, the sergeant held a club in his hand, which he used several times to whack whatever swam beneath the surface. They tied up the skiff at a narrow jetty on the other side and slipped through an opening in the onyx wall.

While they waited, Linden scanned the area for any signs of grihms or dorihms, but the only activity seemed to be the constant thunderstorms above the palace. More than an hour passed before Linden spotted the sergeant and his guard returning in the skiff. She wondered what they'd do if the king asked them to leave. Steal the skiff? Retreat to the cave and regroup? She didn't relish the thought of a return trip through the forest, especially after dark.

The sergeant climbed out of the skiff and nodded at Pryl. "It pleases His Imperial Majesty, the Highest Lord and Most Royal King Roi to offer you his hospitality. He invites your entire troupe to dine with him this evening and looks forward to your performance."

CHAPTER 23

THE DRAWBRIDGE CAME DOWN SLOWLY, LANDING WITH A CLANK OF chains. After securing the bridge to pylons, the guards escorted them across the moat. Linden glanced down, spotting two enormous serpents wriggling in the water. Each creature looked about twenty feet long and at least a half a foot wide. They undulated as they swam, creating long ripples. When the serpents broke the water's surface, sparks of electricity arced in the air above their scaly backs.

"Those are the king's pets," said the corporal, who walked alongside Ashir and Linden.

"They look like dangerous pets," said Linden.

The corporal shrugged. "No more'n anything else around here." Linden thought perhaps she'd underestimated the man. Rather than being slow-witted, he was simply jaded, one of the risks of constant exposure to Fallow magic.

Stewards unloaded their bags and led the horses away to the stables. A servant in a long black robe, his hem and cuffs embroidered with silver runes Linden didn't recognize, beckoned to them from the doorway of the palace. His hood was pulled forward, obscuring his face. Linden assumed the man served one of the necromancers or mages mentioned by the corporal. Stepping back from the door, the servant ushered them into the palace itself.

Despite its all-black exterior and constant drizzle overhead, the palace's interior looked surprisingly normal and royal. *But looks can be deceiving*, thought Linden, the pain in her side ratcheting up. She swallowed down a wave of nausea, sensing the dark magic that Pryl had described as occupying every nook and cranny of the building. He'd been right. Fallowness was as real and present inside the castle, as the rain and storm clouds outside it.

The imposing entranceway soared five stories above them. Two grand staircases rose on either side of the room, their black teak banisters and railings gleaming with fresh polish. Balconies at each level, constructed of the same dark teakwood, overlooked the inlaid floor of the foyer. Linden frowned at the pattern created in the tiny mosaic tiles under their feet; a swirl of blues, greens, reds, and golds, it reminded her of something just beyond the reach of memory. Overhead, a crystal chandelier the length and breadth of a grown man hung suspended from the ceiling. Linden figured it would take a couple of servants an hour or more to light its several hundred candles. The ceiling itself was comprised of delicate latticework, interlaced with panes of glass. Although the atrium would sparkle like a crown jewel on a sunny day, Linden wondered when the royal family last saw the sun shine.

The servant led them to a guest wing on the third floor, with four bedchambers that connected to a common area. Bowing, he spoke in a gravelly voice, barely above a whisper. "I'll leave you to sort out your sleeping arrangements and will return in two hours' time to escort you downstairs."

Pryl asked, "What is the evening's schedule?"

"You will perform for the king and his guests. If your performance pleases, the king may invite you to join him for dinner afterward."

"And if our performance doesn't please?" asked Pryl.

The man lifted his shoulders ever so slightly and rasped, "I advise you to ensure the performance pleases." He bowed again and left.

"I don't think we rehearsed enough," hissed Remy as he hoisted his bag on his shoulder. "I'd rather be tossed in the dungeon *after* a decent meal."

"Stop worrying," said Corbahn. "Let's meet in an hour for a dress rehearsal."

"I don't think one more rehearsal is going to be enough," muttered Remy, following Corbahn into one of the chambers.

Linden turned to Mara and Jayna. "Since the two of you are the stars of the show, it probably makes sense for you to be rooming together." Nodding, they carried their bags into their chamber.

Wreyn and Linden took the last room in the wing, which they discovered had a back door that led to the servants' staircase. "This is perfect," whispered Wreyn. "We can do some exploring without being spotted on one of the main staircases."

Linden chewed her lip, deep in thought. "Maybe so, or maybe this is a test or a trap of some kind. Even if King Roi and Mordahn accepted our cover story, I'm sure they don't trust us. I know I wouldn't trust us."

"True enough. We'll have to explore carefully." Wreyn paused and then asked, "Are you worried about confronting

Mordahn again? I mean, after killing him, or almost killing him?"

"Oh, I definitely killed him. It was going to be one or the other of us, and I was lucky enough to get some help from Kal. But to answer your question, I am worried about facing the undead version of Mordahn. That seems even worse somehow."

"I don't blame you, especially after seeing those undead riders and their horses." Wreyn noticed Linden holding her hand against her side. "Is your pain back again?"

"It's pretty constant, now that we're deep inside Fallow territory."

"When we're back in Faynwood, let's have a fay healer take a look."

"What could a fay healer do that a Faymon healer can't? They're both using Serving magic in their healing rituals," said Linden.

"Fay healers have deeper, almost primal knowledge of how to counteract Fallow spells. Our healers may be able to give you relief."

Linden sighed. "I wish I'd known that earlier, although I suppose it does offer the benefit of providing an early warning of pending Fallowness."

"The benefit doesn't outweigh the cost. You'd be much better off being able to breathe without pain."

"You've got me there. I'll definitely see a fay healer when, or should I say if, we walk out of here."

Wreyn cocked her head to one side and gave Linden an appraising look. "When the time comes, use Serving magic to wreak havoc. Chaos may help create the means of escape."

"But Serving magic creates order, not chaos," protested Linden.

Wreyn shrugged. "Our magic serves order and beauty and truth. But if necessary, it can serve through chaotic activity."

Linden narrowed her eyes and nodded slowly. There was wisdom in Wreyn's words, the kind of wisdom Linden had only encountered twice before, in Nari and Pawllah. "Are all Pryl's scouts so wise, or is there something you haven't told me about yourself?"

Wreyn gave her a shy smile. "My father is one of the teaching monks on Sanrellyss Island. I've inherited a small portion of his prophetic abilities." Linden tucked away this fact to think about later, pleased to learn she wasn't the only seer in their group. Wreyn had visions as well that could be consulted.

"Did you grow up on Sanrellyss Island?"

Wreyn nodded. "I attended school in the cloisters." Wreyn stared at the opposite wall, her eyes slightly unfocused, the hint of a smile on her lips. "I sang in the Sanrellyss Chorale and even performed for Mage Mother Pawllah a few times. Anyway, that all changed when my father had a vision of my calling as a fay scout. The vision appeared to him three times, each time when the moon was full. He sent me to Pryl immediately after the third occurrence."

"When was that?" asked Linden.

"Four years ago. I was sixteen at the time."

Linden arched her eyebrow. "You started spying at sixteen?"

Wreyn giggled. "I prefer to think of it as careful listening. And I didn't operate solo until I completed my apprenticeship at eighteen." Wreyn added, her voice low, "Serving magic calls us early, my Liege. You know that as well as anyone."

ALTHOUGH THE GROUP rehearsed for an hour in their full costumes, most of them still flubbed an occasional line or forgot a cue. Linden hoped their comical play, based on a well-known folk story, would be diverting enough to overcome their mediocre acting abilities. Corbahn seemed to be suffering the most from stage fright, while Linden's anxiety mostly revolved around meeting Mordahn again. She wondered what he would look like—based on the undead riders she saw in the forest, how much of him would be left? She also worried he'd recognize her immediately, before she and the others could neutralize the place of power. If they were going to be caught and punished anyway, she wanted it to happen *after* they'd done some damage to the Fallow king's power base.

Precisely two hours after he'd left them, the robed servant returned to escort them to the great hall for their performance. Wincing at another spike of pain in her side, Linden slowed her breathing until the pain subsided to a dull throb. Her stomach churned as she followed behind the servant. She planned to blend into the background when she entered the hall, hoping to draw the least amount of attention. As Linden descended the grand staircase down to the ground level, she found herself staring at the design in the tiled floor again, convinced she'd seen the same pattern elsewhere. With a start, she realized that a map of the entire continent had been artfully designed into the flooring. However, Valerra and Faynwood were not identified as independent nations. This was an idealized map of the continent, with one nation, Glenbarra, ruling over everything. Linden didn't know what bothered her more, the arrogance of the king to commission the floor map, or the realization that it might come to pass, especially if they couldn't find a way to stop the Fallow sorcery inside that castle.

Their escort paused at the threshold of the great hall to confer with the butler before entering the hall and making his way over to the king. The group clustered in the entrance, waiting for the butler to direct them. Corbahn hovered next to Linden and gave her hand an encouraging squeeze. She flushed at his touch and squeezed his hand in return.

"Samish the Storyteller and his Merry Troupe," intoned the butler in a loud voice and waved them into the room.

Murals depicting various scenes from Glenbarran history covered the walls and ceiling of the great hall. A smaller version of the atrium chandelier hung suspended in the center of the room, its candles flickering in the drafty space. A raised platform with a heavy damask curtain drawn across it occupied the far end of the great hall. Two rows of velvet-covered chairs were arranged in a semicircle in front of the platform, which would serve as their stage for the evening. The butler directed them to the front of the semicircle, where King Roi sat with his advisors and guests.

Pryl glided to the front row of chairs, the rest of the group in his wake. Linden's pulse raced in anticipation of finally meeting the king and his Fallow sorcerers, Mordahn among them. They lined up, and holding hands as if they were already on stage, bowed low before the king.

King Roi nodded languidly and drawled, "We look forward to being entertained." Linden thought this sounded more like a veiled threat, which did nothing to steady her nerves. She glanced briefly at the men and women in the audience but didn't recognize anyone, other than the robed man, who obviously was an advisor rather than a servant, sitting to the king's right. A pretty dark-haired woman, one of the king's concubines, sat on his other side. Linden began to wonder whether Mordahn was even in the palace. In his past life, he'd served as the king's high commander, spending most of his time overseeing military operations. She wasn't quite ready to relax, but she did feel relieved that her confrontation with Mordahn had been indefinitely postponed.

"Thank you, your Highness. We will not disappoint," said Pryl. The king waved his hand dismissively, a signal to get the show rolling. The group bowed again and followed the butler behind the damask curtain. Their props, which Pryl had given to one of the servants shortly after their arrival, sat in center stage. Remy and Efram quickly set up the stage for the first scene, and everyone else scattered to take up their positions.

They were performing a comedy about a wealthy merchant's search for husbands for his three unmarried daughters, played by Mara, Jayna and Wreyn. Remy, Corbahn, and Efram played the various suitors, all unsavory characters in the first act. Eventually, the father, played by Pryl, agreed to allow his daughters to make their own choices. Mara and Jayna, the daughters known for their poise and beauty, fell in love with Remy and Corbahn, princes from neighboring kingdoms. Wreyn, the smartest daughter, started managing her father's business so he could travel to visit her sisters. Efram, the neighbor's son returned from war, courted her with many comical twists, finally winning her heart by the end of the story. Linden played the extra in various scenes, from maidservant to old crone. None of her lines were longer than a few words, such as, "Aye, sir," "No, mum," or "It's that way."

Once they were on stage, Linden became so absorbed in

the performance that she stopped worrying, at least temporarily, about everything else to come. A part of her mind made note of the laughter coming from the audience, especially the king, which she took as a good sign. At least Remy would get a decent meal.

The great hall fell silent as the final scene, with Efram and Wreyn holding hands, wrapped up. Linden held her breath, waiting for applause or censure from the king; she knew no one else would dare applaud until the king decided whether he liked the performance. King Roi slowly lifted his hands in front of his face and gave a few loud claps, nodding and smiling his approval. The rest of the audience joined in a round of applause. Pryl and the group held hands once more, bowing in appreciation as one of the servants pulled the cord to close the curtain.

Still holding Linden's hand, Corbahn whispered, "Now our real work begins."

Linden nodded. "Almost. We need to get through dinner." They waited as Remy and Efram packed up the stage props.

"That's what I meant. More play-acting. It's exhausting," hissed Corbahn.

Linden murmured softly, "You'll be breaking things soon enough. Just a bit longer, and you can be your true self."

Corbahn grinned. "It's gratifying to know how well you understand me."

The butler had slipped behind the curtain and now stood center stage. He waited until everyone fell silent before he said, "His Imperial Majesty, the Highest Lord and Most Royal King Roi, invites you to dine as his guests. Please follow me." Pointing to the props, he added, "My staff will store these for you."

Linden's face fell when she stepped into the dining hall, a formal room that most royal families would have reserved for state dinners. Corbahn had called it correctly; they had hours of roleplaying ahead of them. One false move, their mission would be finished, and they'd likely not live to see morning. Or if they did, they'd be tortured or crossbred into some grotesque version of themselves. Linden plastered an innocuous smile on her face while she shuddered inwardly.

A long table, large enough to seat at least fifty guests, took up most of the dining hall. Luxurious ivory linens, embroidered with the king's family crest, covered the length of the table, which the servants had set with gold plates, goblets, and flatware. Candelabras dotted the table in regular intervals, the light reflecting off the table settings and casting a golden glow over everything. Tapestries draped the walls of the dining hall. Like the murals in the great hall, these also depicted historical scenes.

Linden hoped the group would be seated as far away from the king and his advisors as possible, but no such luck. Samish the Storyteller and his Merry Troupe were inter-mingled with the other guests, surrounded on all sides by Glenbarrans loyal to the king. Everyone at the table either practiced Fallow magic or at the very least, was not repelled by it. Linden wondered whether she'd be able to keep her food down.

The king naturally sat at the head of the table, while his robed advisor anchored the opposite end. Linden was seated adjacent to the advisor and across from Corbahn, who was blinking rapidly. Something was spooking Corbahn, but he was too far away for her to nudge under the table. Pryl and Jayna sat somewhere in the middle, while the rest of the group wound up closer to the king's end of the table.

Linden didn't like the close proximity to the black-robed man, or to anyone with so much influence at the palace. A necromancer who introduced himself as Folcrim, wearing a gray robe with silver braiding at his shoulders, sat on Linden's left. Something about the man's profile looked familiar. When one of the servants referred to him as "master chief," she realized he was the chief necromancer who'd raised Mordahn from the grave, which made him Stryker's wayward uncle. The pain in her side spiked again. She twisted the napkin in her lap, longing to be anywhere but at that table in the heart of Fallowness.

Liveried servants delivered the first course, a creamed soup. The king picked up his spoon, the signal everyone had been waiting for. Spoons clinked against bowls and conversation buzzed around the table. Linden decided she would not attempt to make small talk with the necromancer or the advisor. Her own roleplaying skills could only take her so far. She would respond to direct inquiries but otherwise remain silent.

Linden had been waiting for the advisor to pull back his hood when he ate, but he didn't touch his soup. He didn't taste the next course either, field greens dressed with lemon, herbs, and olive oil. His gloved hands remained folded in his lap as he observed the length of the table. Folcrim asked Linden and Corbahn questions about their work as performers, which they managed to answer credibly enough. The advisor continued to ignore the food on his plate.

Linden thought perhaps they'd manage to make it all the way through dessert without being discovered. She wasn't prepared when the robed advisor turned to Corbahn and rasped, "Tell me, nephew, how fares your father?"

CHAPTER 24

LINDEN FROZE, HER HEART IN HER THROAT. FRESH JABS OF PAIN jolted her side, each one like the twist of a knife. *Could this really be Mordahn?*

Corbahn paled but otherwise didn't react. He slowly wiped his mouth with a napkin and placed it carefully on the table. Linden noticed a small tremor in his right hand, which he curled into a loose fist beside his plate. This was all the evidence she needed. Corbahn knew his great-uncle better than anyone. Mordahn was back from the dead and sitting a few feet away. Linden swallowed hard to keep her food down, her insides quaking from a combination of fear and indignation that the man hadn't stayed dead.

"My father is dead," replied Corbahn icily. "As I have no living uncles, I can't be your nephew."

Mordahn ignored the last part of Corbahn's statement. "I'm sorry to hear it. Haydahn was a sweet lad and a faithful clan leader." Linden almost fell out of her chair. Mordahn, this strange, undead version of the man, sounded genuinely sympathetic, almost human.

Corbahn gritted his teeth. "Glenbarran arrows killed my father."

"Unfortunately, politics divided our clan in the end."

"The politics of magic, you mean. Arrowood follows Serving magic. But you chose the Fallow path, and many of our clansmen followed after you."

Mordahn shrugged. "Two sides of the same coin. Magic is magic, but I chose the stronger of the two."

"You chose the shadier of the two, the side of dark sorcery and necromancy."

"I chose power," said Mordahn simply. "And now you and your lovely companion here have a choice to make. Join me and serve the Fallow way or spend the remainder of your days in the dungeon. Given its inhospitable climate, your stay with us will be quite short-lived."

Corbahn leapt to his feet, his voice booming across the room. "I choose the Serving way!"

While the king and his guests exchanged startled looks, some shouting, "He's a spy," and "Curse him," Pryl raised his hands above his head. His voice hissed out a fay incantation that Linden couldn't translate, but she knew was a mighty spell when a bolt of lightning shot out of the ceiling, splitting the room in half. A crack opened up in the middle of the dining hall. It started down the marble tiled floor, ran across the width of the table, and continued up the walls, tearing the tapestries asunder. The center of the table collapsed in a loud crash, sending the plates, goblets, and flatware sliding down from each end and smashing into the ground. The guests pushed back from the table, screaming, but no one attempted to approach Pryl just yet.

As the entire room rattled and shook, Mordahn roared out a counterspell. Instead of calming Pryl's storm, the two spells exploded, splitting wide open the crack in the floor.

Pryl and their group stood on the far side of the opening, separated from Linden and Corbahn by an ever-widening chasm. Eddies swirled about, lifting table linens, robes, and gowns. Linden backed away from the table, intending to run around to Corbahn, but Folcrim grabbed her. The necromancer clamped one hand over her mouth so she couldn't incant out loud and held her tightly against his chest with his other arm. Corbahn leapt onto the broken table to come to her aid, but Mordahn tipped the table over, sending Corbahn tumbling to the floor. He smacked his head when he landed and sprawled out on the tiled surface, knocked unconscious by the fall.

Vaporous tendrils swirled through the air, as Efram, Mara, Wreyn, and Remy vanished into the traveling mists. Guards poured into the room, drawn by the commotion and screams. Swords drawn, several burly guards dashed toward Pryl, who grasped Jayna's hand firmly in his. She cried out, "No, I'm not leaving without..." and they vanished into the mists as well.

One of the guards ran over to Linden, struggling to free herself from Folcrim, and slapped twisted steel manacles onto her wrists. The ensorcelled metal dulled her senses, taming her magic into submission. Folcrim released her into the guards' custody. Linden felt a cold metal clamp on her right ankle—a leg iron—and she kicked the nearest guard with her free foot. He backhanded her in the face as another guard locked the second leg iron in place. Connected by a three-foot chain, the leg irons made it impossible for her to kick anyone, let alone run away.

Linden stopped struggling against the guards, hopelessness overwhelming her. A trickle of blood ran from her nose, where the guard had hit her, into her mouth. Where did she think she'd run off to, even if she got away? She'd never leave Corbahn behind, and he was still lying on the floor, handcuffs and leg irons firmly in place. Two guards transferred him to a stretcher, and lifting him with a grunt, moved toward the doorway.

Mordahn raised his hand and the guards stopped. He looked down at his great-nephew. "He'll come to soon enough. Take him to the cages." The guards shuffled off, Linden's heart sinking even lower at the thought of Corbahn being sent to some cage.

Mordahn walked over to Linden and cocked his head to one side, as if trying to decide what to do with her. Now that Mordahn stood directly in front of her, Linden could peek under his hood. Instead of finding his cold eyes staring back at her, she saw a gray veil pinned firmly in place. He obviously didn't want to shock the king's guests with his undead appearance. Linden decided if Mordahn looked that bad, she didn't care to see him either. He'd caused her enough nightmares already.

"The little Liege of Tanglewood," rasped Mordahn. Linden clamped her mouth shut to keep her lips from trembling. He'd recognized her after all, and here she was, encased in twisted steel, unable to lift a finger against him. Not that it would do any good. Surrounded as she was by Fallow magic, what could one Serving mage hope to accomplish? She sagged between the guards holding her upright. What was the point of fighting against the dark tide surrounding her?

"Your family has been thorns in my feet long enough. First Nari, and now you and your brother."

A tiny sliver of light, the barest glimmer of hope, pierced through the darkness enshrouding Linden's heart. *Was Matteo still alive?* "My brother? What do you know of Matteo?"

Mordahn snorted. "He's a nuisance who will be routed soon enough."

"What sort of a nuisance?"

Turning away, Mordahn waved his hand. The guards shoved her to the doorway. "Tell me!" she screamed at him. "It can't hurt you to tell me the truth. You've won."

"You are correct, little Liege." Mordahn turned back around and walked toward the door until he loomed directly over her. Beneath the cologne he wore, Linden smelled rotting flesh, the odor of death, which she hadn't detected earlier. In whatever form Mordahn had been raised by Folcrim, it was not without a cost. He said, "It matters not, as you'll never see him again. Your brother leads the resistance in Valerra, along with several close allies. A mere nuisance, who even now is being tracked and targeted for extermination, along with the rest of the vermin who follow him."

Despite the leg irons and manacles and complete failure of their mission, Linden felt lighter than she'd felt since fleeing Valerra. Not only was Matteo alive, but he was also doing what he'd been trained to do all his life, protect Serving magic and fight back against the Fallow way. Some memory stirred, something Pryl had said, about a resistance leader named Tam, a man who'd been severely burned on his face, neck, and arms.

She realized in that instant that Tam and Matteo were one and the same person; her brother's nickname as a boy had been Mat. He'd simply flipped around the letters to create a new identity. If Matteo, with whatever injuries he'd sustained during the war, could fight back, then so could she. She needed a plan, one that would ensure she and Corbahn could escape and live to fight another day.

Mordahn added with a snarl, "Now off to the cages with

you." The guards tossed a burlap sack over Linden's head and half-dragged, half-carried her away.

ONE OF THE guards shoved her hard, and she landed face down in a heap on the ground. Whipping the sack off her head, he backed away and slammed the door. Linden heard the sound of a padlock clicking in place and lifted her head, brushing her tangled hair from her eyes.

Mordahn had not been exaggerating. She sat in a box-like wire cage, about six feet high and wide and deep. The place smelled like a kennel, of too many dogs or wolves living in cramped quarters. A lone torch lit the area. She squinted through the gloom, looking to see where they'd deposited Corbahn. His still form lay in a crumpled heap two cages away from her. The cage between them was empty, but the row of cages across from them housed gray wolves, pacing and panting, their yellow eyes staring back at her. Linden counted twelve wolves in the row, each in a separate cage. She and Corbahn appeared to be the only humans in their row of cages. She heard other sounds down the line, growls and snarls she couldn't identify but didn't think were made by wolves.

"Corbahn," she hissed, afraid to speak too loudly. "Can you hear me?" She heard him grunt. He lifted his hand and rubbed his head.

"Aye, I can hear you," he said, slowly pushing himself upright. "My head's killing me. What happened? Where's everyone else?"

After Linden filled him in, Corbahn said, "So we're sitting in a couple of cages with no means of escape. We probably have a few hours, max, before we're crossbred into a couple of horrific creatures. Oh, and my Uncle Mordahn is here, undead and more powerful than ever. Is that about right?"

"Pretty much, except we don't have to worry about the rest of the group. They've escaped. That's a bright spot."

"With all the bad news, it slipped my mind," grumbled Corbahn. "Pryl and the others will bring word of our demise back to the other clans. Then the fays will abandon us, and Faynwood will succumb to Fallowness. The entire continent will go dark."

Linden rolled her eyes. "I, for one, am relieved to know our friends aren't sitting in cages down here with us." She knew Corbahn had a killer headache, but she hadn't expected him to be this grouchy and unhelpful. "And you forgot the other bit of good news."

Corbahn rubbed the back of his head and grimaced. "Sorry, I'm not particularly good at handling failure. And I'm finding it hard to concentrate. What was the other bright spot?"

"Matteo—my brother—is alive. He's fighting back inside Valerra, and he's not alone. There are others who are resisting the Glenbarran occupation."

"I'm glad to hear it, truly I am. I know how much you've missed your brother and your family."

Linden's eyes started to well up and she sniffed. This was not the time for tears. There was work to be done. If Corbahn couldn't help her think through a strategy, then she'd have to do it alone. But he could at least listen and be a sounding board. "We need to prevent the fays from leaving Faynwood, and we need to help my brother. But first we need to get out of here."

Corbahn sat up straighter. "How? This twisted steel on our arms and legs renders our magic useless. And we're caged like animals." A creature roared somewhere inside the room, and he lowered his voice. "Speaking of animals, that definitely wasn't a wolf. Sounded more like a panther. There's a regular menagerie down here."

Linden leaned forward, grabbing the bars of her cage. "I think you're onto something." She dropped her voice to a whisper. "This twisted steel not only dulls our magic; it interferes with Fallow spells as well."

Corbahn scratched his beard and thought about the implications. Nodding, he whispered, "They'll have to remove these manacles and leg irons sooner or later, if they intend to crossbreed us. They're no fools, though. They'll gag us so we won't be able to incant out loud."

"Wreyn recommended we use chaos to our advantage when the time comes to act."

"Chaos? But there aren't any spells I can think of that invoke chaos," hissed Corbahn. "And we need to be silently incanting the same spell if this will work."

Linden sighed. "I know. We'll have one chance to get this right." She regretted not spending more time studying *Timely Spells* before she left Arrowood. She'd been recovering from her injuries and easily distracted. And if she were being absolutely honest with herself, she hadn't really felt like studying. Now her laziness might get them both killed. "I'm running through spells in my head, but so far, I've got nothing. If my grandmother were here, she'd snap her fingers and already have a plan."

"I wish I could have met her. She sounded like quite a lady."

"Nari was amazing." Linden shifted on the hard ground, trying to find a comfortable spot, which was proving impossible inside the cramped cage. "Whatever we're going to do, we better figure it out fast, because I don't think we've got much time."

"Time is definitely in short supply," grumbled Corbahn. He ran his hand through his hair and seemed to be making up his mind about something. He cleared his throat. "Before we completely run out of time, I want you to know that I can't think of anyone I'd rather be stuck in a cage with."

"Huh?"

He cleared his throat again. "That came out all wrong. What I mean is that if it's all going to end here and now, well, there's no one else I'd rather be with than you. At the end, I mean."

Linden canted her head to one side. She wasn't going to make this easy for Corbahn; if he had something important to say, then he would have to say it. "You'd rather be with me than anyone else at the end. Thank you, I think?"

Corbahn waved his hand in the air. "You're being intentionally obtuse."

"*I'm* the one being obtuse?"

He squared his jaw and tried one more time. "Linden, please listen to me. There's no one else I'd rather be with, in good times or in bad, than you." His voice grew husky. "I want to take you in my arms right now and—"

"I hate to interrupt this touching scene, but time is up for you both." Mordahn's hoarse voice reverberated down the row of cages. "Guards, prepare them for breeding."

CHAPTER 25

Panic-laced adrenaline pounded in Linden's veins, her insides churning with fear. Three guards strapped her onto a table inside King Roi's crossbreeding suite. By the time they were finished, she was unable to move her arms, chest, or legs. The final strap, which they wound underneath her jaw and tied off at the top of her head, clamped her mouth shut. The guards removed her leg irons, but the twisted steel cuffs around each wrist remained firmly in place. Linden knew the cuffs would have to come off in the end, but Mordahn would have his hand on the lever of his elaborate crossbreeding equipment, poised to send a painful surge of energy through her body the moment the cuffs were removed. She'd have a split second to silently invoke a spell, and she still had no idea what spell to use.

Linden stared up at stalactites hanging forty feet above her head. Glendin Palace had been constructed centuries earlier directly above an enormous cave, effectively hiding the fay place of power from the outside world. The king had set up his crossbreeding equipment *inside the cave itself*, a true desecration of the ancient fay burial site. Unfortunately, the long-dead fays didn't notice or care—their latent magic amplifying the energy and spells of anyone who could harness it—Fallow sorcerer or Serving mage.

Twelve rows of fay coffins, arranged in a semi-circle around a dried-up pool where a spring once flowed, occupied the center of a cavern spanning sixty feet wide. Two pairs of tables sat on either side of the room. Each pair of tables connected to their own bank of five machines via tubes and wires. The machines, covered as they were with twisted steel plating, would be able to function despite the presence of magic. The equipment looked identical to what Linden had encountered in the prison camp, except there were two sets of everything. The place of power beneath the palace amplified Mordahn's Fallow sorcery to such an extent he could perform two crossbreeding operations at a time.

There was a commotion across the cavernous space, as Corbahn struggled against the four guards attempting to position him onto the table. They finally secured all his straps and withdrew to the perimeter of the room. Linden glanced over at Corbahn stretched out on the table, the muscles of his arms and chest straining against the too-tight straps. The look he gave her, one of utter defeat and something akin to shame at his own helplessness, shattered her heart.

Linden recalled the first time she met him, tall, muscular, ruggedly handsome, and shockingly arrogant. The only feeling that Commander Corbahn Erewin had provoked in her was anger. Seeing Corbahn like this made Linden want to reach her arms around his broad back and pull him close. She wished she'd said something before now, to let him know she had feelings for him as well, and just how strong those feelings had become. Linden had been too afraid of falling in love again after Stryker, unwilling to recognize all the signs with Corbahn, and now here they were, about to die, and she couldn't offer Corbahn even a single word of comfort.

Mordahn, Folcrim, and King Roi entered the room, followed by most of the mages who'd been in the audience earlier that evening, watching their troupe's performance. Now those same mages would be watching Corbahn and Linden as they were tortured into something hideous, less-than-human.

"Bring in the animals!" ordered Mordahn, and the guards disappeared to retrieve the wolves. But when they wheeled two carts into the room, neither cart contained a wolf. Instead, the guards lifted a sedated doe onto the table next to Linden, and a black panther next to Corbahn. Linden twisted her head back and forth, trying to shout "no," but she made nothing more than a muffled noise. A flashback to her nightmare vision, of being turned into a doe half-breed, came to her. She could almost script what Mordahn would say next. Her blood ran cold as she trembled all over, fear driving all rational thought out of her head. Her mind blanked out; she couldn't even summon a child's spell at this point.

Mordahn leaned over her and said, "You'll make a pretty little doe soon enough, perfect prey for the panther next to you."

"After you've been crossbred, we'll lock you in a cage together and watch as your panther-boyfriend tears you limb from limb. It'll be the final performance of your traveling troupe, and what a show," said Folcrim, rubbing his hands together. Corbahn moaned from across the room, his eyes round with terror.

"Let's get started then," said the king, who seemed anxious to be done with the show and retired to his bedchamber before dawn.

Mordahn nodded and got to work, ordering his mage-assistants to establish the blood connections. They attached probes to Linden's chest, inserting needles with tubing into her arms and legs. Linden squeezed her eyes shut, each needle sending a jolt through her limbs. She prayed for inspiration, for the smallest inkling how to stop this horror show. She wanted the ground beneath these Fallow cretins to open wide, swallowing up everyone inside the cavern. Linden's eyes flew open. She turned over the thought, mulling various incantations, and wondered whether any of them could possibly work.

When the mage-assistants finished working on Corbahn and Linden, probes, needles, and tubing connected each of them to the sedated animals by their sides. Linden swallowed down the bile rising in her throat and focused on her plan, her last-ditch effort to stop the insanity beneath Glendin Palace. It meant the destruction of everything, including her and Corbahn, but death was preferable to the half-life of a crossbreed. She lined up the incantations in her mind, hoping she could complete the spell before she lost the ability to formulate sentences. Either way, she and Corbahn wouldn't be walking out of that cave.

"Everything is in place, sir," said the lead assistant with a slight bow to Mordahn.

Mordahn addressed the small crowd of curious mages milling about. "Step away from the tables, ladies and gentlemen. Find a spot along the back wall to observe. We need room to work." Everyone cleared the area, other than King Roi, Folcrim, and Mordahn. The king stood between the two banks of machines, where he could observe each step of the torturous crossbreeding process.

Folcrim moved to Corbahn's side of the room, and Mordahn remained where he was, standing near Linden's table. He placed one gloved hand on the lever that would initiate the crossbreeding process. Linden took a deep breath to steady her nerves. She turned her head to look one last time at Corbahn and gave him the slightest nod. He seemed to understand, nodding back.

"Ready," said Mordahn. Two assistants ran forward, ready to remove the twisted steel cuffs from Corbahn and Linden. The assistant assigned to Linden removed the first cuff from her wrist, moved around the table to the other side, and waited for his cue.

"Now!" shouted Mordahn. Linden had a single, small advantage over Mordahn. She would know the moment the assistant released her magic from its twisted steel shackles, whereas Mordahn would be watching for the assistant to step back from the table, the cuff in his hand, before throwing the lever. She calculated she had two, maybe three precious seconds to cast her spell.

Linden felt the assistant's hands on her wrist and sensed the instant her magic was freed. She felt as if a symphony was playing inside her head, each chord a siren song to Serving magic—her magic, as well as the dormant power of Serving fays long gone—and she silently called out to the fay magic inside that cave. The faintest of whispers, the soft exhalation of breath, stirred the air around her. The words of an incantation formed inside her head, not a single spell so much as a concatenation of separate bits of spells, strung together for this specific purpose.

Remarkably, unbelievably, the fay magic responded to her call. As if the magic knew she was a Serving mage, the

269

magic chose *her*. Linden indwelled the magical energy inside the cave and cast the mightiest spell she'd ever attempted.

> *"Ancient fays, your bones disturbed,*
> *Help us now with power restored.*
> *Blot out all evil in this spot,*
> *Break down this wicked breeding plot.*
> *Destroy each port of Fallowness,*
> *Purify what's dark and sorcerous.*
> *Ensure not one vestige stands,*
> *Crush and crumble 'til none remains!"*

The earth rumbled deep beneath them. As the assistant stepped away from the table, the cuff in his hand, Mordahn flipped down the lever, sparks flying from the equipment. Jolts of electrical energy coursed through Linden's body, her back arching as pain wracked every fiber, muscle, and sinew. Her injured lung felt on fire, the searing pain worse than when Mordahn's dagger had first pierced her side. She screamed inside her gag, even as she concentrated on her incantation.

Although the fays' magic responded to her call, Mordahn and Folcrim were powerful Fallow masters, wielding their own brand of magic. The crossbreeding process had begun, but Mordahn immediately noticed something was wrong. He ran over to the machines, turning dials and pushing knobs, which seemed to boost the current, wracking Linden's body with agonizing shock-waves. She saw a slow trickle of blood flowing through the beakers on top of the machines and wondered how much time she had before she would forget who she was, before she could no longer incant or even formulate a sentence.

Beads of sweat formed on her brow as she focused on the spell.

The rumbling beneath them intensified, and the equipment began to shake. The mages in the back of the room murmured among themselves, not sure whether to remain in the room or run. A powerful crash boomed across the chamber, and the walls shook violently. The fay coffins rattled and tumbled to the ground, spilling dust and bones onto the floor. Stalactites dropped from the ceiling overhead, smashing to the ground and impaling one of the assistants. Mages ran shrieking from the room, King Roi sprinting after them.

A stalactite fell into the bank of machines behind Folcrim. The largest machine toppled forward, crushing the man. Mordahn shouted an incantation to shift the equipment off the necromancer, but nothing happened at first. Mordahn threw his arms into the air, repeating the incantation even more loudly. With so much magical energy swirling inside the place of power, the addition of one more spell created a chain reaction. The machine lying on top of Folcrim imploded, immediately turning to molten ash. Sparks jumped from the blackened machine to the others, each one melting into itself and continuing down the line.

Several sparks flew onto Mordahn's robe, and he hastily swatted at the small flame with his gloved hands. Glancing about, he seemed to realize he was the last remaining mage. Another rumble deep underground caused him to lose his balance and tumble to the floor. He attempted to stand up, but a tremor knocked him down again. The tables drifted from side to side, pulling out tubes and wires, severing the blood connections. Mordahn crawled on his hands and knees, as quickly as his legs and arms could take him, out of the quaking cavern.

Linden managed to wriggle her arm free from one of her bindings, and quickly loosened the remaining straps. She lowered her legs to the ground and fell onto her knees, a combination of her weakened condition and the roiling ground. Scrambling to her feet, she stumbled over to Corbahn's still form on the opposite table.

"Corbahn!" she screamed, shaking him. His head lolled from side to side. *You can't die, I won't let you*, she thought wildly, wondering how she could carry him out before the entire ceiling fell down, crushing them both. Another stalactite dropped nearby, piercing the panther lying next to Corbahn.

Linden flung the straps off him. Leaning her head on Corbahn's chest, she heard his heart beat slowly, erratically, several times and then stop. In full panic mode, Linden pounded the center of his chest with both her fists. With each thump of his chest, she shouted, "Corbahn, come back!" Giving a final thump, she cried, "I need you."

Corbahn made a gargled sound, the air hissing through his lungs, and coughed. He looked at Linden's tear-stained, dirty face as another shockwave rocked the room. "What are we waiting for? This place is falling apart," he mumbled, swiveling his legs from the table onto the ground and promptly collapsing in a heap.

"Here, put your arm around me," Linden said, grabbing his right arm and helping to hoist him to a semi-standing position. Two more stalactites dropped to the floor behind them. "We need to run, now!" she said.

They ran together, Linden half dragging Corbahn over to the dark stairway leading out of the cave. As they climbed, an enormous crash shook the entire foundation of the palace. "We need to go faster, I think the ceiling just collapsed behind us!" she yelled, pulling Corbahn along with all her might.

They staggered out of the stairwell onto the main floor of the palace, which was deserted, and dashed toward the front entrance. The magnificent crystal chandelier that hung above the atrium fell onto the tiled floor as they dashed past, smashing into a thousand shards of glass. Linden felt a sharp pinprick on her cheek from a glass splinter and swiped at her face. Looking down at her fingers, she found a thin ribbon of blood.

The five-story atrium tilted precariously to one side, as if the entire palace were about to be swallowed up by the earth. Linden and Corbahn ran out the front door, which had been flung wide open by the departing mages and servants. The pre-dawn sky was turning from shades of deep blue to gold and pink, the moon fading as the sun prepared to peek above the horizon. "Over here!" said Linden, running toward the stable.

"Wait," hissed Corbahn. "Let's make sure there isn't anyone on the other side of that stable door, ready to run us through with a sword."

Corbahn gave the stable door a tug and stepped back. When no one came charging through the opening he shrugged and peered inside. "Looks like they cleared out of here in a hurry. The stalls are empty."

Linden's heart sank. She'd grown fond of Ashir and hated to lose him, especially to some ill-mannered Fallow mage. And while she didn't relish the thought of riding across Glenbarra by horse, she couldn't imagine traveling all the way to Faynwood by foot. Then she heard a whinny, followed by a snort, which sounded surprisingly familiar. She ran toward the far end of the stable. "Ashir! What a good boy to wait for me." She opened the stall door and threw her arms around the stallion's neck. He snorted again, flicking his tail. As Linden saddled him, she heard Corbahn speaking in dulcet tones a few stalls down; he'd found Chestir. Linden led Ashir into the stable yard, followed by Corbahn with his horse.

Linden felt a tremor beneath them and looked at the palace. The entire structure was trembling. One of the onyx turrets tumbled from its perch above the courtyard and crashed into a bubbling fountain, spraying water every-where. "It's going to come down any minute!"

"Let's cross that moat while there's still a functioning drawbridge," shouted Corbahn, mounting his horse. They rode around the stable yard and trotted to the drawbridge, which the fleeing palace staff had left in the down position.

As they approached the bridge, Linden saw a flash of dark green pass underneath. "Wait a minute," she called out to Corbahn.

"Wait for what?" he asked, pointing at the palace behind them, its black turrets and high walls leaning even farther to the right.

"There's no sign of Mordahn or Roi, and they've assumed we're dead, right?"

Corbahn nodded. "So?"

"But if you were Mordahn, wouldn't you set a trap, just in case we survived?"

Corbahn scratched his beard. "Without a doubt. What sort of a trap, do you think?"

Linden nodded at the moat. "Those things down there were the king's special pets, which means they're Fallow creatures. I think they've been instructed to prevent anyone else from exiting the grounds."

"What do you have in mind?" asked Corbahn, glancing

behind them at the palace. "Glendin Palace is going to collapse any minute."

"A small test." Linden reached back into her saddlebag and withdrew a cooking pot. Handing it to Corbahn, she said, "Could you fling this onto the center of that drawbridge? Make as much noise as you can."

Corbahn took the pot wordlessly from Linden's outstretched hand. His aim was perfect, the pot landing with a thud in the center of the bridge, and bouncing a few times before skidding to the edge. A dark green tentacle whipped out of the water and smashed into the bridge, sending the tin pot tumbling over the side into the water.

"Well that was interesting," said Corbahn.

"We have no choice but to use Serving magic on that thing."

"And draw every other Fallow creature within range to our location." Another tremor shook the ground beneath them. The horses snorted, anxious to be gone. Corbahn added, "Whatever we do, let's do it quickly."

Nodding, Linden said, "Do you know your kitchen spells?"

"I never spent much time in the kitchen," said Corbahn. "Other than to snatch biscuits as they were cooling on the sideboard."

Linden sighed. She'd have to do this on her own, despite her massive headache, the result of invoking the fay magic inside the cave. Every one of her muscles ached from the crossbreeding process Mordahn had attempted and thankfully, the fay magic had thwarted.

"Be ready to dash across that bridge!" said Linden.

"I'll not leave you on this side of the moat by yourself," Corbahn objected.

"I need to cast the spell, and I promise I'll be right

behind you." Drawing his eyebrows downward, Corbahn gave her a curt nod, clearly unhappy he would be crossing first. Linden waited for Corbahn and Chestir to get into position at the end of the drawbridge before she shouted, "Change liquid form to solid ice, freeze this moat from side to side." Invoking a simple kitchen spell for freezing water, she altered it slightly to account for the moat. As the water began to freeze, the twin sea creatures rose up from the surface, waving slimy tentacles toward the sky and screeching in protest. Icicles formed on the tentacles, and the surface of the moat turned opaque. As the moat froze solid, the creatures let out one final scream, temporarily trapped in the ice. The spell wouldn't last long on a body of water the size of the moat.

"Go now!" hollered Linden. Corbahn and Chestir thundered across the bridge. Linden and Ashir started to cross as another tremor rocked the ground, the buildings, and the bridge. She heard an ear-splitting crash as the palace collapsed behind her, sending up a plume of dust and rubble that rained rocks all around them. The bridge creaked beneath them, knocked off its moorings, and a gap of several feet separated the bridge from the land. Ashir reared up, the whites of his eyes showing.

Corbahn yelled, "You've got to jump; it's the only way!"

Linden leaned forward, her knees pressing into Ashir's sides. "Come on, boy, we can do this," she shouted, her heart in her throat as she urged him on. Ashir gathered speed and leapt across the gap, his rear hooves scraping the frozen moat as he scrambled up the bank to safety.

"You did it! You're a genius horse," said Linden. Ashir snorted in agreement. She patted his quivering neck and turned him around for one final look at the rubble of Glendin Palace. Not a single sleek onyx wall remained standing. Everything, from the pointy turrets to the outer courtyard and stables, had collapsed. The sky above the palace, which had been so dark and stormy when they'd arrived the day before, had cleared. Instead of gray skies and thunderclaps, puffy white clouds scuttled across a blue sky. Linden wasn't sure whether the improvement was due to the aftereffects of so much fay magic being released into the atmosphere, or the routing of Fallowness from the palace. In either case, the air around them felt lighter, cleaner, more normal somehow.

Corbahn pulled Chestir alongside her. "When I was a young lad, and Glenbarra still followed Serving magic, I visited this palace with my father. I remember being enchanted by the place, it's beauty and history. I even developed a crush on one of the queen's ladies-in-waiting."

Linden tilted her head and smiled. "I suspect you've broken many hearts in your day, Corbahn Erewin, Chief of Arrowood."

He grinned. "Given that I was a boy of twelve, and the lass was eighteen, it was the other way around." Something shrieked from deep inside the woods, causing Linden to shiver despite the warm weather.

Corbahn peered down the road and shook his head. "I don't like the sound of that. And we've no weapons. They're all back at the hideout in the hills, which is on the other side of those woods."

"At least we can use Serving magic now. They already know we're here," said Linden.

"I'd prefer to use both magic and weapons when I'm fighting Fallow beasts," grunted Corbahn. The shrieking grew louder, and Linden wondered whether they'd be attacked by undead riders, grihms, or dorihms. Her eyes alighted on the abandoned guardhouse at the same time

Corbahn spotted it. He said, "Do you think the guards left anything behind in their haste?"

"Whatever we do, let's do it quickly," said Linden, running through defensive spells in her head, unsure which would work best against a horde of Fallow creatures.

Corbahn dismounted and ran into the guardhouse, coming out a minute later with a sword for each of them. He'd slung a bow across his back and carried a quiver of arrows, which he attached to Chestir's saddle. Linden pointed down the road and said, "Take a look. That's more than a pack of grihms. Mordahn knows we've survived." A dark, swirling cloud spanned the width of the road, shrieking and quivering as it moved toward them. Thunder rumbled as the cloud progressed on the road toward them.

"What did the guards say ran along that road, besides the undead riders we encountered?" asked Corbahn. "Grihms and something else?"

"Howling grihms and swarming dorihms," replied Linden.

"It sounds like Mordahn has called down all of them." Corbahn squinted down the road and glanced back at Linden. "I reckon they'll be here in a couple of minutes. I don't think two swords and a few arrows are going to make that much of a difference to this assortment of creatures. I'm hoping you have a spell in mind, kitchen spell or otherwise. None of my military spells will do the trick against that mass of Fallowness."

Linden had been turning several spells over in her mind, wondering which would be best. She couldn't rely on a defensive spell alone because they'd never outlast Mordahn on his home turf. They'd have to go on the offensive. "I think we need to divide and conquer."

"That's a sound military tactic, but not a spell, at least

not one I'm familiar with." Corbahn nodded at the looming cloud before them. "And we have about a minute before they're here at the guard house." Flattening his ears against the squawking and yelping, Ashir whinnied in protest.

Linden patted Ashir's neck and then pointed to a copse of trees on either side of the palace road. "If we split up, the swarm of Fallow creatures will split up as well. We can use impenetrable fog to confuse them."

"That's a good start. Then what?"

"I'm still working that part out."

Corbahn locked his eyes on hers, his expression softening. Despite her pounding migraine, throbbing limbs, and aching side, Linden's heart lifted at the look Corbahn gave her. "I trust you. Now go!"

Linden and Ashir peeled off to the right, Corbahn and Chestir to the left. Linden shouted the incantation for impenetrable fog, Corbahn echoing her words from the other side of the road. Great puffs of thick-as-wool fog drifted across the road, enveloping the woods on both sides, and muffling somewhat the screeches and grunts coming toward them.

Mordahn's dark cloud of Fallowness collided with the impenetrable fog, and for a moment, Linden saw nothing but a massive gray swirl. Then the blank faces of undead riders and the oddly formed muzzles of grihms peeked out from the whirlwind, their screaming mouths open wide as they spun around. Dorihms, their beaks snapping at empty air, circled overhead. They dived toward the fog and then pulled up in frustration, unable to penetrate the shield.

Linden continued incanting to maintain the fog in place, all the while formulating the next spell. Mage Mother Pawllah had taught her the spell, one that she'd insisted Linden memorize before she would declare Linden to be a proper master mage, since the spell couldn't be found in any books. Pawllah had actually called it the *chaos spell*. Linden had never used the spell and had all but forgotten about it since leaving Sanrellyss Island. Linden ran through the incantation in her mind, waiting for the right moment to invoke the spell.

The right moment came soon enough, when two dorihms broke through the fog on Corbahn's side of the road, and Linden saw a pair of arrows slice through the air, piercing one dorihm in the chest and the other in its wing. The fog shield was thinning over Corbahn, likely due to his weakened state. She felt a trickle of blood running from her nose onto her upper lip and knew she wouldn't be able to sustain the shield much longer herself.

Linden took a deep breath and perching forward in her saddle, raised both arms in the air. She had to get the chaos spell right, not one word out of place. She wouldn't have a second chance, since she'd lose the threads of the impenetrable fog spell once she began the new incantation.

Throwing her head back, Linden used her commanding voice to cry chaos into the whirlwind. "Serving mages and fays, long since passed, call down chaos upon this place. A rift of disorder, a spark of power, pure pandemonium 'til evil's thrown over."

She repeated the incantation, wondering how and where chaos would slice through the Fallowness, allowing Serving magic to reign. The defensive fog thinned rapidly into wispy tendrils, and now she could see into the center of the Fallow cloud. Mordahn sat on top of a skeletal horse, at the head of a long column of undead riders, his robes flapping about him. He didn't seem to notice the chaos spell, instead grunting out his Fallow incantations, ordering his crossbreeds to destroy anything living in their way.

The swarm of dorihms flew above Corbahn and Chestir, their large wings whirring as they flew. Howling and growling, the grihms charged toward Linden and Ashir. The pack quickly surrounded them, and as they drew closer, Ashir reared up, neighing and pawing at the air. Two of the grihms jumped up, one grabbing Linden's leg, snapping his jaws at her, the other attempting to wrest her hands from the reins. She swung her sword, her aim less precise than usual, but the blade made contact. Whining, the grihms withdrew out of range of her sword.

Linden's throat went dry as she continued to incant, keeping an eye on the grihms as they paced around her, preparing to attack again. She wondered whether she'd forgotten something important, something that would soon prove fatal to both her and Corbahn. Then she remembered one of Pawllah's final lessons. Mage Mother had told her to never, ever, doubt herself in the midst of a spell. More master mages had failed due to self-doubt than to erroneous incantations. Pawllah told her to trust herself, her instincts, and her magic.

Linden heard a loud tear, as if a curtain had been ripped open, and a spike of bright white sunlight penetrated Mordahn's dark cloud. The light zeroed in on the source of Fallowness, and shimmering sparks rained down on the old sorcerer, his undead riders, and the crossbreeds. True to the name of the spell, chaos exploded along with the sparks of light.

The grihms yelped, as if in pain, and began chasing the glimmering spots, completely ignoring Linden and Ashir. The last she saw of them, they were running through the trees to her right, yipping after the dancing light. The dorihms flapped their enormous wings, soaring up and away from the bright light, as if fleeing from danger.

Mordahn and the undead riders looked up at the sky, screeching at the bright sparks, which made small hissing sounds when they landed. The undead horses bolted, running off the road and away from the glittering lights, their riders screeching in fear whenever a spark landed on their ragged clothes. Mordahn's horse tossed him to the ground and bolted along with the rest. Mordahn threw his head back and howled like a grihm, screeched like a rider, and squawked like a dorihm. Then he started running down the road, a sword in each hand, ready to take on Linden and Corbahn. She jumped down from Ashir and ran toward Mordahn. Corbahn jogged next to her, both of them holding their swords aloft. Linden continued to incant the spell and noticed that whenever a fresh spark fell onto Mordahn's robes, it burned a hole.

Mordahn pointed his sword at Corbahn and screamed a Fallow spell. Corbahn clutched his chest and crumpled to the ground, his sword clattering out of his hand. Mordahn turned to Linden, repeating his incantation, but she pivoted mentally, switching to the most basic of all protection spells, one she'd learned as an apprentice to ward off evil magic. "Protect us from magical harm, keep us safe from Fallow charms."

The spell would keep her and Corbahn temporarily safe from Mordahn's Fallow magic but not from his physical weapons. Linden didn't have the stamina to muster anything more, and she wouldn't last long at this rate. Mordahn's Fallow spell still sent a jolt of pain through her chest as it passed by, and she coughed but continued running toward him. She had no choice now but to maintain the protection spell to safeguard Corbahn, and charge Mordahn with the borrowed sword.

Mordahn pointed his sword at her a second time, but instead of incanting, he brought his arm behind his head and threw it, the blade winging through the air and spearing Linden's left shoulder. She cried out, pulling the blade from her flesh and flinging it on the ground. Linden dropped onto one knee as the pain radiated from her shoulder down her arm and torso. Screaming, she used her sword to push herself upright again and immediately resumed incanting the basic protection spell. Her nose was bleeding as heavily as her shoulder, an aching weariness seeping into every muscle of her body. She staggered forward, raising the sword in her trembling hand and pointing the tip of the blade at Mordahn. Linden shook her head, wondering why Mordahn wasn't noticing the sunshine spilling from the cloud above him, raining light and life all around them. The sun's rays sparkled like shafts of diamonds as the dark cloud surrounding Mordahn dispersed, winking out in a plume of pure bright light.

Mordahn screamed as his robes and veil dissolved, the light stabbing the sinew and bones of his undead frame. Linden grimaced at the sight of his face, the skin hanging in strips, his mouth a gaping hole full of pointy teeth, his nose two narrow slits. Roaring, he flung his second sword at Linden, the blade grazing her right side as it whizzed by. She cried out in pain but managed to remain upright.

Determined to stop him or die trying, Linden stumbled toward Mordahn, struggling to maintain a grip on her blade. She was eight feet away when a volley of arrows whizzed through the air, piercing the flaps of skin on Mordahn's neck and torso. He howled, turned, and fled off the road, in the direction of his horse and other riders.

Before he dropped behind the ridge, passing out of sight, he hollered down at her and Corbahn, "You will be forever looking over your shoulder, wondering whether today is the day that Mordahn returns to seek his revenge!"

Linden fell to her knees, unable to take one more step. She heard footsteps running up behind her and turned her head. "I think I'll need some help getting on my horse." She felt herself pitching forward onto the road as Corbahn shouted her name.

CHAPTER 26

LINDEN'S EYES FLUTTERED OPEN. SHE WAS LYING ON A BEDROLL inside a cave that looked vaguely familiar. A small fire burned nearby, casting an orange glow on the walls. Something bubbled over the flames, a hearty stew by the smell of it. She breathed a sigh of relief, recognizing the fay-ensorcelled hideout in the hills near Glendin Palace.

"You're finally awake!" said Corbahn, who knelt beside her and felt her forehead, pursing his lips in concentration. "I was beginning to wonder whether my healing skills had utterly failed you. Here, have some water." He gently lifted her head so she could sip from a small mug.

"Thank you," she said after swallowing the cool water. Corbahn helped her lean against the wall, putting a blanket behind her for extra support. She grimaced with every move. "How are you feeling? I saw you take a direct hit."

Corbahn rubbed his chest. "It wasn't a direct hit, otherwise I'd not be here. I was able to deflect most of the damage from Mordahn's Fallow spell with one of my own. A fay healer will be able to leach out the rest when we're back home."

"Home is a luscious-sounding word. But how will we manage to get there?" Linden paused, trying to calculate the distance back to the Arrowood border. It was simply too far, and she was too injured, to make that trip without fay traveling mists to help them. "You need to go without me. We're deep inside Glenbarra, and I'm not up for traveling through Fallow territory. I'll wind up getting us both killed."

Corbahn squared his jaw. "I'm not leaving you behind. We'll figure something out."

Linden winced as she reached out her hand, which Corbahn grasped in his much larger one. "You are the Chief of Arrowood. You have to get back to your clan, your people."

Corbahn brought her hand up to his chest. "And you are the Liege of Faynwood. You are my Liege."

Linden shook her head. "We both know the five chiefs, Reynier included, are the real leaders in Faynwood. The Liege is more of a ceremonial title."

"You can't possibly be serious," said Corbahn, sounding indignant. "My father would never have pledged his allegiance to a mere ceremonial title. He pledged his allegiance to you, Linden Arlyss, Liege of all the Faynwood clans, because of who you are. You managed to unite us after fifty years of strife."

"The clans were weary of war, ready for peace."

"But we needed you to help reconcile our factions," said Corbahn. "Look, when I first pledged my allegiance to you, I did it because my father expected it. I did it because it was my duty. I didn't know you, the real you. But now I do. And today, I pledge not just my allegiance, I pledge my—"

A loud clatter, of clay jars smacking together and a few pots tipping over, interrupted Corbahn. He grabbed his sword, which he'd laid on the ground beside him, and sprang up. Linden felt completely useless, so weak she couldn't muster even a child's spell.

Tendrils of vaporous haze wafted by, fay traveling mists by the look of it, and she cried out, "Wait, I think it might be Pryl!"

"Pryl! What a welcome sight you are," exclaimed Corbahn, lowering his sword and hugging the shorter man. In a rare display of emotion, Pryl hugged him back.

"It's good to see you—both of you," said Pryl, amending his statement when he saw Linden was unable to stand. "Although I'm sorry to see you're injured. I came as soon as I could. There was so much hullabaloo among the fay council members that I had to call an emergency session first."

"What sort of hullabaloo?" asked Linden, wincing as she shifted against the wall. Although her poisoned lung felt better inside the fay-spelled cave, her physical injuries made any movement excruciating. Pryl sat down on one side of her so she wouldn't have to crane her neck to speak, and Corbahn sat across from him on her other side. She felt safe, truly safe, tucked inside the snug fay hide-away, despite the fact they were deep in Glenbarran territory.

"The fay council is in an absolute uproar that we did it, that you and Corbahn did it."

Corbahn frowned. "Did what, precisely?"

"Accomplished the mission! Neutralized the place of power, brought down Glendin Palace itself," said Pryl. "King Roi and Mordahn are on the run, thanks to the two of you."

Corbahn picked up Linden's hand, "'Tis Linden who did it. I don't even know how, exactly, but she's the one who rescued me from the crossbreeding table. Her magic was magnificent."

"And you're the one who stopped Mordahn in the end, with your arrows," said Linden. "My magic wasn't enough against him."

"But how did you know?" asked Corbahn. "And the fay council as well?"

Pryl grinned. "We fays always know when there's a disruption of magical energy, and this was more like a major eruption, an explosion of magical forces, Serving and Fallow, that most of us have never experienced in our lifetimes. It's something for our bards to sing of one day, a story for the ages."

Linden thought of the fay history books in her grandmother's library at Delavan Manor, and smiled to think that her story, their story, might be recorded in a future edition. But Valerra was still occupied, besieged, and her brother was fighting back with a small group of resistance fighters. Would the fays now agree to help them?

"You called an emergency meeting of the fay council. What was the outcome? Will the fay council keep their word?" asked Linden.

Corbahn chuckled. "I think you may be feeling better."

"How so?" said Linden.

"Whenever you start talking politics, it tells me you're on the mend."

Pryl nodded. "Aye, and that's a good thing too because I bring the best of news. The fay council has voted, unanimously, to come to Valerra's aid. We will help to drive out the Fallow occupiers there."

Linden exhaled the breath she'd been holding as she waited for Pryl's answer. "That's wonderful news! I just hope we're not too late—to help my brother and the other resistance fighters—and to save the remaining Serving mages who didn't manage to escape."

"We will do this thing," said Corbahn. "We'll restore Valerra, and the entire continent, purging the stench of Fallowness that has hung about us for too long. And then, perhaps, we will have earned our rest."

"Our rest?" repeated Linden. "When have you ever rested, Chief Corbahn Erewin of Arrowood?"

Corbahn threw back his head and laughed. "True enough. Let's say respite, then. A respite so we may enjoy the simpler pleasures of life." Corbahn lifted her hand to his lips, and Linden smiled.

"Ah yes, I perceive your meaning," she said.

Pryl coughed. "Well then, first things first. Let's have some of that stew on the pot over there, the only pot I managed not to knock over, and let's get you home."

An hour later, Corbahn carefully lifted Linden into the saddle. She gritted her teeth, determined not to cry out, although her shoulder and side throbbed with every movement. Corbahn climbed up on Ashir, wrapping his arms around her to keep her from falling. Linden gratefully leaned against Corbahn's chest, relieved to have someone else take charge for the moment. "We're ready," he called out to Pryl, who was sitting on Chestir. Pryl raised his hand and said, "Alright then, follow me!"

It took four jumps, and one short sprint to escape from a roving band of Glenbarran troopers, before they landed safely inside the Arrowood campgrounds. Linden hoped to be able to get to a soft bed immediately, and bypass any sort of welcome from the clans, as well as prodding and poking by Jayna and her healers, but no such luck. Efram and Wreyn had alerted everyone of their arrival, even before they'd actually crossed the border.

As soon as word spread they'd touched down near the Tanglewood campsite, a clamor of trilling and cheering could be heard from one end of the bowl-shaped field to the other. Jayna and Mara threw their arms around Linden, who was leaning against Corbahn for support. Linden flinched and sucked in her breath, prompting both of them to ask what was wrong. When Linden didn't answer, Corbahn described her injuries, and Jayna ordered Linden to the healer's tent immediately, but not before Reynier and Remy shook her hand and Corbahn's, shouting their congratulations. Then Kal arrived in a flutter of wings, foregoing his usual aloofness whenever Linden returned home from a trip without him. Instead, Kal nestled up against her legs, clicking his beak happily. Corbahn's sister, Carissa, kissed her brother and then Linden. She cradled Zeena, Linden's small black cat, in her arms.

Rubbing the soft fur behind Zeena's ears until the cat purred, Linden said, "It's good to be home."

Corbahn glanced at her and smiled. "Aye, and now it's time for you to go with Jayna. I'll make sure Kal and Zeena are safely delivered to your tent."

Kal squawked at the mention of his name, and Linden said, "Kal's not going to leave my side. Jayna doesn't mind, do you?"

Jayna shook her head. "Of course not, so long as Kal doesn't fly around inside. Now no more stalling, let's go." Corbahn wrapped his arm firmly around Linden and escorted her to the healer's tent. It took them three times as long to make the short trip, because of the number of people milling about, cheering and clapping for them.

Linden slept straight through the next day, Zeena at the foot of her bed and Kal curled up on the rug nearby. She had no dreams, no visions, nothing to disturb her rest. When she finally woke up, the sun had set, and she enjoyed a light supper in bed. Linden still had a lot of pain in her shoulder and her side where Mordahn's swords had wounded her, but the achiness whenever she took a deep breath was gone. Wreyn had sent a fay healer to Jayna, and the fay healer used ancient magic to dispel the seeds of Fallow sorcery inside Linden's lung.

As Garlan removed the remains of Linden's dinner, she said, "You have a visitor, mum."

"Who is it?" asked Linden.

"The Chief of Arrowood."

Linden ran her hand through her tangled waves. "My hair, could you help me brush it please?" Grabbing a hairbrush and comb, Garlan worked out the worst of the knots in Linden's hair, which hurt almost as much as the pain in her shoulder.

"Your lovely blue streaks are showing through again; the coppery color's mostly worn off," said Garlan, as she draped a delicate ivory shawl around Linden's shoulders. Linden smiled to recall how much teasing her blue highlights had caused her as a girl in Valerra. Now, she was relieved the fay-inspired blue streaks ran through her hair again.

Garlan invited Corbahn inside the tent and drew closed the curtain to afford them some privacy. Linden noticed he held something behind his back, but he clearly wanted to reveal his secret in his own way, so she waited as he pulled a chair up beside her bed. He'd trimmed his beard and his hair, which was still longer than Reynier's or Remy's, but he'd combed it back from his forehead, much more kempt than usual. Wearing flowing robes, in the rich green and brown of the Arrowood clan, Corbahn looked every bit the chief, handsome, proud, and serious. Linden was now beside herself with curiosity, but she also knew from experience Corbahn couldn't be hurried.

He pulled two roses out from behind his back, one white and one red. The thorns had been removed from the smooth stem of the white rose, but not the red one, which was wrapped in fabric to protect Linden from pricking her finger.

"I understand that in Valerra, a white rose symbolizes new love, its sweetest hopes and dreams. It's customary to remove all the thorns, all the imperfections before gifting the rose." Corbahn handed her the white rose with a small bow from the waist.

Linden tilted her head and said, "Thank you. It's lovely, a perfect rose."

Corbahn nodded and continued. "In Arrowood, a red rose symbolizes the deepest, strongest love. We leave the thorns on the rose as a reminder that despite our weaknesses and foibles, we're still capable of the profoundest sacrifices in the name of love. We love fully, without holding back. When we love, it's thorns and all." Corbahn handed Linden the red rose and cleared his throat to let her know he wasn't finished. "Back in the cave, we were interrupted by Pryl's arrival, as welcome as it was. I'd like to finish what I was trying to say."

Corbahn hesitated, and Linden gave him a nod of encouragement. He took a deep breath, his sea-green eyes serious. "I repeat my pledge of allegiance to my Liege, Linden Arlyss, of Tanglewood and Valerra. And I pledge my love to you, as well." Corbahn took Linden's hand in his much larger one. "Now that we are home, and you are on the mend, I'd like to, ah, I want to...that is, may I kiss you, my Liege?"

Linden smiled at the strong, dependable clan chief

who'd captured her heart with his gruff ways and tender looks. Nodding slowly, her voice catching in her throat, she whispered, "Aye, Chief Corbahn, aye."

Corbahn rose from the chair and leaned over Linden, taking her face gently in his calloused hands. He kissed her softly on the lips and sat back down. Linden's heart fluttered inside her chest and her stomach lightened. Corbahn looked at her expectantly, waiting for her response.

Tomorrow, she thought, the battle plans would resume. They had a war to run and a nation, her former homeland, to retake from its Fallow occupiers. Her feelings for Corbahn, and his feelings for her, would have to wait. But tonight, this very moment, she'd enjoy her much-earned reprieve from war and worry.

Linden inhaled the sweet scent of both the roses and then with a smile, crooked her finger at Corbahn. He arched an eyebrow and moved over to sit on the edge of the bed next to her. Linden wrapped her good arm around Corbahn's neck and brought his lips down to hers for a longer, deeper, more satisfying kiss. Linden's kiss was a red-rose, thorns-and-all kind of a kiss, and it was all the answer that Corbahn, Chief of Arrowood, needed from his Liege.

BOOKS BY TONI CABELL

A fast-paced adventure full of magic, romance, humor, sword fighting, dangerous creatures, and the power of light versus darkness, **Serving Magic** is a YA Epic Fantasy series with Steampunk and Regency vibes. Winner of The Wishing Shelf Book Awards and recognized by Indies Today as a Top 5 YA Fantasy series by an indie author:

- *Lady Apprentice, Book 1*
- *Lady Mage, Book 2*
- *Lady Liege, Book 3*
- *Lady Spy, Book 4*
- *Lady Reaper, Book 5*

In the arid hills of Toresz, there's one thing more dangerous than divining for water... falling in love with the enemy. **Water Witch** is YA Romantasy duology packed with action, danger, intrigue, royal politics, and romance. Winner of The Wishing Shelf Book Awards:

- *The Lightness of Water, Book 1*
- *The Way of Water, Book 2*

If you're looking for sweet, slow-burn romance with swoony kisses, second chances, and funny, heartwarming characters, don't miss the complete **Faeries of Door County** series. Winner of Best Paranormal Romance, each novel is a standalone story set in the same cozy small town:

- *Rhyme, Riddle, and Romance*
- *Half a Faerie*
- *Return to Mooncrest Inn*

Find all Toni's available books and upcoming new releases on tonicabell.com and Amazon. All her novels are also available in audiobook format on Audible and Apple Books.

ABOUT THE AUTHOR

When Toni told her fifth-grade teacher that she wanted to be a writer, neither of them expected Toni's journey to include stints as a nurse's aid, personal banker, instructional designer, real estate broker, systems analyst, and youth director. Toni is thrilled to be an indie author and does at least half her writing in the middle of the night, which may explain her wild plot twists and unforgettable characters.

Today, Toni writes award-winning fantasy stories filled with spunky gals, protective guys, imaginative magic, and romance that sizzles without the spice. Whether you're a fan of fast-paced, YA fantasy adventures with a dash of swoon or cozy paranormal romance packed with heart-stealing kisses and small town charm, you're sure to find something to love.

Toni's novels have earned Silver and Bronze Medals in The Wishing Shelf Book Awards, two Gold Medals in the Global Book Awards, and Best Paranormal Romance from Indies Today.

She makes her home in a small village along the shores of Lake Michigan with her handsome husband, where she enjoys generous supplies of strong coffee, too many pastries, and more books than she can ever read.

Want a free novella and to stay current on Toni's upcoming releases, sales, and giveaways? Then visit tonicabell.com and sign up for her newsletter.

Toni posts regularly about her indie author journey, life lessons, what inspires her, and her books on Instagram and Facebook. Also consider joining her Reader Group on Facebook, @onceuponaswoon, where she hangs out with some of her closed-door author friends and readers like you.

Soli Deo Gloria.